Two Teens. A Vast Cosmos. One Ancient Mystery to Solve...

THE
COORDINATE

M A R C   J A C O B S

By Marc Jacobs © 2019

Two teens...
A vast cosmos...
One ancient mystery to solve...

Logan West and Emma James grew up together but are now high school seniors going in totally opposite directions after graduation. When they are assigned to work together on one last history project, they hardly expect the monotony of high school life to change. Instead, as they decode a series of unexplained clues hidden within their history project itself, Logan and Emma manage to unfold an ancient mystery that has baffled scientists and archeologists, one with powerful implications for the present day. As they embrace the adventure they've stumbled upon, and a growing romantic attraction to each other, Logan and Emma find themselves caught up in a dangerous, high-stakes race across the globe to decipher mankind's past in order to save humanity's future, not to mention their very own lives, with a mystery that just might reach towards the stars...

The Coordinate by Marc Jacobs

Printed in the United States of America

First Printing, 2019

eBook ISBN: 978-0-578-51959-3
Paperback ISBN: 978-0-578-51960-9

Publisher: Marc Jacobs

marc@marcjacobsauthor.com
www.marcjacobsauthor.com

To My Loving Family, Friends and Editors

This book is dedicated with love and appreciation to my supportive family, friends and editors who have inspired me, challenged me and helped me to make this journey to the stars a reality.

Contents

Chapter 1 – Chamber of the White-Eyed Star God

Leaning on one knee halfway up the outer steps of the Copán Temple, Dr. Jonas Arenot squinted at the Mayan hieroglyphs as if doing so might pull more information out of them that years of study by previous scholars failed to extract. Time was running out on his team's grant from Harvard University where he was a professor in the Archeology Department. Considering what Harvard was paying for his team's two-month summer trek to the Copán ruins in western Honduras, they expected results. He knew his reputation was on the line given his repeated failure to turn up anything notable on any of his prior costly expeditions.

Frustrated, Dr. Arenot wiped the sweat from his forehead, running his hands through his thinning brown hair and graying sideburns.

Puzzled by Dr. Arenot's intense scrutiny of the hieroglyphics, graduate assistant Martin O'Brien felt compelled to ask him, "What are you looking for?"

"A clue, Martin, a clue."

"A clue?" Martin replied, confused.

"Yes, a clue. A clue as to how they did it."

Martin did not follow. Although he had been studying under Dr. Arenot for years, he still hadn't mastered the skill of interpreting the hidden messages woven into the professor's vague responses implying Martin should know what he was talking about.

"How they did what?" asked Martin.

Dr. Arenot looked at him quizzically, surprised he didn't understand. At this point, Dr. Arenot stood up on the steps and explained, "The United States, a world superpower, has only been around a couple hundred years. The Roman Empire lasted, what, 1,500 years?" Dr. Arenot put his hand on one of the sixty-two steps leading up to the flat top of the pyramid-shaped temple. "But here, we stare at a longevity beyond compare. The Mayan civilization lasted for *thousands* of years. Don't you ever wonder how they did it? Despite modern society's supposed sophistication and technology, never a day goes by that I don't wonder how we're going to make it another 50 years much less thousands like the Mayans. There's a thing or two we can learn from these hieroglyphics… and if I don't come up with *something* in the next two weeks, Pushire is pulling the plug."

Martin, stunned, did a double-take. "But… but how can he do that? We've still got two months left on our funding."

"There's a new rock star in town and her name's Professor Jill Quimbey, daughter of Lord Quimbey of the, um, *something* Isles overseas. And the Department's ready to give our funding over to her and her cyber-technetic archeology."

"I thought she wasn't coming until January?"

"Well, it appears they lured her six months early with my grant money," griped Dr. Arenot, still smarting from last year's International Archeology Symposium when organizers bumped him from his speaking slot to fit in Professor Quimbey. Dr. Arenot was not looking forward to working with her, at all. Still, he couldn't help but admit that he found some of her theories fascinating. Not 'groundbreaking' like others did, but intriguing, nonetheless. "Here, look at—"

Before he could finish his sentence, the ground started shaking, the result of a small tremor common in these parts. Dr. Arenot and Martin steadied themselves to avoid falling down the steps. After fifteen seconds, the minor earthquake stopped. When it was over, Dr. Arenot returned his attention to the hieroglyphs, seizing the opportunity for a teaching moment for his grad student.

"Look at these," he said to Martin, leaning back down on one knee to point out a series of hieroglyphs carved into the steps, which archeologists referred to as the Hieroglyphic Stairway of Copán. Martin leaned down beside the professor who continued, "Here, this sequence is one of my favorites, and it's a perfect example of what I'm talking about. Can you read it?"

Martin gave it a shot. "The God of the Heavens—"

"Stars," Dr. Arenot interrupted, helping Martin with the translation. "The God of Stars."

Martin tried again. "The God of *Stars* lights the heavens, revealing the secret truth hidden within."

"Good… keep going," Dr. Arenot approved.

"A truth that will learn…"

"*Teach*," interjected Dr. Arenot, correcting him again. "A truth that will *teach...*"

Martin started over. "The God of Stars lights the heavens, revealing the secret truth hidden within; a truth that will *teach* man the way to the gods."

"Excellent," said Dr. Arenot as he sat down on the steps and looked at Martin. "Now, what do you think that means?"

"It represents…" Martin paused. The professor appeared distracted. "Dr. Arenot?" he asked.

The professor remained lost in thought for a moment, and then blurted, "Martin, grab the others and bring the infrared thermographer, cosmic particle detector, and 3D laser scanner into the temple and meet me at the Kneeling Wall."

"Why? What's up?"

"Just meet me down there!" exclaimed Dr. Arenot.

Dr. Arenot dashed down the steps to the Copán Temple's ground-level entrance. With a flashlight in hand, he proceeded into the narrow mouth of the temple and down a dim corridor to the relatively insignificant 'God of Stars Kneeling Wall.'

He gazed upon the wall's perfectly-etched stone blocks, the time-tested work of masterful Mayan stonemasons. Most walls inside the temple had multiple hieroglyphics on them, each telling a complete story, but the Kneeling Wall had only one hieroglyph on it standing for the "God of Stars." As a result, over the years, it had attracted far less attention from scholars than the others.

This wall had been catalogued years ago, and Dr. Arenot had walked by it countless times over the last six weeks. But today, something occurred to him that he had never thought of before: did the hieroglyphics which read, 'the God of Stars lights the heavens, revealing the secret truth hidden within,' refer to the metaphorical guidance the gods gave to the Mayan people that could be found in their culture's constellations, or did it mean something else entirely?

The God of Stars lights the heavens, *revealing the secret truth hidden within*, pondered Dr. Arenot. Was there a secret truth hidden within? He knew there was nothing behind the wall because his team had scanned it when they first arrived. But as he thought about the Copán people's historical references to the Kneeling Wall describing how the gods instructed them to kneel *down* at the God of Stars, today, for the first time, Dr. Arenot considered whether there was something hidden *down* below ground. He had not scanned the floor for subterranean spaces in this corridor yet.

Dr. Arenot's team of six grad students arrived with their flashlights in hand. "Here you go, Dr. Arenot," said Maggie Samuels, handing him the infrared thermographer, cosmic particle detector, and 3D laser scanner. The state-of-the-art equipment was brand new, the latest in stone scanning technology. When it became available in handheld form, at Dr. Arenot's request, the Board of Trustees authorized the purchase for this sabbatical, banking on his expedition turning up *something* of interest.

"Thank you," said Dr. Arenot. "Keep the thermographer," he said to Maggie. He handed the 3D scanner to Martin and kept the cosmic particle detector for himself. "Let's give it a whirl."

"What are we looking for?" asked Maggie.

"To see if the Copán people have been trying to tell us something for five hundred years," answered Dr. Arenot.

Maggie and Martin turned on their devices. Dr. Arenot bent down and pointed his cosmic particle detector toward the stone floor.

The particle detector used subatomic particles known as muons, to identify gaps and hidden chambers behind stone. Muons traveling in open space move quickly while muons traveling through rock move slowly and eventually stop. By monitoring the speed of the muons, the detector, after syncing up with the 3D scanner, could formulate a rudimentary image of what was behind or below the stone.

Dr. Arenot began moving the particle detector along the floor's stone surface, surveying several stone blocks in the corridor in front of the Kneeling Wall. When he got to the block at the foot of the Kneeling Wall, he lingered a bit longer. After thirty seconds, renderings from the cosmic particle detector started registering on the 3D scanner.

"Dr. Arenot, you've got to see this," said Martin. "The 3D scanner is showing a space below the stone in front of the Kneeling Wall."

"Let me see that," said Dr. Arenot, surprised he might actually have been right. Martin leaned over to show him. "Would you look at that!" exclaimed Dr. Arenot. "There's something down there." Dr. Arenot suddenly felt validated by his instincts. "It's showing what appears to be a corridor below us."

"Where does it go?" asked Maggie.

"I don't know, it leads out of range," replied Dr. Arenot, still analyzing the scanner. How had he missed this, he chided himself.

"What do you think's down there? A tomb?" asked one of the other grad students.

"Only one way to find out; we've got to find the way in," said Dr. Arenot, examining the floor. "Here, let's clear some of the mold and dust from the seams around this stone block."

The professor's grad students did as asked. When they finished, the seams around the stone looked like the seams around the other stone blocks in the temple wedged together to form a solid floor; but there was an increased depth to the ridges around this one that Dr. Arenot had not noticed before beneath the dust and mold.

"Hand me a wedge," he said. One of the students handed it to him. Very carefully, Dr. Arenot inserted the wedge into the seam, and it sunk farther than he expected. There was *definitely* something different about the seams surrounding this stone. "Martin, Justin, bring in the crowbars."

Excited, the students ran outside to fetch the crowbars Dr. Arenot requested. It was not long before Martin and Justin returned with the tools. Once they did, Dr. Arenot's team went to work inserting the crowbars on each side of the stone in order to lift the block up. Dr. Arenot had one grad student photo-document the process while another student filmed it. After half an hour, they

12

carefully extracted the stone block from the floor, revealing an opening with ledges set down below that were holding the stone up.

"Shine some light down there," said Dr. Arenot.

One of his students pointed a flashlight into the opening. They could see steep stairs.

"Someone grab the PicPro," directed Dr. Arenot. He wanted to lower a camera down for a closer look before climbing in. Martin grabbed the expanding stick with a video camera affixed to the end. "Okay, lower it in," Dr. Arenot instructed him.

Martin extended the PicPro down into the opening. Maggie provided illumination with her flashlight. With the PicPro's wireless signal syncing up with the PicPro app on Dr. Arenot's smartphone, the professor watched the live stream feed as Martin slowly rotated the PicPro camera 360°.

"It's a passageway. Looks okay to me," said Dr. Arenot. With a flashlight in hand, he took a deep breath and started lowering himself into the passage.

"Be careful, it could be booby-trapped," warned Martin.

"What do you think this is, an Indiana Jones film??" snapped Dr. Arenot, tired of archeology students who were overly influenced by Hollywood movies. Ignoring the warning, Dr. Arenot lowered himself the rest of the way in. "Come on down," he called back up to the others.

His students eagerly climbed down into the opening. They found themselves in a low-ceilinged corridor filled with cobwebs. They followed the passageway until coming to an abrupt end at a stone door approximately five and a half feet tall. The door was already partially ajar. Etched above it were more hieroglyphic symbols.

Although Dr. Arenot deciphered the hieroglyphics immediately, he asked the grad students accompanying him, "Does anyone want to take a swing?" They all failed to venture a guess, too overwhelmed by the excitement of the moment. After all, none of them had ever made a 'discovery' before. Sighing with disappointment, Dr. Arenot said, "It reads 'Chamber of the White-Eyed Star God.'"

"That's odd," said Martin, unfamiliar with the Copán's reference to the Mayan God of Stars as the 'White-Eyed Star God.'

Dr. Arenot smiled and said, "'That's odd,' is usually what people say right before something interesting happens." He pushed open the inner door and then, unexpectedly, paused to allow the nerves ripping through his stomach to work their way out of his system. When ready, Dr. Arenot ducked below the stone threshold leading into the Chamber of the White-Eyed Star God. One by one his students lowered their heads and followed, unaware that they were all about to make a profound discovery that would finally pique the interest of Harvard's Board of Trustees, not to mention change the course of human history.

Chapter 2 – *Five Years Later...*

When the alarm went off, MegaWave's 'Jagged Edge of the Sun' blasted out of the radio. Logan West groaned at the thought of starting another school week. It was October 17th. Only eight more months and thirty-four Mondays to go in his senior year at Jersey North High School before graduation.

After graduating, Logan planned to attend community college. His grades were good enough for a four-year college, but his mother didn't make much money managing a restaurant over the river in Manhattan. And while his grades were solid, they certainly weren't scholarship worthy. As for his father, he was completely out of the picture, taking off shortly after Logan was born. According to his mom, signing Logan's birth certificate was just about the only thing his father did right before splitting.

Logan got ready for school, threw on blue jeans, black high-tops, and a gray sweatshirt, roughed up his already disheveled, brown hair, grabbed a protein bar for breakfast, and shot out the door. His mother was already long gone, having caught the 5:30 a.m. train into the city for the start of her fifteen plus hour day. Sometimes, she wouldn't return home until well after midnight and text messages were the only way they communicated. When he texted his mom, he always promised to take her away from this someday, and she always responded the same way:

"# U R worth it @ I ♡ U #now go to school#"

Her misuse of hashtags never failed to make him laugh, but he did not have the heart to tell her she was doing it wrong or that hashtags were totally useless in private text messages. She wanted so badly to be the "cool mom" and to relate to Logan better, a feeling he knew stemmed from her guilt from all the time she spent at the restaurant away from him.

Logan rode his bike to school, barely beating the 8 a.m. bell. This Monday was just like any other, a snooze fest in English lit, a pop quiz in calculus, a failed experiment in science because the school's equipment was twenty years out of date, and that was all before lunch. When Logan got to 4th-period history, he hardly expected the brutal Monday monotony to change.

Logan sat there patiently, waiting for another predictable class to start. He chatted with friends seated nearby trying to soak up every last second of freedom before the bell rang. When it finally did, Mr. Jackson, the quirky history teacher with oversized glasses and out-of-control, floppy brown hair, snuffed out the remaining conversations the bell failed to cut short. It was time for class to start.

"I hope you all had a nice weekend," said Mr. Jackson in his usual energetic tone that, immediately after lunch, always took a few extra seconds to get used to. Logan looked around at his classmates, who all appeared dazed. Undeterred, Mr. Jackson continued.

"As we so often talk about, history, not me, is the greatest teacher," he said in a distinctly academic voice. "It provides civilized society with a rich compendium of information about the past, guiding us to learn from our mistakes and enabling us to make better choices in the future than our ancestors made. A great historian once said, 'Our past actions define our future plans, so we better pay attention to our history.' Who said that?" The question had a rhetorical ring to it.

Beck Raymer raised his hand like always, and Mr. Jackson, after surveying the room to see if anyone else was doing the same, called on him. "Mr. Raymer?"

"You did, Mr. Jackson," answered Beck.

"Right," Mr. Jackson chirped. "Sometimes, however, history can't explain everything, like how things happened or why." The class already seemed bored, but Mr. Jackson kept going, determined to win over the students with his enthusiastic and interactive approach to teaching. "Who can come up with an example where history tells us what happened without the how or the why?"

No one's hand went up, not even Beck's this time, so Mr. Jackson called on a terrified Elise Holden.

Elise meekly squeaked out, "The dinosaurs?"

"Was that a question or an answer, Ms. Holden?" asked Mr. Jackson, critiquing her uncertainty.

"The Bible," shouted Beck confidently.

"Interesting, and yes, a great example of how history permeates everything from religion to culture to science. Even the Bible, which some consider the greatest historical document ever, poses questions that can't be answered. Anyone else?" No one took the bait, so Mr. Jackson, after pushing back a few drooping strands of hair that had fallen over his face, moved on.

"For the next few weeks, we are going to study historical mysteries where the only thing historians have been able to definitively answer is the *what* of it all, without the *how* or the *why* − oddities in history historians and scientists can't quite explain; where theories diverge on geographical, cultural or religious grounds. Each of you will study those theories, draw your own conclusions, test them, and the part I am sure you will all love the most, prepare a written report and give an oral presentation for the class on the topic assigned to you."

The class moaned out loud.

"Don't fret, you won't have to go it alone on this one. Consider it my gift to you lazy seniors. I will be putting you in groups so you can share the workload and complain to each other. Written reports will be due the week of Thanksgiving, and you will give your group oral presentations immediately upon your return from Thanksgiving break."

Mr. Jackson turned around and walked back to his desk to pick up a stack of papers for the class. "The dinosaurs. Religion. Those were good answers from Ms. Holden and Mr. Raymer, but too obvious for you. These group projects will focus on smaller scale mysteries that I hope will be a little more fun, like the Great Pyramid of Giza, the oldest and largest of the great Egyptian pyramids."

Mr. Jackson punched up a picture of Giza on the overhead projector for the class. On the pull-down screen appeared the 455-foot tall pyramid surrounded by several smaller pyramids. The Great Sphinx of Giza, a long statue of a reclining sphinx with the body of a lion and the head of a human, guarded the Great Pyramid.

"Built around 2,560 BC, the pyramid was the tallest man-made structure in the world for over 3,800 years. Millions of tons of limestone blocks hoisted impossibly high above the ground. How did they do it? Slaves? Machinery? Pop culture claims aliens built it. Why did the Egyptians, or perhaps, the '*aliens*,' build it? Your group will report back to me on the historical and scientific theories, the cultural and pop-culture theories, and lastly, your own theories as to the how and the why."

Mr. Jackson moved on from Giza and clicked over to a new slide depicting another ancient monument…

"What about the ancient Trilithon in the Temple of Jupiter within the mysterious ruins of Baalbek in Lebanon? Never heard of it? Imagine this: a monumental stairway and platform surrounded by three massive retaining walls held up by twenty-seven limestone blocks, each larger in size than any other limestone blocks in the world. All of the limestone blocks weigh more than 300 tons. There are three weighing over 800 tons, and one on the temple's southern end which weighs more than 1,000 tons, or more than *three 747 airplanes*. These are some of the most amazing engineering achievements of all time, and they not only carved these stones, located and stood them up, they managed to move them over to the temple from locations far away. How did they do all of this without machinery thousands of years ago? And again, why?"

Mr. Jackson pulled up another picture on the overhead projector of a solid stone arch, square in appearance. "We will be looking at the Gate of the Sun, multiple 40-ton stone blocks lifted off the ground and fashioned into a free-standing doorway by the ancient Tiwanaku people of Bolivia. These blocks were carved, hoisted off the ground, notched, and interlocked together perfectly in three dimensions, yet they bear no chisel or chain marks whatsoever. How these stone blocks were shaped and lifted remains a mystery. And like the other examples we've been talking about, these blocks were taken from rock quarries more than 50 miles away. How were these enormous blocks, weighing as much as ten elephants each, moved that far at a time in history before horses were used for transport in South America?"

Jen Erickson raised her hand. "Do we get to choose the topic we want to cover?"

"No, you do not," replied Mr. Jackson. "I will be assigning the topics."

Ugh, the class collectively groaned again.

Mr. Jackson ignored the griping and kept going. "You will study the ancient Nazca Lines," he said, pulling up a picture of a 150-foot long giant spider carved into the Nazca Desert. Mr. Jackson explained, "The Nazca Lines in southern Peru consist of ancient geoglyphs carved into the ground rock, visible only from high in the sky. There are hundreds of them ranging from simple lines to geometric shapes to animals to trees and flowers, some hundreds of feet long or wide. There's even one with near-parallel straight lines that looks like an airport landing strip." Mr. Jackson conjured up a picture of the 'landing strip' on the screen for the class to look at. "Again, who built them and what was their purpose? For their gods in the sky?"

Mr. Jackson rapidly flipped through a few more pictures, talking as he did so. "We will study the Sacsayhuamán in Peru, world-famous Stonehenge in the United Kingdom, and many other ancient sites. I've selected a dozen of these for you. I'm hoping you will all roll up your sleeves and dive into this. Studying these ancient achievements should be a fun way to explore history and culture in many different parts of the world.

I want your reports to tell us what scientists and historians have to say about these amazing accomplishments built by early civilizations achieving engineering feats that would be hard to accomplish even by today's technology. I want to know what pop culture says and I want your theories, who do you agree with and why. Don't worry about how preposterous any of it sounds. A thorough, well-balanced project with a properly formed thesis is all I am looking for.

Because there are 35 of you in this class, there will be 11 groups of three and one unlucky group of two, to cover my 12 selected topics. As for the smaller group, just do your best. I'm passing out the assignment sheets now."

The sheets circulated down the aisles like wildfire with students anxiously scanning for their names, group, and topic. When the list reached Logan, like everyone else, he searched for his name. He scanned the first eleven groups with no luck. *Oh no*, he thought, he was in the two-person group. He cursed his luck until he saw who he was paired with... *Emma James*. In the blink of an eye, Logan's misfortune turned into good fortune.

Logan had had a crush on Emma since the 2nd grade. He liked *everything* about her, from her caring yet carefree personality to her sandy-blond hair, green eyes, and dimples. In 2nd grade, they were the best of friends, but as they grew older, they'd drifted apart. Logan never really understood why that had happened, and he'd always regretted it.

This project was his chance to rekindle a connection before senior year ended and they both went their separate ways after graduation. And it didn't hurt that Emma was a terrific student. She was in Calculus with him, and was among the smartest students, if not *the* smartest, in the entire class. If Mr. Jackson was going to assign Logan a partner to work with on this project, Emma was the perfect one, at least from *his* perspective.

Logan was so excited that he almost forgot to look at the topic they had been assigned. He skimmed the page until he found it: The Secret Chamber of the White-Eyed Star God found inside the Copán Temple in Honduras five and a half years ago. "Hmm," he uttered quietly. He had never heard of the Copán Temple before.

Logan glanced in Emma's direction. Her hair was pulled back in a tight ponytail, and she was wearing dark navy-blue pants and a long-sleeve white blouse. For a brief moment, their eyes made contact. She acknowledged him, smiled, and returned her attention back to Mr. Jackson. From their brief exchange, Logan could not tell if she was happy Mr. Jackson had paired them together or not. When class ended, he decided to walk up to her to talk about their project.

Emma, still seated, was busy gathering her things and preparing to head to 5th-period when Logan approached.

"Hi, Emmy," he said.

"Emmy," she laughed, looking up at him. "You know, you haven't called me that since we were like, what, seven?" Nowadays, her close friends called her "Em," but it had been a long time since Logan qualified as that.

It was too late for him to take it back. "Right, sorry. I was wondering if you wanted to get together later for coffee or ice cream, so we can start on the project." *Ice cream*? What was he thinking? Like Emma said, they weren't seven anymore.

Emma smiled and replied, "Did you just ask me out on a date or to get together for the class project because when a guy asks a girl out for ice cream, it's usually a—"

"No, no, for sure for the project, I meant for..."

"I don't know Logan, it sounded like you asked me out on a date..."

"I, um..."

"Logan, chill. I'm messing with you."

Logan laughed awkwardly, partially relieved, partially embarrassed, and partially disappointed she didn't just say, "Yes."

Emma stood up. "I can't today. I have AP test prep after school and too much homework tonight."

"How about tomorrow?"

"Can't. I've got plans with Chad."

Ugh, Chad Peters, the 6'3" hunky, blond-haired, blue-eyed football team captain with a football scholarship to the University of Virginia Southern. Logan looked over at Chad who was busy fist pumping his buddies. Chad bragged around school about dating Emma although it remained an unconfirmed rumor. Emma's comment suggested there might be truth to it.

"Why don't we figure it out later?" she said, trying to break the scheduling stalemate.

"Yeah, we can text or something..."

"You're going to need my number for that," Emma replied. She hesitated for a second, then said, "Here, hand me your phone." He unlocked his phone and gave it to her. She quickly programmed her number into his phone and sent herself a text message so she had his number, too. "There! All done. We'll figure it out later, then."

"Great, it's a date," responded Logan. "I mean, um, text me later and we can figure out what *date* is good for you." *Good save, you idiot*, he said to himself.

Emma grinned. "You are so weird sometimes." She always found Logan awkward, in a cute harmless kind of way. "Okay, I'll text you tonight after my AP class. Bye." She grabbed her things, waved and walked off.

Before he could make things worse, Logan left class and headed to 5th-period P.E. where a grueling push-up-a-thon awaited him. He hoped his last few words had made everything less embarrassing. It could have been worse, he considered, not much, but definitely worse.

Chapter 3 – A Head Start

Monday evening wore on and still no word from Emma, not that she promised to text Logan at a specific time or anything. Rather than stare at his phone, Logan focused on his homework. Later, when his text message chime sounded, he scooped his cell phone up from the kitchen counter only to see that it was his mom:

> "Hi dear. #Home late again# There r leftovers in fridge. #Hugs N kisses when I get home# luv you ♡#"

Logan sighed. He felt bad for her. Here it was, a random Monday night in October, and the restaurant *still* had her working late… and they had not even gotten to the holidays yet. Once Thanksgiving rolled around, forget about it. Logan doubted he would see her at all. He decided to cheer her up:

> "Got it, mom. Too sick to my stomach to eat from all the drinking and smoking going on over here. Crazy party!! Will try to kick everyone out before you get home so you can get some sleep. Luv u 2"

Logan put down his phone, amused by his own response and hoping he put a smile on her face. She deserved a break time grin.

It was time for dinner. Logan went to the refrigerator in search of the leftovers his mom had mentioned. If his mom working at an upscale Manhattan restaurant had one perk, it was the nightly leftovers. Tonight, Logan would be enjoying a $55 serving of day-old butternut squash tortellini with dates and chestnuts. When the microwave beeped, he retrieved his fancy reheated entrée and plopped down at the kitchen table with his laptop.

He decided it was time for him to look up this Copán Temple thing, so it at least sounded like he knew what he was talking about the next time he spoke to Emma. He wanted to be ready to bring *something* to the conversation besides awkward comments, given how well that had worked out for him earlier in the day. He cringed every time he thought about it.

Starting the project was easy enough. He simply typed the words, "secret chamber white-eyed star god copán temple honduras" into his browser's search bar and his project was underway. The results were more plentiful than he expected, pulling up three pages on a subject he had never heard of before today.

The top result was a *National Archeology Digest* article from December, five years ago, called "Ancient Mystery Found in the Honduras Rainforests - A Real Life Chamber of Secrets." "Interesting," he said out-loud.

The next search result read, "Mayan Mystery Uncovered, Without Uncovering the Mystery." Hmm, catchy title, intriguing. Several additional results followed, including an odd one called "Ancient Aliens and Ghosts - the Conspiracy at the Copán Temple," from the fringe website **www.aliensandghosthunters.com**. Seeing so many interesting links to check out on Page 1 of the search results, he saw no reason to check out the results on Page 2, at least not yet.

While Logan definitely planned to check out the **www.aliensandghosthunters.com** article later since it sounded entertaining, he decided to start with the first one on the list, the *National Archeology Digest* article, because it sounded like a credible source. He clicked the link.

The article started with a brief discussion of the Copán Ruins in western Honduras near the Guatemalan border. It described how the 2,000-year-old Mayan city was *the* capital of the Mayan empire from the 5th to the 9th centuries, and how its population slowly dwindled over time.

The article went on to talk about a Harvard professor by the name of Dr. Jonas Arenot who, during a research expedition to the Copán Ruins, discovered a hidden chamber inside the Copán Temple marked by hieroglyphics that meant, *"Chamber of the White-Eyed Star God."* The article, sparing no flare for the dramatic for the publication's readers, wrote:

> *Earlier this summer, Dr. Arenot's team bravely entered a secret tunnel that wove through the temple's cold, ancient stone into a large spherical room 40 feet in diameter. He led his team out onto an elongated stone platform that stretched all the way into the middle of the mysterious chamber. His team's footsteps echoed from the acoustics of the sphere they found themselves in. Cautiously inching their way toward the end of the stone catwalk and peering over the edge, it appeared like they were floating inside a globe.*
>
> *Closer examination by Dr. Arenot's team revealed even more wonders. Carved into the smooth, curved walls of the chamber were Mayan hieroglyphs - thousands of them - 18,194 to be exact. Not words or depictions of historical events or even deities, but hieroglyphic numbers. Rows and columns of numbers filled the entire sphere, up above, down below, to the left and right, everywhere, sparing no inch of rock within the cavern. Each of the numbers consisted of a unique four to seven-digit number between 0 and 3,600,000. For example, one segment of one row of Mayan hieroglyphs read, when deciphered: 13,780; 2,496,987; 2,702,337; 1,113,456; 873,056; and, 2,845,778.*

Dr. Arenot's revelation, unveiled at this year's International Archeology Symposium in Edinburgh, Scotland, drew praise and captured the imaginations of scholars across the entire international stage. Symposium attendees found the randomness of the numbers in the chamber, which appeared to have no order, sequence, or correlation to one another, particularly mesmerizing. On the opposite end of the cavern, across from the farthest tip of the platform, was a hieroglyphic doorway carved into the curved wall and the Mayan number glyphs for 0000 and 0000 etched above it. Experts at the Hieroglyphic Institute of North America estimate the hieroglyphs to be 500 to 700 years old. But what do these numbers mean? Why are they there? Why is there a hollowed globe hidden inside the Copán Temple? Who was the White-Eyed Star God?

According to the Dean of Harvard University's Archeology Department, Professor William Pushire, answers are forthcoming: 'Dr. Arenot is one of our finest and has always had our complete support. With the full weight of this University's resources, solving this age-old mystery is a certainty given Dr. Arenot's dedication to the pursuit of truth.' In an interview with Dr. Arenot himself, the professor reported that his team is working around the clock and that he hopes to decipher the meaning and purpose behind the numbers in the Copán Temple within the next six months. Dr. Arenot can be assured the international archeology community will be counting on it, no pun intended.

For a closer look at the photographs of the numbers recovered from the Copán Temple, <u>click here</u> and see if you can unscramble the ancient mystery. Discovery awaits you."

"*Wow*," Logan muttered to himself, echoing the same sentiment probably shared by scholars at the Symposium five years ago. He suddenly understood why Mr. Jackson had included this topic among the twelve he chose. If he was looking for topics where history could explain the *what* without the *why* or the *how*, the Copán Temple was a perfect choice.

Logan clicked on the article's link to the photographs of the number glyphs, wanting to see what they looked like. Unfortunately, the link took him to a page that said, "Page Not Found."

Undeterred, he hit the back button until he reached the original search results. He clicked on the next link. Oddly, the same thing happened. The page displayed the message, "Page Not Found." In fact, the only two links that didn't were the last two – "Ancient Aliens and Ghosts – Further Evidence from Beyond – the Conspiracy at the Copán Temple," and "Harvard Professor Discovers a Chamber that Mystifies Anthropologists."

The 'Harvard Professor' article essentially mirrored the *National Archeology Digest* article, pulling from the same source material but without any photographs. The "Ancient Aliens and Ghosts" article, on the other hand, offered some creative theories and another promising link to pictures of all 18,194 number glyphs *and* a page listing in order all of the number glyphs, conveniently translated.

The theories about the Copán Temple's number glyphs in the **www.aliensandghosthunters.com** article included ancient Mayan rituals, numbers counting the days until the end of the world, a portal to another planet through the hieroglyphic doorway opposite the catwalk, and a map to the heavens. All creative ideas for sure, not that Logan expected anything less from a website that once ran a story claiming the White House itself was a UFO. Stories like that made it hard to take anything on the site seriously. Still, it had a comprehensive set of pictures and a list of the number glyphs translated, so he clicked on the link. Incredibly, that link generated a "Page Not Found" message, too.

Unbelievable. Not possible. Logan found it more than coincidental that each of the links was down. Something felt amiss, fueling his interest in unraveling the mystery even more. Perhaps that was the real reason Mr. Jackson chose it.

Logan went back to the search results and clicked through to Page 2, then to Page 3, and onward until he went through them all and there were no more relevant results to look at. In every case, the basic information about the initial discovery was there along with some pictures of the secret chamber, but the few links claiming to have a comprehensive set of photos depicting *all* number glyphs produced the same error message, "Page Not Found." Although Logan did not want to say the word out loud, he couldn't help but think it… this had the look and feel of, well, a *conspiracy*.

As he finished his tortellini and leaned back, his phone rang. Still distracted by the mystery on his computer screen, he casually glanced over to see who was calling. When he saw who it was, he straightened up. Nearly jumped up was more like it. *It was Emma James*.

Chapter 4 – A Good Mystery

"Emma," Logan answered, sounding surprised.

"Expecting someone else?" she teased.

Trying to play it off, he responded, "No, it's just that…"

Emma did not wait for his answer. She was too excited. "Have you checked out our project? It's fascinating! A secret chamber, a mysterious set of numbers, and—"

"Missing webpages," interrupted Logan.

"I know, right? It's like straight out of a movie or something. But rather than knocking off all the witnesses, someone's knocked off all the webpages that might provide more information."

Logan laughed, finding her analogy entertaining. "Watch a lot of those dopey crime dramas where they solve everything in an hour, do you?"

"Actually, I do, thank you very much," she replied, her voice hardening.

"*Um...*" It was suddenly apparent to Logan that he had stuck his foot in it. It was one thing for him to be awkward, another thing entirely for him to be a jerk. "Sorry about that. I didn't mean to, um, what I'm trying to say is, sorry."

"Forget it," she said. "My dad's a huge mystery buff. When I was little, I used to watch the shows and read Nancy Drew mystery novels with him. He got me hooked on them, and lately, I've even gotten hooked on cryptography mysteries, too."

"Cryptography... what's that?"

"It's the study of codes and ciphers, writing, and solving them. I've always loved that stuff. Remember those decoder rings in the cereal boxes? I used to make my mom buy box after box just so I could collect those things. And when I was 8, I drove my dad crazy because I wanted to learn Morse code... I wouldn't leave him alone until he taught me how to do it. He seriously had to buy a book to teach himself first, just so he could show me how." Emma giggled slightly as she recalled the memories.

Logan chuckled. "You're like a teenage Sherlock Holmes," he commented.

"I'll take that as a compliment," responded Emma, smiling on her end of the line. "I was actually thinking of going to school to become a cryptologist someday."

"That's a thing? There are jobs out there for that?"

Emma laughed. "Yes, Logan, it's a thing... They don't make a lot of money, but whatever. It sounds interesting to me."

"Wow, that's awesome," he replied. He was impressed, impressed by her choice and by the fact that she already knew what she wanted to do with her life. He had not remotely tackled that question yet.

"I wish my parents thought so," said Emma.

Logan immediately picked up on her downtrodden tone. "What do you mean?"

"Let me put it this way," said Emma. "My dad's already lined up law internships for me over the winter and summer breaks with his law buddies." Emma's father was a big-time partner in a New York law firm. "He wants me to go to law school and take over his legal practice someday, whatever that means."

"Have you told him you don't want to do that?"

"I've tried a few times, but he always says the same thing… 'You can't live in New York on a cryptologist's salary,' or 'Time to grow up,' or his favorite, 'If I'm paying for college, you're going to law school.' And my mom kind of just goes along with it."

"Ouch," said Logan. He could hear the frustration in her voice. He did not know what it was like to have parents dictating his future like that. Logan and his mother were basically just trying to get by, and his father had always been totally out of the picture. Whatever he did after graduation was going to be based on what was in his bank account, not pleasing a parent.

"I know they just want what's best for me, but sometimes I just wish they…" Emma stopped herself, then abruptly changed the subject. "So, why do you think all of the sites are blocked?"

"I don't know," replied Logan. So much for him preparing in advance to be able to bring *something* more useful to the conversation than an, 'I don't know.'

"I read in an old online post in a user chat room on the **aliensandghosthunters.com** website that those numbers form a map."

"A map for what?" wondered Logan. "Hidden treasure?"

"Who knows. I also read that all of the webpage links going down is part of some government conspiracy to prevent us from learning the truth."

As crazy as it sounded, it wasn't that far-fetched. Logan had been thinking precisely the same thing only a few minutes earlier. "The truth about what, though?"

"Well, that's why we've got to get a look at the number glyphs," Emma responded.

"I've already poked around and all the links with pictures or transcriptions of the numbers are down, unavailable, or missing."

"Yeah, I had the same problem," replied Emma. "What about emailing that professor at Harvard? What was his name, Dr. Arenot?"

Logan thought about it. "That's not a bad idea." He loaded up Harvard's website, clicked through to the homepage for the School of Archeology, clicked on the faculty list and then, on Dr. Arenot's name. After finding his email address, they composed an email together:

To: Professor Jonas Arenot [jarenot@harvarduniversity.edu]

From: Logan [Logan33rocks@eznet.com]

Cc: Emma James [immj@zahoo.net]

Subject: School Project

Dear Dr. Arenot,

I am working on a high school history project with my partner, Emma James, about the secret chamber you discovered inside the Copán Temple. We can't find any links to view more than just a few pictures of the chamber. Do you have any recommendations as to where we can look to find pictures and a list of all the number hieroglyphs? Any help you can give us would be greatly appreciated. Your discovery is very fascinating, and we look forward to learning more about it. Thank you, Logan West and Emma James"

He hit send. Fifteen seconds of optimism later an *Out of Office* reply came back saying, "Dr. Arenot is currently out of the office on sabbatical. If you need immediate assistance, please contact the Office of Graduate Affairs."

"Well, that was short, sweet, and painful," lamented Logan. "Now what?"

"Do you always give up *this* easy? Come on, it's our first day on the job. There has got to be a way for us to look back at some of these old links."

Logan, spurred by her challenge, was determined not to disappoint. In fact, her comment had actually sparked an idea. Look back... *of course*, that was the answer.

"What about an archive site?" asked Logan.

Emma was not familiar with the term, so he explained.

"Archive sites store information found on webpages from the past for anyone to view. It's like they take a digital picture of the webpages by sending out 'robots' or 'web crawlers,' saving mirror images of the webpages as of the date the robots 'crawled' the site. I've looked back at sites on the internet several years old on one of those archive sites."

"That's great!" exclaimed Emma.

"Well, it doesn't always work. They don't catch everything. There're too many websites out there, or sometimes a webpage's coding prevents the robots from doing their thing, and most archive sites only store information dating back a couple of years because of the huge space requirements. But it's worth a try."

"See, that wasn't so hard. That's the type of thinking that's going to crack this case."

Emma's moderate compliment made Logan proud. Perhaps he was a worthy partner, after all.

"So how do we look at one of those archive sites?" asked Emma, more optimistic than she was a minute ago.

"I know a few. Hold on, let me email 'em to you so we can check them out together." He sent a short list of archive sites to her.

Simultaneously, they looked at the first couple of sites with Logan browsing on his laptop and Emma on her tablet. As Logan half-expected, the first three on the list did not go back far enough in time. The fourth did not capture any of the websites they needed because it was geared toward major sites, newspapers, and mainstream digital. But they scored with the last one, an archive site called www.thearchiver.com.

That one went back far enough in time and, according to its search index, captured the *National Archeology Digest* article and the **www.aliensandghosthunters.com** webpage on the Copán Temple. However, when they proceeded to the archive's links for the pages on the Copán Temple, nothing happened, *again.* The archive links were not working, either.

"Crap," Logan muttered.

"Damn it!!" cursed Emma.

Clicking through the site a little more, they realized none of thearchiver.com's "look-back" links for *any* archived websites worked anymore.

"How can that be?" complained Emma.

Poking around the site a bit longer, they found an "About Us" page saying the site was last updated three years ago. *Another dead end.*

"But the information's there, or, at least, it *was*. There's got to be a way to get it," griped Emma. "What if we just email whoever ran the site?"

Logan clicked back to the "About Us" page where he recalled seeing a "Contact Us" link. There was no phone number or physical address, which was typical for a website like this, but there was an email address - **info@thearchiver.com.**

"How about this?" asked Logan, sending a draft email to Emma that read:

"To Whom It May Concern,

We are interested in accessing information that was once available on your archiver.com webpage, but the links aren't working. Is there still a way for us to see the links? It's for a school project. If you could please let us know, we would greatly appreciate it.

Sincerely,

Emma and Logan"

"Looks good to me," she replied.

Logan sent the email. It took only thirty seconds to receive the dreaded bounce-back email:

An email you addressed to: info@thearchiver.com has not been delivered. Email Not Deliverable. Bad address or recipient email address is incorrect.

"*That* was predictable," Emma grumbled. In a weird way, that was precisely what both of them expected to happen.

Logan had another idea. "Why don't we check out who the website is registered to? Maybe we can track them down that way."

"Good idea," replied Emma.

36

Logan went to the trusty WhoseSiteIsItAnyway.com webpage where people could check out who a website's registered to. Entering thearchiver.com into the search bar, the information popped up. He read it out loud to Emma. "Bryan Callister, Website Design Solutions, 2709 S. 24th Street, Philadelphia, Pennsylvania."

After searching online for Callister and Website Design Solutions, they could find no active telephone numbers for him or for the company.

"Why don't we just go pay Callister a visit," suggested Emma.

Her comment caught Logan off-guard. "Are you serious? Really? Now?"

"No, not now, dummy. It's 11:15 p.m."

"Oh," Logan laughed, "because for a moment there..."

"Tomorrow, after school. We have an address. Philly's only an hour and a half from here by train. We could totally do this." Emma was excited by this project, and clearly, she loved a good mystery.

"I guess we have nothing to lose," said Logan, although he was confused about something. "But I thought you said you were hanging out with Chad after school tomorrow?"

Emma remained silent for a moment. Then, she responded, "Well, now I'm hanging with you, but on one condition: no questions about Chad. No dating talk. Friends, okay?"

After processing the not-so-subtle and mildly disappointing hint behind her words, he reluctantly replied, "Okay."

Emma was jazzed. "So, we're really doing this?"

"Yep." Logan could hardly believe it himself.

"It's late," said Emma, fighting back a yawn. "I'm going to sleep."

"Yeah, me too," Logan said, although he doubted he was going to get much sleep tonight.

"Good night," she said.

"Night."

Chapter 5 – Dewey's Lair

When the final bell rang at 3:15 p.m., Logan packed up his things and hightailed it out of class. He and Emma had agreed to meet in front of school so they could catch the 3:30 train to Philadelphia from Journal Square Station. Easterner 2197 would reach Philly's 30th Street Station at 5:17 p.m., leaving only a short fifteen-minute walk over the Market Street Bridge to their destination on 24th Street. Emma told her parents that she was getting together with her group to work on their history project after school and that she would be home late. She conveniently left out the small detail about how she was jumping on a commuter train to Philadelphia with Logan, but she figured as long as she got back by 9:30 p.m. or so, her parents would be none the wiser. As for Logan, given the hours his mom worked, she would never know.

Leaving school with Emma, Logan felt like the high bidder at an auction, meaning all eyes were on him, especially Chad's. Logan did not know what Emma had told Chad about their outing, but he didn't look happy. Logan caught a glimpse of Chad standing near his friends on the lawn outside of school, carefully watching them walk away. Emma, on the other hand, stared straight ahead. She never looked back.

Maybe it was luck or just a perfect plan, but they jumped onto Easterner 2197 just as the doors were closing. They made their way down the middle aisle until they found two unoccupied adjoining seats. With huge smiles on their faces, they sat down next to each other and started talking as the train pulled away from the station.

"That was fun!" said Emma, slightly winded, referring to their quick escape from school and mad dash to the train station.

"Just like when we were kids running around the neighborhood," replied Logan, "well, until your family upgraded to the better side of the tracks, anyway."

"God, that seems like such a long time ago," reminisced Emma. "Those days were fun. How old were we back then?"

"I don't know, maybe 8 or 9. When did your family move away?"

"End of 5th grade, I think," said Emma.

"Hey, last night when you were talking about reading Nancy Drew novels with your dad, that totally reminded me of the birthday party you had in 3rd or 4th grade, the Nancy—"

"Wow, you remember that?" A huge grin blossomed on Emma's face.

"How could I forget the Nancy Drew Mystery Birthday Party, where we all had to solve the mystery of the missing birthday cake."

Emma giggled. "That's so funny you remember that party. My dad planned it all out. He hid clues around the house, created little maps for everyone, and broke everyone up into pre-arranged teams… boy girl… boy girl…"

"And you got paired with Chad, if I recall," said Logan.

"Oh my god, I can't believe you remember that, too. You've got a good memory."

"Yeah." In truth, Logan had never really forgotten it. After all, Emma was his first crush. Watching Chad get paired with her was not the kind of thing a brokenhearted 9-year-old forgets.

"I think my dad had an agenda for me, even back then."

"Totally. Everyone was pretty convinced your dad planned everything out to try to make sure you found the cake first."

"I guess not much has changed," said Emma, only half-joking. "So, who'd you get paired with?"

"I think it was Kate... what was her name, the red-headed girl... Kate O'Kelly?"

"O'Reilly!" said Emma excitedly. "Kate O'Reilly, that's right, I remember her. Didn't you guys get stuck in the closet looking for the cake, in the complete dark?"

"Yep, but only because someone locked us inside and turned out the lights. We never did find out who did it. We were stuck in there for forever because no one could hear us."

"That's because my dad was blasting his music over the radio. He was definitely having fun, almost like it was his own party!"

"No one even realized we were gone until your parents started cutting the cake."

"Kate always used to tell everyone that you guys kissed when you were in the closet, at least, that was the rumor among the girls, anyway. She was pretty possessive over you for the rest of the school year. Actually, I think she claimed you for the following year, too!"

Logan laughed. "I guess that explains why all the girls stayed away from me. Whatever happened to her, anyway?"

"I don't know. I think her parents got divorced and she moved to California with her mom. Let's look her up on Instagram or Facebook, see if she's on there." Emma immediately pulled out her phone and started scanning various social media apps. After searching for a minute, Emma said, "Ooohh, I found her. She's pretty. I'm going to send her a friend request and a DM about you, see if I can rekindle that flame." Emma laughed and started typing away.

"Would you stop it!" snapped Logan, reaching over to try and grab Emma's phone out of her hands.

"Hey, I'm just..." Emma was now laughing too hard to finish her sentence. "Okay, okay, I'm just kidding." Emma chuckled some more. "So, what really did happen in the secret closet?"

"Oh, you know, we talked about politics, about the future, what kind of girl I wanted to marry..."

"Really?"

"No! I was 9. I have no idea what we talked about. All I know is that there was no kissing."

"Too bad. You missed your chance, because I really did find her, and she's gorgeous now."

Suddenly, Logan was curious, and he started reaching for her phone. "Okay, fine, let me see her..."

"Nope, too late, I've already closed the apps," teased Emma with a smirk, pulling her phone far away from him. "You snooze, you lose."

Logan was grinning.

"What?" asked Emma, noticing the conspicuous expression on his face.

"Nothing, it's just, it's been a long time since we hung out like this."

"Yeah, it really has..." Emma felt guilty. She knew it was partially her fault. After her family "upgraded" to a better neighborhood, as Logan put it, her parents, but really more her dad, discouraged her from spending time with her old friends on the "wrong" side of the tracks, and they certainly didn't make it easy for her. Then, they sent her to a fancy new private middle school starting in 6th grade. The only reason she was back in public high school, at all, was that her dad had heard from one of his partners that attending a public high school would make it easier for her to get into a fancy college because it would make her look like less of a silver-spoon kid. After sharing a brief moment of eye contact with Logan, Emma asked, "Uh, so, are you going to the college fair next Monday night?"

"Nah, I don't think so."

"Why not?"

"If I go to college, I'm going to Jersey CCC next year. Don't really see the point in going to the fair."

"What do you mean, 'If I go'? You've to go to college. You're way too smart."

"Bill Gates, Steve Jobs, they didn't graduate from college..."

"So, you think you're Bill Gates, huh?"

"I'm pretty good with computers, if I may say so myself." If there was one thing Logan was good at, it was computers. They had always been an interest of his.

"Logan, I'm serious. Gates, Jobs, those guys are, like, one in a trillion."

"It's a money thing. I'm going to start at community college, take some computer classes, and see where I'm at after two years.

Maybe transfer if I can or start my own company so I can make some money to help my mom out."

"Have you talked to Mr. Grove about scholarships?"

"Yeah. He says my grades are good, but they're not good enough for a scholarship, and I don't really have any extracurriculars on my resume besides occasionally tutoring elementary school kids in math."

"Didn't you used to play soccer? You were like the best one in the neighborhood."

"Not as good as you," Logan responded, throwing her a compliment. Emma was, by far, the best soccer player out of all the girls on the block. It was one of the first little things about Emma that made Logan crush on her, that, and she was also his first friend when he moved to the neighborhood, and always, his most loyal.

"Hah, right. Thanks. Still not as good as you. Do you play in a league? Maybe you can put that down."

"No. I stopped in 8th grade." Just another thing that fell by the wayside when money got tight at his house.

"Oh."

"I've actually applied for a few scholarships that Mr. Grove thought I had a chance of qualifying for—"

"Well, that's good!"

"...but I didn't get any of them."

"Ugh. That stinks," replied Emma. "What about financial aid?"

"Paying back student loans for the rest of my life? No, thank you."

She didn't know what else to say. She felt bad for him, and even a little embarrassed, considering the expensive private colleges her parents had her applying to, which they were more than willing to pay for. After a short period of awkward silence, Emma said, "Speaking of computers, what should we say when we get to Website Design Solutions? I was thinking that you know more about these archive sites than I do, so maybe you can start with some of the technical talk and then, we see what happens."

"*If* the address for Website Design Solutions is even good." Deep down, Logan worried it wasn't.

"Hey!!" snapped Emma. "Come on, let's think positively. You're putting a bad vibe out there."

"I'm just saying the chances that this company is still at this address aren't great. Web companies like this don't use real addresses most of the time. It's probably a mailbox place or something like that."

"You know, Logan, that would have been useful feedback *last* night," uttered Emma. For a moment, they sat there quietly. Then, Emma had an idea. "Hey... why don't we pull up a street view image of the address? Maybe we can see what's there."

Logan quickly pulled up the street view image on his phone. "*Phew*, it's a storefront for a place called Dewey's Comic Books and Hobby Shop. Looks like the kind of place a web designer might hang out."

They exhaled a sigh of relief.

Emma smacked Logan's arm playfully. "You see? I told you, you've got to be more positive. Stop assuming everything's going to go wrong all the time."

Emma was, without a doubt, right. She was one of the most positive people he had ever met. He, on the other hand, always tended to assume the worst, a bad habit probably ingrained in his subconscious ever since his father abandoned him. He tried to make light of it. "And now you're gonna tell me you've got good parking karma, too?"

Emma smiled. "Well, *actually...*"

"Okay, okay. I get the point. Positivity. I'm going rogue positive." He was not quite sure what he meant by that, but it sounded good, so he just blurted it out.

"That's the spirit. I like that, 'rogue positive.' I've got to remember that one."

The rest of their train ride, they reminisced about the past, talked about the future, and about everything in between except Chad Peters and dating. Logan steered clear of those topics, honoring Emma's request from last night, and as it turned out, he was glad he did because, for the remainder of the train ride, they were friends again just like old times. Logan almost imagined some sparks between them at times, but he figured it was just his imagination.

They arrived at Philly's 30th Street Station at 5:14 p.m., a few minutes early. They got off the train and headed for 24th Street, crossing the Market Street Bridge over the Schuylkill River underneath a darkening late afternoon sky with the sun beginning to set. Right around 5:30 p.m., they arrived at Dewey's Comic Books and Hobby Shop. It was open until 8 p.m.

When they entered the store, it was like walking into another world. Shelves stacked with action figures and brightly colored comic books organized by genre, theme, and superhero took up one side of the store. On the other side, model trains, dollhouses, miniature furniture, paints, board games, figurines, remote-controlled cars and planes, you name it. If it had a subculture or underworld, it was in here.

A young, dark-haired, twenty-something-year-old male wearing jeans and a Grateful Dead t-shirt stood at the counter in the middle of the store. Emma and Logan approached him, futilely trying to remain inconspicuous among the two or three other customers milling about.

"How can I help you?" asked the shop clerk whose name tag read "Zack." He eyed them up and down.

"Is Bryan here?" Logan politely inquired.

"Maybe," Zack replied.

Really, Emma thought, finding Zack's caginess completely unnecessary. After assessing the situation, she decided to apply some female charm.

"Is Bryan here? I really need to talk to him." Emma gave him a favorable glance.

"Are you his girlfriend?"

Taken aback, Emma responded, "*What?* No. I just want to talk to him."

"Because it'd be really cool if you were." He snorted under his breath.

Emma was running out of patience. "Seriously, can I talk to him or…"

"Yeah, let me call him." He buzzed an intercom, then spoke into the phone, "Hey dude, there's a *girl* up here to see you."

A tall, skinny, curly-haired blond kid, only slightly older than Zack, walked out of an office at the back of the store and headed toward the counter. He wore tennis shoes, blue jeans, and an untucked black Metallica t-shirt. After checking out the two teenagers who were asking to see him, he inquired, "How can I help you?"

Emma replied, "Are you, Bryan Callister?"

"Yeah, I'm Bryan Callister."

Logan shot right into it. "We were hoping you could help us access some information on your archiver site."

Zack jumped back in, asking, "Are you guys with the Feds?"

Bryan backhanded him in the shoulder. "Dude, they're like teenagers, you idiot." He looked back at Logan and Emma. "Sorry about my watchdog. It means well." Zack cowered slightly and stepped back.

Logan and Emma exchanged a glance. Perhaps there was more to their conspiracy theory than they thought.

"We need to see some archived website pages for a school project," Logan said, thinking his request was easy enough.

Bryan appeared to consider helping them but then said, "I'm sorry. I haven't operated that site for years."

Logan wasn't satisfied. "Don't you have the server tucked away somewhere on an external hard drive or something like that?"

Although Emma was sure Bryan nodded his head *yes*, he responded, "Nope, I don't have it anymore. I deleted it for storage reasons to house other projects. Sorry, I can't help you. If you need anything else, Zack can assist you." Without saying another word, Bryan started walking away toward his office at the rear of the store.

Logan looked at Emma and shrugged his shoulders as if to say, "What now?"

Emma mouthed back the words, "Let's go," and motioned with her green eyes and a subtle head nod in Bryan Callister's direction. Once Logan realized what she was trying to convey, they took off after Bryan who had a twenty-foot head start.

They caught up to Bryan in his office and followed him inside. After they entered, Bryan shouted, "Hey, look, I told you I got rid of everything," while at the same time closing the "Employees Only" door behind them.

Once the door was fully shut, Emma asked, "What's with all the cloak and dagger stuff?"

Bryan ignored her question and responded with one of his own. "So, is the school thing really true? What school do you guys go to?"

Hoping to smooth things out quickly, and seeing no harm in answering Bryan's question, Logan replied, "Yeah… Jersey North High School in Jersey City."

His response surprised Bryan. "You sure came a long way just to talk to me about a school project."

"Can you help us?" asked Logan, sensing he could.

"Well, that depends," Bryan replied, looking at them both very carefully, "on whether you can help me."

"Um, how?" asked Emma. "I mean, this is only for a school report, it's not like we're going to do something illegal or anything like that for a grade."

"Nothing illegal… at least, I don't think it is." Bryan paused to think about it, giving Emma and Logan even more cause for concern.

"You're not sure if it's illegal?" Emma wondered, worrying about doing something that might hurt her ability to get into college.

"It's simple. $50 and if I help you, you promise to keep it a secret. I could get in trouble."

Staying quiet? That's it? Logan and Emma looked at each other. $50 and silence didn't sound so bad, so Logan responded, "Yeah, sure, we can do that. No problem."

"I'm serious, no one can know."

"Fine, whatever," said Emma, looking at Bryan, "but *why?*"

Bryan appeared hesitant to answer, but after enduring a few seconds of her gaze, the floodgates opened.

"Three or four years ago, I got a nasty letter from the U.S. Department of Justice – Internet Fraud Division, packed with a whole bunch of threats about how thearchiver.com was archiving information for illegal websites, aiding and abetting illegal activity. I really didn't understand what they were talking about, but they cited a long list of Federal criminal statutes and FCC regulations my website was supposedly violating. They said they were going to impose a $100,000 fine against me as the website operator for the first violation, but that they would suspend enforcement and put nothing on my record if I agreed to disconnect all of my archive links. They said a second violation carried a $500,000 fine and up to five years in prison."

The revelation stunned Logan and Emma.

"Did you get a lawyer?" asked Emma. With her dad being a lawyer, she knew he had rights.

"No, I was seventeen at the time. My mom freaked out and made me take the archives down like the Feds asked. Honestly, I'm not even sure which website in my archives caused the problem. Occasionally, my archive robots picked up sites that were gateways to the dark web. Figured it was probably one of those."

"Damn, that's messed up," said Logan.

"Tell me about it. I wasn't making any money with the site anyway, so I didn't fight it. I just deactivated the links and the Feds confiscated the primary and backup servers. The only reason the base mainframe's still up at all is because the site still pulls in a good amount of traffic. I have advertising for a few of my other websites on there and sometimes I get some click-throughs."

"Do you still have *any* archive servers left, if they took everything?" asked Logan, concerned their trip to Philly was about to be a bust.

Bryan looked at him slyly. "They never asked me whether I had a backup for the backups."

Logan grinned. Emma smiled.

"Well, I promise we won't say anything to anyone," said Emma.

"So, what are you guys looking for anyway that caused you to travel two hours by train after school on a weeknight in rush hour?"

Logan handed him a piece of paper with the *National Archeology Digest* and the **www.aliensandghosthunters.com** information written down. Bryan stared at it for a moment.

"Unfortunately, I can't help you with the *National Archeology Digest* one. I held a marathon Dungeons & Dragons tournament in here one-weekend last year and idiot Zack spilled soda all over the server for archived sites starting with the letters L to Z. Corrupted the whole thing. But I should still have this other one you're looking for."

Bryan stood up and reached for a printer supplies box sitting on an upper shelf behind his desk. He brought the box down to desk level and started removing toner cartridges until he found what he was looking for, an external server for archived sites starting with the letters "A to K."

"So why do you need my archives anyway?" he asked.

"Because all of the website links we need for our project are missing, deactivated, or unavailable. It's like they're gone."

"Hmm, that's weird. Let's see what I've got." He sat at his desk, pulled a cable from the back of the computer and plugged it into the server.

"How long have you worked here?" asked Logan, trying to make small talk.

"I've been working at Dewey's since I was 13 and hanging out here even longer than that. Practically grew up in this place."

"You the manager?" asked Logan.

"Nope," replied Bryan, "I'm the owner."

"Owner?" uttered Logan, surprised. The comment also piqued Emma's interest.

"Yep. When Dewey died a year and a half ago, he left the whole store to me. I don't think he had anyone else to leave it to, and I was the closest thing he had to family. He trusted me to love this place."

"That was really cool of Dewey to do that," Logan replied.

"Thanks. Dewey was *very* cool," said Bryan. Right after the words left his mouth, his computer screen turned on. After a few hyper-fast keystrokes, the server lit up. He typed in the website and date parameters, and up popped an archived version of the **www.aliensandghosthunters.com** webpage.

"Is this what you guys are looking for?" asked Bryan.

"Yes!" exclaimed Emma. With some finger pointing, she directed him to the pages about the Copán Temple, and sure enough, pictures of *all* the number glyphs and the list transcribing all 18,194 numbers, were there. "That's it, they're all there! Can you get those for us?"

"Of course," Bryan replied with confidence, as if there was never a doubt. With no trouble at all, he downloaded the files and copied them onto a small thumb drive for them to keep.

"Is that it, then?" Bryan asked.

"Yes, this is awesome! Thank you so much," said Logan. "Can I Venmo the $50 to you?"

Bryan waived him off. "Forget about it, you guys are cool."

"Really?" asked Emma. "You're so sweet." She gave him a hug, which he seemed to appreciate way more than $50. He blushed.

"Hey, let me know how it turns out, okay?" said Bryan.

Logan gave him a final fist pump.

And that was it. They took off and raced back to the train station, catching the 7:15 p.m. to Journal Square Station with an expected arrival time of 9:00 p.m. The whole way home, Emma could not be more pleased with how well their plan had worked out. Logan actually thought she was giddy.

"Good job tonight," she said to Logan, running her fingers through her hair.

"You, too," he replied. "We make a good team." Logan held his breath anticipating her response. She just looked at him and smiled, and she didn't disagree. They did not talk much for the remaining ride home, each of their minds wandering and both a little tired, too.

When they got off the train at Journal Square Station, they called an Uber. The Uber driver proceeded to Emma's house first because it was on the way, although Logan would have insisted they do so even if it wasn't.

As Emma got out of the car, Logan called her name before she closed the door. "Emma," he said, causing her to poke her head back into the door which was still slightly ajar. "I had a lot of fun today."

"Me too," replied Emma, smiling, "but my friends call me Em."

Chapter 6 – 18,194 Questions

Tuesday evening after dinner, while seated at the kitchen table, Logan copied the files off Bryan Callister's thumb drive to his laptop, uploaded them to a file-share link, and emailed them to Emma. In the email's subject header, he wrote "Clues for the Cryptographer in You." He figured she'd appreciate the reference.

Although they had agreed to go over everything after school tomorrow, Logan could not wait to look at the files. With his empty dinner plate still sitting beside him, Logan pulled up the photographs of the hidden chamber. The photographs included, in high-res detail, pictures of the spherical room and hundreds of close-ups of the hieroglyphic numbers ranging from 0 to 3,600,000.

Logan found it astonishing how scholars had learned to decipher Mayan number hieroglyphs over the years. Curious, he decided to try a few himself. He toggled back and forth between the Copán Temple photographs and a Mayan number glyph website that showed him how to do it. After attempting to convert a couple on his own, and having 18,194 to go over, Logan eventually decided to check out the list with all of the number glyphs translated that someone else had already prepared.

Looking at the list, like previous scholars, Logan wondered why none of the numbers exceeded 3,600,000. What was the significance of 3,600,000? Did it refer to the number of days left until the end of the world or something like that? Logan recalled reading once that the Mayans had a doomsday calendar and he even remembered Hollywood making a movie about the end of the world based upon that doomsday myth.

He looked it up online and found an article explaining how Mayan mythology referred to the lifecycle of humanity beginning and *ending* on the Mayan calendar every 1,872,000 days. The last lifecycle ended on December 21, 2012, with a new 1,872,000-day cycle commencing the following day. Whatever the mythology was behind the doomsday calendar, humanity obviously survived, and the number 1,872,000 did not correlate with any of the numbers found in the Copán list.

Logan considered whether 3,600,000 indirectly referred to 360 and whether that was the number of days in a Mayan calendar year, although what would he do with all of the extra zeros left at the end after 360? Ultimately, it did not matter because, according to the internet, the Mayans followed a "Haab" cycle of 365 days just like modern calendars, except theirs was spread out over nineteen months. So that wasn't the answer either.

Logan stared at the numbers, muttering to himself, "Think, Logan, *think*." He was frustrated, coming up with the same dead-end ideas, going around and around in circles. And then it hit him...

"*Circles*... that's it!" he yelped. A full rotation around a circle was 360°. But again, with the number 3,600,000, what would he do with all of the extra zeroes after 360? Perhaps there was supposed to be a decimal point after the 360 instead of all the commas everyone just assumed were supposed to be there. Maybe the numbers on the list reading 3,600,000 and 98,768 were really meant to read 360.0000 and 9.8768, with a decimal point in the thousandths place, leaving four digits to the right.

With this new theory in mind, he studied the numbers again. This time around, he noticed a *pattern* he had not previously picked up on. Logan noticed that the numbers alternated in range. *Without exception*, a number in the range of 0 to 90 or 270 to 360 *always* preceded a number from 0 to 360. Why would that be, he wondered?

Logan got up and walked over to the counter to grab a piece of paper and a pencil. He returned to the kitchen table and wrote down a few of the numbers in order so he could look at them on paper, a technique that often helped him to solve problems in math more effectively. He inserted the decimal point, leaving four digits to the right, and after doing that, the numbers read:

9.8768
1.3363

86.2019
314.5775

279.8108
187.8447

66.7778
231.2845

5.2748
341.0906

True to form, the first number in the alternating pattern fell in the range of either 0 to 90 or 270 to 360, while the second number ranged from 0 to 360. Logan called back up the high-res pictures of the Copán Temple on his computer screen to look at them again. Then, it occurred to him...

"It's a sphere," he said, having his second epiphany in the span of five minutes. Was the shape of the room itself a clue? Remembering back to his geography days, plotting points around a sphere or a globe required *two* numbers, not one, including a latitude (for north-south) and a longitude (for east-west). Were these Copán numbers coordinates for plotting points around the globe?

He immediately went to **www.geography.com** to brush up on plotting coordinates. Based on what he was reading, if these numbers were coordinates, the alternating pattern would make sense for several reasons.

First, when plotting coordinates around the globe, 360° represented a full rotation around the planet, explaining why the numbers never exceeded 3,600,000 or 360.0000.

Second, if the alternating numbers really were latitudes and longitudes, geography.com explained why the first alternating number *always* fell in the range of 0 to 90 or 270 to 360. Cartographers, when plotting a northerly direction to head up from the equator to the North Pole, used a directional plot of +0 to +90 degrees N (which converted to 0.0000 to 90.0000 using the modified Decimal Degree System (*m*DDS)); and a directional plot of -0 to -90 degrees S to head down from the equator to the South Pole (which converted to 270.0000 to 360.0000 on the *m*DDS). *That* was why the first alternating number in the pattern always fell between 0 to 90 or 270 to 360. It had to be.

Likewise, geography.com explained how cartographers plotted the east-west direction as + or - 180 degrees (which converted to 0.0000 to 360.0000 on the *m*DDS). According to the website, the zero degrees east-west point on the globe was based on the Prime Meridian which divided the planet in half, located at the equator in the Atlantic Ocean in the Gulf of Guinea off the west coast of Africa. Everything west of that was the Western Hemisphere and everything east, the Eastern Hemisphere.

It all added up... these were *coordinates*, 18,194 of them, he was sure of it. There could be no other explanation. And that is exactly what he texted Emma at 11:45 p.m. Tuesday night.

Chapter 7 – Technical Difficulties

"**AR**E U SURE???" texted Emma.

"+ Positive +" he responded.

His cell phone rang. Logan answered without looking who it was. He knew.

"Hi," he said.

While still lying in bed, Emma quietly said into the phone, "I was almost asleep, so I hope this is as interesting as it sounds, otherwise—"

"It is."

Emma sat up. "Okay, I need to understand this... why do you think these numbers are coordinates?"

Logan explained, walking her through everything he had just reviewed, looked at, and concluded. Emma listened patiently, yawning a few times. After considering his reasoning, she agreed. He was right, these numbers appeared to be coordinates… but for what?

"I guess there's only one way to find out and that's to enter them into a coordinate database or something like that," said Emma softly, trying to keep her voice down so she didn't wake her parents.

"It's not that easy," Logan replied. "If these numbers really are coordinates, then we first have to figure out what point on the globe represents absolute zero degrees latitude and longitude, so we can determine where to start from."

Emma didn't see the issue. "What's so hard about that? Can't we just look at a map?"

"When I was looking this up earlier, I read that cartographers established the modern-day Prime Meridian at an International Meridian Conference in 1884. I'm just assuming, but I doubt they had the Mayans' worldview in mind when they voted on it one hundred and thirty years ago, especially when the Mayans had been gone for hundreds of years by then." Logan punched up details for the modern Prime Meridian on his computer screen and read a portion out loud:

> *Modern cartographers use an 'absolute zero' point reflecting zero degrees latitude and longitude, at the equator, 611 km south of Ghana, 1,078 km west of Gabon off the west coast of Africa. This is the reference meridian point of the Global Positioning System (GPS) operated by the United States Department of Defense and the International Terrestrial Reference System.*

"See what I mean?" asked Logan rhetorically.

"Yeah," replied Emma. "So, where on the globe do we start from, then? We definitely can't plot out these coordinates using... what did you call it a second ago, an 'absolute zero' point, chosen at some conference hundreds of years after the Mayans vanished."

"Exactly," stated Logan.

"Let's pull up the pictures of the Copán Chamber," suggested Emma. "There's got to be something in there that helps us." Emma got out of bed and walked over to her backpack lying on her bedroom floor to retrieve her computer. She pulled it out and returned to her bed. Sitting on top of her covers with her legs crossed, Emma booted up the computer and opened the files Logan had sent earlier. She started looking through the photographs of the Copán Chamber.

Logan did the same. He scanned the walls, following the spherical chamber's hypothetical equator all the way around. He stopped when he got to the hieroglyphic doorway carved into the wall opposite the stone catwalk.

"What about the 0000 and 0000 carved above the hieroglyphic doorway?" asked Logan. "Think about it, why are those there? All the other numbers in the chamber are hyper-specific down to the thousandth decimal point, randomized like someone dropped the digits into a blender. But above the doorway etched into the stone are two perfect numbers, 0000 and 0000, separated from the rest."

Emma was intrigued. "Are you suggesting we treat the Copán Temple as 'absolute zero'?"

"That is exactly what I am suggesting. Maybe they intended the 0000's carved above the hieroglyphic doorway as an instruction to treat the Copán Temple as absolute zero, .0000 by .0000."

"That would make sense, but... can we do that?" wondered Emma.

"Sure, why not?" Logan looked up the Copán Temple's location on Google. "The Copán Temple is located at 14.8487 by 270.8532. All I need to do is adjust the coordinates to plot out using the Copán Temple as absolute zero rather than the modern point. It's a simple adjustment really." He did a few quick calculations, and then explained, "I can just copy the numbers from the list and paste them into Excel, and then enter a formula into Excel that subtracts 14.8487 from the latitude coordinates and adds 89.1468 to the longitude coordinates."

"You know how to do that?" asked Emma. "I suck at Excel."

"I'm pretty good with it," Logan bragged. "I'll go in and do it tonight. And then, we just need to enter all 18,194 numbers into a coordinate plotting program."

"Oh," said Emma, less impressed than she was a few seconds earlier, especially after realizing the time-consuming catch. "That could take weeks and with school... it's not like either of us has time to do that. I mean, think about it. Even if we enter in, say, eight numbers a minute, with 18,194 numbers, that's going to take us like, what, forever." She pulled up the calculator app on her phone, divided 18,194 by 8, and said, "It's gonna take us more than 2,275 minutes... that's almost *forty hours* of typing time alone, assuming we can maintain an eight numbers-a-minute pace without our fingers falling off and without interruption."

She had a point. Logan thought about it some more. "I've got a great idea," he said.

"I do love great ideas."

"We've already got all of the numbers on a list, right?"

"Yeah, I suppose."

"After copying and pasting the numbers into an Excel spreadsheet, Excel will do the math and then, maybe there's a way I can just upload the spreadsheet into a coordinate plotting program so we don't have to type all of the coordinates in."

"I do like the sound of that, and not just because it's midnight," said Emma.

"I thought you might," replied Logan.

"Okay, if there's nothing left to talk about, let me just say you're a rock star, but I'm going to bed. And you should, too. We've got a pop quiz in English Lit tomorrow."

"Crap, how do you know that?"

"Ms. Silvestri tells me everything. It pays to be the teacher's fav sometimes."

"Seriously, no kidding. Thanks for the heads up. I won't stay up too much longer."

"I'll talk to you in the morning," said Emma.

"Yeah... same." He hung up.

Tempting his English Lit fate, Logan did exactly the opposite of what he told Emma he would do... he stayed up nearly all night working on the project. First, he copied the numbers on the Copán list and pasted them into an Excel spreadsheet. Then, he changed the numbers to treat the Copán Temple as 'absolute zero' by programming two formulas into Excel, one to recalibrate the latitude numbers and the other to recalibrate the longitude numbers. While it took him longer than expected, that proved easy enough.

The bigger challenge for him was finding a coordinate plotting program that allowed him to upload the Excel spreadsheet. He searched for hours. By the time 4 a.m. rolled around, he still had not found the right one. With his eyes getting blurry, he decided to take a quick five-minute break, resting his forehead in his arms...

Click!! When his wake-up alarm popped off at 6:45 a.m., he lifted his head. "Crap," he mumbled. He had fallen asleep, with his face ending up right on top of his keyboard. It seemed like he put down his head only seconds ago. He wiped the drool from the side of his mouth, hoping none of it leaked through the keys.

Logan got ready for school, dreading the English Lit quiz waiting for him when he got there. Unfortunately for him, English Lit was first-period, leaving no time for last-minute test prep triage. He was exhausted, hardly prepared, and it showed. He crashed and burned on the quiz as a result, not that he cared. He had other things on his mind, like making good on what he told Emma he could do.

Passing *that* test was the only test he really cared about, as the last two days had reignited his feelings for Emma in a big way. He couldn't stop thinking about her.

He spoke to Emma briefly throughout the day updating her as to his progress, but he really didn't have time to search the internet for plotting programs while at school. It was not until he got home later that he started looking again. Early Wednesday evening, he found it: a vacation planning program that allowed travelers to input or upload multiple-destination itineraries on a map using addresses or coordinates.

Within minutes, he successfully uploaded the Excel spreadsheet and watched with pride as the vacation program plotted out 9,097 coordinates over the entire global map. Since plotting coordinates required two numbers to compute, i.e., a latitude and a longitude, using all 18,194 Copán numbers, the program came up with exactly half, or *9,097* plotted coordinates. After cross-checking a few to confirm they plotted out correctly treating the Copán Temple as absolute zero, Logan emailed Emma instructions, his Excel spreadsheet, and a link to where she could download the vacation planning program.

She quickly responded, "Like I said, U R A ROCKSTAR!!! Will look at tonight. Having dinner now with my dad and some of his law buddies he wanted me to meet for the summer internship. Yuk (:"

Logan laughed, although dinner sounded like a good idea to him, too. He walked over to the refrigerator in search of Tuesday night's unsold restaurant special courtesy of his mom and pulled out a healthy piece of pan seared salmon with roasted fennel, Brussel sprouts, and a lemon potato purée. He reheated it, sat down on the couch, and began studying the coordinates map. There were 9,097 coordinates scattered around the world representing 9,097 intriguing possibilities. He did not yet understand how they all related to one another, but the night was young, and he was determined to find out.

Later that evening, after getting home from dinner, Emma checked out the instructions that Logan had sent. Once she got the coordinates up on her screen, she too marveled at the points plotted all over the world, seemingly sprinkled about the globe at random. She spent hours analyzing them from every conceivable angle, looking for some indication, *any* indication really, that they were coordinates. At 2 a.m. in the morning, she finally found what she was looking for, *proof*, and a little something extra… one of the 9,097 coordinates was *not* supposed to be there.

Chapter 8 – An Unexpected Answer

Logan was planning to talk to Emma about their project after school, but when he saw her sitting at her usual outdoor table with friends during lunch, he decided he could not wait. Instead of heading to where his friends were sitting, he stopped by Emma's table first.

"Hi," he said, failing to come up with anything more original.

Caught off guard, Emma responded with a subtle wave and a short *"Hi"* back. Her friends immediately began dissecting what was going on. Chad Peters, who was sitting right next to Emma, seemed very interested in the situation.

"Figured some cool stuff out for our project last night," said Logan, just now picking up on the stir his decision to approach Emma was causing. "Just wanted to let you know."

Emma said, "That's great. Talk later?"

"Um, yeah, that works," responded Logan, turning around. Bad timing. He should have just texted her. As he walked away, he heard Chad ask her what that was all about.

When Logan reached the table where his good friends Patrick and David were sitting, he sat down beside them, and threw his backpack under the table. "What's up?" he casually said, oblivious to the bewildered expressions on their faces.

"For a second there, I thought you were ditching us for some new friends," teased David.

"Who says I wasn't?" Logan countered.

"What was that all about, anyway?" asked Patrick.

"You know, the, um, the Mr. Jackson history project," responded Logan.

"Yeah, right," doubted Patrick. "You've had a thing for her since elementary school. You finally gonna do something about it?"

"Like Chad's ever going to let that happen," blurted David.

"Hey, what's Chad got that our boy, Logan, doesn't?" responded Patrick, coming to Logan's defense.

David was quick to reply, "Um, *everything*..."

"Thanks, man," said Logan.

"No problem," replied David with a grin, patting Logan on the back.

"So, what'd *Chad* say when you walked up?" asked Patrick.

"He didn't—"

"Hi guys," said Emma unexpectedly, sitting down next to Logan, catching the three of them off guard.

"Hey, Emma," responded Patrick and David in unplanned unison.

She immediately turned to Logan and said, "Hey, I'm sorry about that. It's just that everyone's a gossip at this school. I know, it's stupid. I should have—"

"Seriously, don't sweat it," interrupted Logan. "I know how people can be," he added, giving Patrick and David a subtle accusatory look.

Relieved, Emma said, "Thanks. Do you want to talk now?"

"Sure," Logan nonchalantly replied, trying to play it cool.

"Bye, guys," said Emma.

She got up and started walking over to an empty table off to the side of the lunch patio under a tree. Logan followed with his backpack, leaving his food and friends behind. As he walked away, Logan looked back and Patrick gave him a thumbs up. Logan quickly caught up to her.

"So, what did you find out last night?" asked Emma as she sat down at the table. Logan sat across from her.

"You first," he said, trying to be chivalrous. She didn't put up a fight.

"I didn't believe it when I saw it at first, but seriously, how did the Mayans do that 500 years ago, come up with that level of sophisticated math to plot out such precise coordinates to do this?"

"I know. Mapping out geographic coordinates around the Earth like that, it's incredible."

Emma looked at him and smiled. She had noticed something he missed. "Map of geographic coordinates around the Earth? Is *that* what you think it is?"

With a perplexed expression on his face, Logan responded, "Um… yeah, what else would it be?" He scratched his head trying to figure out what she was getting at.

She did not leave him hanging for too long. "Well, if you look at it—"

Emma was interrupted by, who else, Chad Peters. "Em, you forgot your food," he said in an assertive tone that sounded more like he was announcing himself. He placed her lunch down in front of her, trying to simultaneously process what they were talking about based on the few words he overheard.

Emma looked up at him and replied, "Thanks, Chad. So sweet."

"How's it going here?" Chad asked, sitting down without waiting for an invitation.

"Fine, good," Logan answered, not quite sure yet what Chad's intentions were.

"How've you been, Logan? We don't talk anymore," said Chad.

Logan's mind raced. His nerves kicked in along with some adrenaline. "Good!!" he exclaimed, trying to pretend everything was normal. Of course, it wasn't.

"What's it been, 2 or 3 years?" asked Chad.

"7 or 8, but who's counting..."

"Okay, boys, I think that's enough," Emma interjected, sensing the conversation escalating in tension. "Chad, thank you for my food. We'll talk after lunch, okay? Logan and I are just going to finish up really quickly."

Chad stood up, smirked and walked away.

"Don't worry about Chad," Emma commented. "He's just—"

"It's cool. I'm cool. All good," said Logan. "So, you were saying...."

Emma got right back on track. "Okay, I wasn't sure at first that we had it right or that these Copán numbers really were coordinates, but after studying them for a while, now I'm sure. They're definitely coordinates, but not for mapping out geographic coordinates around the Earth, even though they do plot out using Earth's geography."

"I don't understand," replied Logan, confused.

Rather than try to explain it to him, she decided to show him. She pulled her computer tablet out of her book bag and opened the vacation planning program with all of the coordinates displayed over the Earth's surface. She zeroed in on a small section of plotted coordinates over the Pacific Ocean. Pointing at them, she asked, "What does that look like to you?"

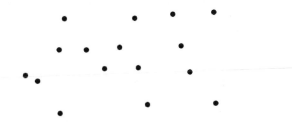

"I don't know. They look like random coordinates plotted out over the Pacific Ocean to me."

"The Big Dipper," she replied. As soon as the words left her mouth, he suddenly saw the pot-shaped constellation, too, in the middle of the cluster of coordinates. Using her index finger to connect twelve of the coordinates like she was painting by numbers, she ran her finger over each coordinate until she finished drawing the asterism that looked like a pot with an extended handle.

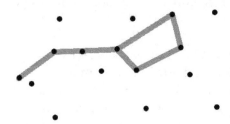

"Maybe it's a coincidence. There are more than 9,000 coordinates in this map," Logan said. "I'm sure if you look at chunks of them long enough, they will all start to look like something. It's like when you stare up at the clouds, there's always a shape to imagine up there."

"Alright, then what about this section of the map?" She zoomed in on another portion of the map showing approximately 21 coordinates grouped together over the southern tip of Brazil.

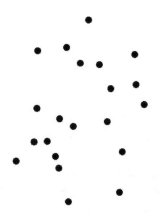

Looking at the pattern of coordinates, although Logan already suspected she was going to tell him there was another constellation in there, he still couldn't make out which one. "Who can tell?"

"It's the constellation Canis Major," she replied, referring to the Latin-named constellation that meant "greater dog." Like she did before, using her finger, she drew out the canine-shaped constellation by moving from coordinate to coordinate until it looked like a dog.

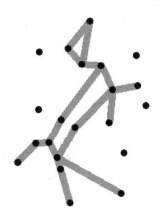

Emma now had Logan's complete attention. Somewhat shocked, he said, "Okay..."

"And what about this one right next to it?" She pointed to a collection of coordinates over the Atlantic Ocean with three coordinates in a row inclining slightly up to the right, in the center.

"Orion," said Logan, recognizing the three stars of Orion's Belt, all lined up in a row at the waist of the cosmic hunter known as Orion. Orion was a constellation depicting a hunter standing in set position, with a bow held in the hand of his outstretched left arm, and his right arm cocked back and up. He did not need her to finger-paint this one out for him. He could see the mythical warrior Orion clearly.

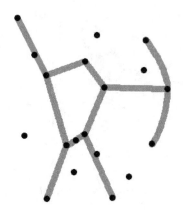

"Exactly." Emma closed her tablet. "This isn't a map of coordinates around the Earth. This is a star map created using the Earth's geography to plot it out. I compared it to a star map I found online and checked out a few more constellations and star clusters. The Copán map of coordinates plotted out over the Earth mirrors the star map, at least the sections I looked at."

"Holy crap," said Logan, astonished. "But how is that possible?"

"This is bigger than random numbers on a wall inside the Copán Temple, don't you see that? How in the world did the Mayans come up with the perfect geographic coordinates to map out the entire night sky using the Earth's geography, 500 to 700 years ago? Do you remember the name of the secret chamber discovered by Dr. Arenot?"

Logan replied, "Yep. Chamber of the White-Eyed Star God. Does the Copán map show all of the stars?"

"Glad you asked," she replied. "I looked that up last night, too. There are literally billions of stars in the night sky visible from Earth using telescopes and technology, but do you want to guess the number of stars visible in the night sky on a perfectly clear night with no light pollution, using only the naked human eye, according to the Academy of Stellar Sciences and Cartography?"

"That can't be," Logan uttered, anticipating what she was about to say.

"Yes, it can. *9,096…* and that's assuming your eyes can see the entire night sky at once from wherever you're standing, which, of course, you can't because on any given night, nearly half the stars are on the other side of the planet."

"9,096… but how did the Mayans get *that* right 500 to 700 years ago?"

"There are actually 9,097 coordinates in this Copán map, meaning one of them is not supposed to be there. After school today, you and I are going to come up with a plan to figure out which one."

Emma was calling the shots now and Logan kind of liked it. "Okay. Where do you want to talk?"

"Actually, I think you owe me an ice cream," she replied with a suggestive smile. He smiled back, and their plan was set.

After school, they went to Scoops, a popular self-serve ice cream shop a few blocks from school. As they ate their personalized ice cream creations, Emma asked, "Do you know how big this Copán story is?"

"Yeah, I do, but that Harvard professor who made the original discovery probably figured all of this out already, right?"

"Maybe," said Emma. "But if that's true, why isn't there any mention of it on the internet? I mean, how is it possible a discovery like this can go unmentioned anywhere online?"

"Maybe they took down those websites, too," speculated Logan.

"Yeah, probably," said Emma. She paused. "I have a question, but don't laugh at me. Promise you won't, okay?"

"I won't, I promise," agreed Logan, although he wasn't quite sure what he was getting himself into.

"Do you think this Copán map might be evidence that...," she stopped, too embarrassed to say what she was thinking. Then, she just let it out. "That aliens visited the Mayans hundreds of years ago? I know I sound crazy like I've spent too much time on the aliensandghosthunters.com conspiracy site, but this stuff is really incredible."

"You're right. Waaaayyyy too much time on that site and totally crazy."

"Hey, you jerk!!" she exclaimed, smacking him. "Shut up, I'm serious."

"Okay, okay. I'm just kidding," laughed Logan. "In all seriousness, from the little I've read, the Mayans were way advanced for their time. So, is it possible they actually solved the math to do this? Maybe. Wikipedia talks about the Mayans developing some of the most accurate pre-telescope astronomy in the world, but there's obviously something more to this... something interesting enough to cause someone to erase all of the evidence and websites."

"Then, you and I are going to figure out exactly what that *something* is, and to do that, we have to start by comparing the Copán map to a star map to figure out which coordinate should not be there."

Logan agreed. "How about this… I'll take the coordinates falling in the Western Hemisphere and you can take the Eastern?"

Emma nodded, and that was it. They had a plan to compare all 9,097 stars in the Copán map, one at a time, to see which coordinates tracked the stars in the online star map, and more importantly, to find the ONE coordinate in the map which did *not*.

Over the next week, the process was painstakingly slow, like looking for a needle in a haystack. They had to review and compare the maps one small quadrant at a time. It took a full seven days for them to complete their reviews. They did not talk much over that week, which disappointed Logan who, if he had it his way, would have talked to Emma every day. Instead, they only texted each other at night to provide short updates on their progress.

A couple of times, they found a coordinate in the Copán map that did not appear to track with the star map. On those occasions, their communications were livelier as they worked together to compare the maps. In both instances, however, the coordinates turned out to be false positives with the Copán map plotting them slightly askew from their actual proportionate locations in the online star map, close to where they should have been among the stars – just not exact.

That all changed on the seventh night of their research project when Emma, while sipping a cup of tea and reviewing one of her final coordinate sections, came upon a lonely coordinate that fell nowhere near where a star should have been. As soon as she saw it, she knew the Copán star coordinate at 29.6518 x 100.4516 was not simply mis-plotted slightly askew from its actual location in the online star map. Instead, it fell in a gap of stars where there should not have been a star.

To confirm her intuition, she opened a more comprehensive online star map, one that showed more than just the stars visible with the naked eye. This map had millions of stars in it, including those viewable only with the aid of powerful telescopes. If 29.6518 x 100.4516 had a home in this small section of the heavens, she would find it. Only, she couldn't.

She looked closely. "Come on Little 29, where are you?"

After more than two hours of searching the more detailed map in the precise quadrant where Little 29 should have been, even with the additional stars to choose from in the higher intensity map, Little 29 still did not correlate with any known star location. Emma was now even more confident this was the extra coordinate.

But it was not until she realized *where* Little 29 plotted out over Earth's geography on the Copán coordinates map that her confidence turned into certainty. Nearly every Copán coordinate except this one fell over an ocean, mountain range, desert, ice plateau, or substantially non-urban area. That wasn't surprising given that, according to Emma's Google search, out of the planet's approximately 197,000,000 total square surface miles, only *.007%* fell in an urban area. Sure, with 9,097 coordinates in the Copán map, there were instances where coordinates fell in urban areas, but the odds were *extremely* rare.

Yet here, Little 29 was not only the one coordinate out of 9,097 (a *.0001%* chance) in the *entire* Copán map that did not correlate with a known star, it *also* happened to fall in that rare .007% category of coordinates which plotted out over an urban area. And perhaps most convincing of all to Emma was the fact that Little 29 didn't just fall within an urban area or near a city; it plotted out squarely on top of the footprint of the city center of *Bologna, Italy.*

At 11:52 p.m., it was Emma's turn to pick up the phone and wake Logan. This call could not wait. Whatever they were looking for was in Bologna.

Chapter 9 – Peer Pressure

"**B**ut why Bologna?" asked Logan, fighting back a yawn. He was half-asleep when Emma called. Sitting up, he added, "It just doesn't make any sense."

"Perhaps it does," replied Emma, who was sitting on her bed with her computer and prepared to offer a theory. "What about the European conquerors who invaded the New World. Maybe there's a connection between the Copán Ruins and Bologna, Italy."

Logan thought about it. "Yeah, but weren't the European conquerors Spanish, like Christopher Columbus?"

"Well, if I remember correctly from World History last year, Columbus was not Spanish. He was Italian. Maybe that's the connection."

"Did Columbus ever visit Honduras?" With the Copán Ruins located in *Honduras*, Logan's question made sense.

"Good question," said Emma. She did not know the answer, so she punched up Christopher Columbus in Wikipedia, and, after some quick and dirty research, read aloud: "'Christopher Columbus was born in Genoa, Italy in 1451.' Yep, definitely Italian," she said before continuing. "'He made four voyages to the New World. His first voyage in 1492 aboard the Santa Maria, the Pinta, and the Nina, funded by the Spanish Crown, took him to lands now referred to as the Bahamas, Cuba, Haiti, and the Dominican Republic."

"That doesn't help us," said Logan.

"Patience and positivity, remember, Mr. Rogue Positive?" She kept reading: "'His second voyage in 1493, also paid for by the Spanish Crown, included 17 ships and 1,200 men to colonize the New World. Columbus visited Cuba, the Dominican Republic, Puerto Rico, and the Lesser Antilles. On his third voyage in May 1498, he took six ships, three to bring supplies to the Spanish settlers and three to explore Venezuela and portions of South America. However, when he returned to Spain in September 1498, the Spanish Crown was so infuriated over his failure to deliver on the promised riches of the New World that they arrested him for deception and imprisoned him for two years. When they freed him in 1500, most thought Columbus' days of exploration were over.'"

"Is there anything in there about Honduras?" asked Logan.

"Give me a minute," said Emma. She scanned down the page. "Okay, here it comes… 'In May 1502, Columbus surprised everyone by embarking on a fourth voyage. Who funded the voyage has remained a mystery to this day, but most believe that the Italians paid for it. The theory stems from a letter Columbus wrote immediately before leaving Spain to the Governors of the Bank of Saint George, Genoa, Italy on 2 April 1502. He wrote *'Although my body is here, my heart is always near you.'* Historians studying the records of the Bank of Saint George, discovered several substantial, anonymous monetary transfers to Christopher Columbus. Seemingly funded by an anonymous benefactor, Columbus sailed for the Strait of Malacca, supposedly to see if it led to the Indian Ocean, but the world's most renowned maritime navigator somehow missed the Strait completely and ended up in the exact opposite direction back in the Americas."

"He missed the Strait of Malacca? Just like that?" asked Logan.

"Yep," replied Emma. "It says 'Most historians to this day doubt Columbus inadvertently returned to the New World. After first visiting some of his prior colonies, Columbus sailed to Central America, arriving in *Honduras* on July 30, 1502.'"

Logan's ears perked up. "So, he *did* visit Honduras."

"Yep, and check this out… 'As chronicled in Columbus' written journal from his 4th voyage, on 5 December 1502, he and his crew found themselves in a storm unlike any they had ever experienced. Columbus wrote, 'Should I survive the insatiable appetite of the waves, I hope to return to the holy sanctuary to pay my debt of gratitude to The Holy See.' Columbus would do just that after returning home, traveling to The Holy See in December 1504.'"

"What's the Holy See?" asked Logan.

"*It's the Vatican,*" replied Emma.

"What do you mean, 'It's the Vatican?'"

"The Holy See's like the government for the Roman Catholic Church, under the Pope's control, and the Pope lives at—"

"The Vatican."

"Yep, in Rome," added Emma.

"Wow," said Logan, surprised by her answers and even more by the speed with which she gave them. "You seem to know quite a lot about the Holy See."

"Well, I'm Italian, so you know, knowing that kind of stuff goes without saying."

"You're Italian?" said Logan, again surprised.

"Yep, on my mom's side of the family."

"I had no idea."

"My mom's maiden name is Rossi, and," she paused, preparing to share something even more personal. "Emma's not even my real first name. It's my parents' nickname for me."

"Really?? A nickname for what?"

"Emma is short for Immaculata. I'm named after my grandmother." Emma remained quiet, gauging his reaction. She grew up uncomfortable with her given Italian name, always fearing kids would tease her for it because of how religious it was. Over time, she had gotten used to her nickname and it just stuck.

"It's beautiful," he said.

"No—"

"No, I mean it, your name is seriously beautiful. It suits you."

Logan knew he was going out on a limb with that comment, taking a tiny leap forward to advance their friendship in a way he had never tried before. If Chad Peters was already in the picture, Logan could not keep being quiet and hiding how he really felt. Despite his best efforts to play it cool, he was falling hard for Emma James.

Emma said nothing. Instead, after several seconds of awkward silence, she changed the subject back to Christopher Columbus. "Hey, look at this. If you search for Christopher Columbus and the Holy See in the same Google search, it pulls up an interesting link talking about Columbus' written journals, do you see that?"

He typed in the information and replied, "Yeah."

"Click on that link and go down to the excerpt from 2 December 1504, where it says: 'I return home now, a man I never thought I'd be, to pay my debt to his Holiness and to deliver my *albino* bounty to the Holy See.' Do you see that?" she asked, focusing on the word albino, which typically referred to a person with white skin, hair, eyes or other features due to an absence of pigmentation.

"As a matter of fact, I do."

They were both thinking the same thing… is there any chance the albino reference had anything to do with the White-Eyed Star God?

It was all starting to add up to something very mysterious indeed: the Copán Chamber of the White-Eyed Star God in Honduras; mysterious hieroglyphic numbers dating back 500 to 700 years, placing their origin in the 1416 AD to 1616 AD range; coordinates pointing to the heart of Italy; a mysterious 4th voyage by Columbus in 1502 under false pretenses to Honduras, seemingly funded by the Holy See; and then, Columbus returned home with an albino and took the "bounty" back to the Holy See in Italy.

"Am I crazy or was Columbus' 4th voyage to the Americas a manhunt to bring the White-Eyed Star God back to the Vatican??" asked Logan. "Was he a bounty hunter for the Holy See? For the Pope?"

"Now it sounds like *you've* been spending too much time on conspiracy sites, but I also think you might be right. We need to see that journal!" declared Emma. "Not just the excerpts, but the complete journal of his 4th voyage."

"Is it downloadable? Can we check it out as a book somewhere?" wondered Logan.

They looked it up. After a few quick Google searches at 1:30 in the morning, they had their answer, just not the one they were looking for. The only official transcription of any of Columbus' handwritten journals was by Bartolome de Las Casas in the 1530's, who transcribed Columbus' writings from his 1st voyage only. All other remaining excerpts of Columbus' journals which had survived over the years were scattered for viewing at different national museums in Spain, Italy, and Portugal.

But that was not the most intriguing part. The only known surviving excerpts from Columbus' *4th voyage to the New World* were not available online or in any book or national museum for viewing. Instead, *those* excerpts were kept in a place that valued secrecy above all else: the Vatican Secret Archives in Vatican City, Rome, Italy. And who ran the Vatican Secret Archives? *The Holy See.*

According to Wikipedia, the Vatican Secret Archives were the central repository for all acts promulgated by the Holy See. The Pope, as Sovereign of Vatican City, owned and controlled the Archives which contained the Vatican state papers, correspondence, papal account books, and other historical documents the church had accumulated over the centuries.

"We've got to find a way to see Columbus' writings from that final voyage," insisted Emma.

"But how?" asked Logan. As he read more about the Vatican Secret Archives, he realized just how difficult that was going to be to do. "Listen to this," he said,

> *"In 1881, Pope Leo XIII opened portions of the Archives to outsiders, but only to select qualified scholars from approved institutions of higher learning pursuing scientific or religious research, who applied for an entry card to view documents maintained in the Archives. The Vatican Secret Archives requires that applications for an entry card be submitted months in advance, and if approved, the VSA requires that appointments to view documents be scheduled at least 30 days in advance. And for all person(s) desiring to view VSA documents, please be advised that it is STRICTLY against VSA rules to make copies, photographs, or scans of original archive documents, or to email or fax original documents. NO EXCEPTIONS, BY PAPAL DECREE.'"*

"Now what?" groused Logan, discouraged by the VSA's rules prohibiting anyone from sending them, electronically or otherwise, a copy of Columbus' writings to look at.

Emma had a thought. "You know, my cousin Enyo is an Administrator at the University of Florence, School of Arts. I know it's a long shot, but maybe he has some connections in his academic circles who can get us into the VSA this weekend."

"This weekend?? Emma, you're not serious? You're talking about traveling to Rome, 4,000 miles away."

"I'm totally serious. We can do this."

"I can't do that."

"What, you have a big date this weekend or something?" teased Emma.

Logan quickly shot that down. "No... it's just that..." He paused and then, somewhat embarrassed, said, "I can't afford a plane ticket to Rome. Not sure how—"

"Do you have a passport?"

"Well, yeah, but—"

"Then I'll pay for it," said Emma without hesitating.

"What? No. I can't ask you to do that."

Emma quickly replied, "It's not a problem."

It was becoming clear to Logan that Emma wasn't going to take *no* for an answer. He could hear her punching away at her keyboard over the phone.

"It's like $1,500 for a round-trip ticket this Friday," said Emma. "Are you in?"

"That's a fortune."

"I've got a nice little bank account thanks to Grandma Immaculata, may she rest in peace. Really, it's no problem. My parents will never know. My dad has his firm's annual partner retreat this weekend and he's taking my mom. They'll be gone all weekend. And you told me your mom works all weekend, right? We could totally do this. What do you say?"

"Um, I suppose, but how do you know we can even get into the Archives? We don't have one of those VSA entry cards *or* an appointment."

"So, you're saying you'll go if we can get in? We could buy plane tickets for Friday and take the 2:45 p.m. flight out of New York on Air Italy, arriving in Rome by early Saturday morning with the time change. And after visiting the Archives, we'll still have plenty of time to check out Bologna which is only a few hours north of Rome. And then, we can catch the 10:30 a.m. flight back Sunday morning. With the 6 hours we gain back in the time difference, we'll be home by midday Sunday. No one will ever know we're gone."

Logan hesitated.

"Come on, this girl is *not* taking no for an answer," said Emma more insistently this time.

"Emma, we're talking about traveling halfway around the world without our parents knowing, and dropping at least $3,000, probably more, just for a history grade."

"Logan, this is bigger than a grade. Don't you see that? There's a mystery here and it is ours to solve—"

"Why do you care so much anyway? It's risky."

"Maybe risky isn't bad."

"What do you mean?"

"I don't know. I guess... I guess I just feel like everything in my life has been really safe so far. Like, my dad plans everything.

84

He's always talking about which college and law school I'm going to go to and what internships I'll do for law school and what I'm going to do after law school, and I haven't even graduated high school yet! And now, we have the chance to do something that matters, something that's bigger than us, something exciting and risky, and I don't want to be the kind of person who holds back just because it's scary."

Hearing her response, Logan suddenly felt the weight of her dad's expectations on his own shoulders. Peer pressure to be more impulsive and go on a whirlwind trip to Europe with the girl of his dreams, what was he hesitating for?

"So?" Emma asked, feeling like this was her one chance to break away from a life that felt constricted and inevitable, thanks to her father. "You need to do this, too, you know. If we uncover something big, it could really open up some doors for you, like college…"

Emma was right. This was about more than just following his boyhood crush to Europe. They were on to something, and if it turned out to be as big as they hoped, and if they broke the story, he would have scholarship offers from every college in the country, maybe even more. This could change his life. If he wanted to help get his mom out of the mess that his deadbeat dad left behind seventeen years ago, this was *his* chance. If he got a scholarship to a good college, maybe he could get a high paying job out of school, help his mom move into a better apartment, help her change to a job with regular hours, and even take her on vacation! After all of the years of growing apart, he and Emma still had something very much in common: a desperate need to re-arrange the cards that their fathers dealt them.

"Emma, do you know how crazy this is?"

"Yeah, *and…*" Emma was waiting for Logan's answer.

"Okay, *yes*," he said.

Emma practically leapt off her bed. "Yes! Yes! This is going to be so much fun." She sounded more excited than he felt, and he felt pretty damn excited.

"I guess the last step before buying those tickets is for you to email your cousin."

"It's nearing 1:45 a.m. now, so in Florence, it's like…" Emma paused to think for a moment. "It's 7:45 a.m. He should be awake by now." She drafted the email and read it out-loud to Logan as she typed:

To: Cousin Enyo [erossi@florenceuniv.edu.it]
From: Emma J [immj@zahoo.net]

Subject: My School Research Project

"Dear Enyo,

Hi there!! I hope you are doing well. My mom is looking more like your dad every day, but don't tell her I said that. I have a question for you, really more of a favor to ask of my favorite <u>cool</u> cousin. I am working on a school project about Christopher Columbus and my research has led me to a dead end. As strange as it might sound, I really need to see a document at the Vatican Secret Archives about Christopher Columbus' 4th voyage to the New World called 'Columbus Journal Excerpts from 1504.' Do you know anyone at the Vatican Secret Archives, or do you have any connections in your academic circles that might be able to help me see the document? You know how crazy I am about my grades!! Please, don't say no.

Love, your little M"

"Good?" she asked.

"Perfect, hit send. Do you think he'll help?" asked Logan.

Emma sent the email and replied, "He'll do anything for me. He's awesome. I stayed with him in Florence three summers ago while my parents were traveling through Europe. At first, I was mad when they dumped me with Enyo and his wife Mimi so they could do Europe without me, but it turned out to be the best summer of my life."

Within one minute, a response from Enyo appeared in her inbox:

> To: Emma J
> From: Enyo R
>
> Subject: re: My School Research Project
>
> "Emmy,
>
> My baby, Emmy, so wonderful to hear from you. Yes, I actually do know a curator at the VSA, my good friend, Paolo Baldassario. You remember him and his wife, Gina? You met them when you stayed with us a few years ago. They were the couple with baby twin girls and I think you might have even babysat for them. As for viewing the document, I'm not sure. A few years ago, I had a 3-month VSA Entry Card to view documents in the VSA Reading Rooms, and it was strictly against the VSA's rules to make copies or photographs of original archive documents. I doubt that has changed, so probably Paolo can't even send, scan, or email a copy of the document to you. And I don't feel comfortable asking him to break rule. So sorry, M."

"What did he say?" asked Logan.

"What we already know, that the document can't be sent to us, but he does know someone. His friend works there."

"Really? Can his friend get us in this weekend?"

"I can't ask Enyo that. The first thing he'll do is call or email my mom to ask questions, like, is she coming, too, or does she want to get together after we arrive, or does she want him to pick us up at the airport, etc. He'll say something to wreck our plan. But I have an idea. First, I've got to thank him." She replied back:

To: Enyo R
From: Emma J

Subject: re: re: My School Research Project

"Enyo,

Totally get it. No worries. Don't want to get him in trouble, either. Thank you anyway!! Never hurts to ask. Tell Mimi I miss her and kiss Lorenzo for me. Remind Lorenzo that I'm still taller than him, Love, M"

"Alright, now we need to find Paolo Baldassario's contact info at the VSA," said Emma. She searched for the "Vatican Secret Archives" online and pulled up the website, **http://www.archiviosegretovaticano.va/**. She proceeded to the Curator Department page and tracked down Mr. Baldassario's email address: **pbaldassario@asv.va**. "Here we go, one more email. What do you think of this?

To: Paolo Baldassario [**pbaldassario@asv.va**]
From: Emma J [immj@zahoo.net]

Subject: My School Research Project

"Dear Mr. Baldassario,

I hope you remember me. My name is Immaculata James. I am Enyo Rossi's younger cousin from the United States. I don't know if you recall, but I met you a few years ago when I spent the summer at Enyo and Mimi's house, and I even babysat your beautiful baby twin girls. I bet they've grown a lot. How is your wife, Gina? I have a question for you. I am coming to Italy this weekend with my family to surprise Enyo. I also happen to be working on a school project about Christopher Columbus' 4th voyage to the New World. My research has led me to a dead end and as coincidental as it sounds, there is a document I would like to see in the Vatican Secret Archives called 'Columbus Journal Excerpts from 1504.' I asked my parents and they said we could make time to visit the VSA on Saturday when we are in Rome if you can help me. Is there any chance you can get me in to see the document for a few minutes? It would really help me out a lot on my school project. Either way, please don't say anything to Enyo. My mom will *kill* me if I spoil the surprise before we visit him Saturday night. Are you able to let me know?"

Sincerely,

Immaculata"

"How does that sound?" she asked.

"Like a bunch of white lies, but I'm all good with it. Whatever works."

"Like Grandma Immaculata always said, 'It's better to beg for forgiveness than to ask for permission...' That's how she stowed away on the ship to America. Grandma Immy was the best." Emma sent the email.

They stalled for a few minutes, waiting for Paolo to respond, contemplating whether it was time to go to bed. Just before calling it a night, Paolo responded:

To: Emma J [immj@zahoo.net]
From: Paolo Baldassario [**pbaldassario@asv.va**]

Subject: re: My School Research Project

"Dear Emma,

Of course, I remember you. How could I forget Enyo's Little M? I am sure my girls are not the only ones who have grown. Are you able to come at 10 a.m. Saturday morning? I do not usually work Saturday but can come in for few hours. I cannot do afternoon, so let me know. If that time works, I will email you the details when I know more. And of course, I won't say anything to Enyo. Sounds like a wonderful surprise.

My best, Paolo"

When Emma saw that, her eyes lit up. "He can do it!" she exclaimed, surprised her scheme had actually worked. She read Paolo's response out-loud to Logan, and then asked, "What are you going to tell your mom so she doesn't get suspicious when she gets home from work on Friday night and Saturday night and doesn't see you there?"

"I'll just tell her I'm sleeping over at Patrick's this weekend or something like that. She'll be cool with it. Since she works all weekend, honestly, I think it makes her feel better knowing I'm not alone."

"Okay then, it's all set. This Friday, we're flying to Rome to see Columbus' journal entries on Saturday, and we'll be back Sunday midday before anyone knows we're gone."

"Emma, you know, at some point, Mr. Baldassario from the VSA is gonna talk to your cousin, to ask him how the surprise went, or to let him know that you visited the Archives… *something*. I mean, they're friends. Your parents are going to find out. And when they do—"

"We'll be back home safe here in Jersey. They'll be pissed off, yeah, I get it. And they're probably going to ground me for weeks."

90

"More like months…"

"Whatever it is, I'll live. I don't care. We're talking about chasing history. And if we find some of that history, I can do interview requests from my bedroom. But this isn't just about me, you know… your mom's going to find out, too. My dad's going to call her, and when he does—"

"I don't care, either," Logan blurted out. If she wasn't backing down, there was no way in the world he was going to.

"So, we're in this together?" asked Emma, knowing full well how much trouble both were going to get in, wanting to make sure he was totally on board and, perhaps, testing him a little.

"Together," he responded without a hint of doubt.

"Good," she calmly replied, hiding a celebratory grin on her end of the line.

"So, we're really going to do this…" Logan concluded.

"We really are. I just bought the plane tickets."

Chapter 10 – The Vatican Secret Archives

On Friday as planned, after turning in their forged notes to get out of school following 3rd-period, Logan and Emma once again raced to Journal Square Station to catch the 1 1/2-hour commuter train to John F. Kennedy Airport (JFK) in New York City. From there, they planned to take the 2:45 p.m. Air Italy flight to Rome's Fiumicino Airport (FCO). Their expected arrival time in Rome with the 6-hour time difference was Saturday morning, a little after 6 a.m.

As they hurried into the airport terminal each carrying nothing more than a backpack, Emma yelled back at Logan who was lagging a few steps behind, "Hurry up, you slowpoke, you're going to make us miss making history." Logan picked up his pace, determined not to let that happen.

Between the hour and a half commute, international check-in, security lines, and the general daily chaos at JFK, they cut their arrival time very close. But as was quickly becoming their modus operandi, they made it to the gate right on time.

They boarded the massive transatlantic airliner and funneled down the aisles until they reached their cramped economy seats in Row 41 near the back of the plane.

As the plane started taxing away from the gate, it took only one glimpse at Emma for Logan to realize flying made her nervous.

"You okay?" he asked, concerned.

"Okay, yes, fine, as long as this 400-ton flying chunk of metal stays in the air." She looked at Logan who had nothing comforting to offer. Emma put her hands over her face, slightly embarrassed. "I'm sorry, I've just always hated flying. I'll be fine."

Logan was not convinced. "Are you sure?"

"Yes. Thank you for asking. I appreciate it."

"You know, if you need a hand to squeeze, I've got a good one..."

Emma smiled and responded, "I was already planning on it. Why do you think I brought you along?"

"Um, because you need my help," he replied, "and because I make better company than Chad."

"Always Chad, Chad, Chad. You need to stop worrying about Chad all the time."

"Does he know you're on this plane with me?"

"Of course, he knows. I tell him everything. He told me to have fun, fly safe, and to be careful."

"Seriously?" said a shocked Logan. Those weren't the words of a jealous jock boyfriend. "And he's totally fine with you taking a two-day trip to Europe with me, just like that?"

"I mean, I think he's a little jealous, but who wouldn't be? It's Italy. He likes you... thinks you're good for me. You're like one of the only guys at our entire school he'd let me do this crazy trip with."

Her words surprised Logan. In fact, they were completely the opposite of what he expected her to say.

"You two aren't dating? But I thought—"

"Chad's gay." Emma waited for Logan to catch up. "He loves me, always has, and I love him, too, like a brother. He's always looking out for me... a little nosey sometimes, but I look out for him, also."

Logan was speechless, overcome with feelings of exuberance over the fact that she was not dating Chad, but also, regret for some of the things he had thought, said or presumed about Chad. "I don't know what to say, I had no idea. I just assumed—"

"Like everybody else, yes, everybody assumes a lot of things about Chad. He's the sweetest guy in that whole school. But if anyone else was to learn the truth, how do you think they'd treat him, the captain of the football team? Chad's not interested in complicating his life right now."

"So, you pretend you two are dating?" asked Logan.

"It's not like I go out of my way to sell the rumor, but yeah, I let people believe what they want to believe, and Chad probably encourages it, which is fine with me. I don't need a boyfriend anyway. Who has time? Because of Chad, the guys stay away. He always reminds me he's saving me from the heartache. He's probably right."

"I had no idea."

"Well, how could you? Like you said the other day, you and Chad haven't spoken in what, 7 or 8 years? By the way, you've got to stop doing that, avoiding talking to people who are good for you. Not a good recipe for happiness in life," remarked Emma.

No truer words had ever been spoken, Logan thought, although that wasn't the only thing going through his mind. Logan wondered, "So, is that why you think you and I haven't talked much the last few years, because I was avoiding you?"

"No, not exactly..."

"Not exactly? Why do you say that?"

"I guess I just wish that I had made a better effort these last few years. Working on this project with you the last two weeks has been a lot of fun and has brought back a lot of great memories. It makes me wish we hadn't waited so long to reconnect like this…"

"Yeah, me too," conceded Logan.

"But, you know, you could've put yourself out there a bit more also." Before Logan could respond, the plane straightened out on the runway and began to accelerate. "Oh, here we go," said a suddenly white-knuckled Emma. "This is the part where I usually close my eyes and hide my face."

"How about my shoulder?" replied Logan, offering her a place to hide.

To Logan's surprise, she did just that, dip her head into his shoulder, shut her eyes, and place her trust in him to get her through takeoff. Now it was Emma who had taken a tiny step forward to advance their friendship in a way she had never done before. Logan closed his eyes and smiled. This weekend was already shaping up to be the best of his entire life, and the plane hadn't even left the runway yet.

ΔΔΔΔΔΔΔΔΔΔ

The flight was long, tiring, and exciting all at the same time. They talked. They planned. They slept. And most importantly, after logging in to Air Italy's midair Wi-Fi, they emailed their parents every few hours to keep all questions at bay, and to confirm their alibies.

Several hours into their flight, they received an email from Paolo Baldassario providing them with details for their visit to the Vatican Secret Archives. He had arranged for them to view 'Columbus' Journal Excerpts from 1504' at 10:15 a.m. Saturday morning. He told them to meet him at the entrance to the Secret

Archives, adjacent to the Vatican Library. He also left his cell phone number in case they needed it.

Their plane landed at Rome's FCO airport right on time, early in the morning. After going through customs, they changed out their money for euros at a Foreign Currency Exchange booth. Emma had brought with her $300, while Logan had brought the money he earned tutoring kids in math. Once they got their euros, they made their way to the airport's outer curb to catch a taxi to Vatican City.

While they were exiting the airport, Logan caught a glimpse of a burly man wearing a dark brown leather jacket and blue jeans, with pale skin and tightly-cut blond hair, standing off to the side of the automatic doors, smoking a cigarette and staring at them. Logan looked ahead without thinking much of it until he peeked again a few steps later, and this time, he thought the man snapped a picture of them.

"That's weird," said Logan.

"What?" asked Emma.

"I might be crazy, but I think we're being followed."

"Where?? Who??" Emma threw a look in all directions. The mere suggestion that they were being followed made her uneasy. "You're not messing with me, are you?"

"No," said Logan. He spun around looking for the man but could not find him. "I swear, I noticed someone watching us. I think he even snapped a picture of us with his phone."

"Maybe all the conspiracy talk and an 8 1/2-hour flight are playing tricks on your mind, making you paranoid. Either that or local thieves are casing the tourists getting off the planes. Let's get out of here."

They ducked into a taxi as quickly as possible. At least for now, as the taxi sped off, it seemed whomever Logan saw snapping photographs of them did not follow. Still, they carefully watched the cars traveling behind the taxi just in case.

When the taxi reached the 110-acre walled enclave of Vatican City in Rome's northwest quarter, they entered its age-old walls and beheld the view from inside St. Peter's Square, a large outdoor plaza in front of St. Peter's Basilica. Despite its name, St. Peter's Square was actually oval-shaped. Paved with an endless sea of cobblestones, the plaza was enormous, over one thousand feet long and nearly eight hundred feet wide. Massive colonnades, four columns deep, framed the outer edges of the elliptical plaza on both sides, with the colonnades symmetrically wrapping all the way around and leading up to the trapezoidal entrance to St. Peter's Basilica at the plaza's west end.

Emma and Logan made their way to the center of St. Peter's Square where an ancient Egyptian obelisk made of red granite reached high toward the sky. Standing in the middle of the plaza and looking back out, Papal structures surrounded them, including St. Peters Basilica with its tall dome towering over Vatican City, the Apostolic Palace, and various other buildings adorned with sculptures and decorative Renaissance-inspired stonework.

Even though it was early in the morning, the plaza still teemed with life. Thousands of tourists scurried about, sightseeing and taking photographs, followed by hundreds of tour guides peddling personal, guided tours of the Vatican. Armed military police guarded all outer entrances into Vatican City, while the Papal Swiss Guard, a small militia force established by the Holy See to protect the Pope, kept watch within Vatican City's interior walls.

Looking out at her surroundings, Emma said, "Grandma Immy always used to tell me about this place, about how beautiful it was and about the incredible feeling she always got standing in the middle of St. Peter's Square looking around at something so much bigger than her, bigger than all of us. Grandma Immy was right."

"Well yeah, you can fit, like, twelve football fields in here," joked Logan.

"Ha-ha, very funny... that's not what I'm talking about. Seriously, look around. We're surrounded by centuries of history, culture and religion. I mean, the Pope lives here! It's just hard to believe that we are actually here."

"You haven't been here before?" asked Logan, somewhat surprised.

"No."

"I guess I kind of just assumed you had, you know, with your mom being Italian and all."

"I know this will come as a great shock to you, but my dad plans all of the vacations in my family, and usually, we go where he wants to go."

"And you didn't come here when you stayed with your aunt and uncle in Florence, either?"

"No, my uncle was working a lot, and we just didn't get the chance. Trust me, there's still plenty to see and do in Florence. But when I'm out of college and paying for my own vacations, I'm going to travel all over the world."

"Not on a cryptologist's salary, you're not," teased Logan.

Emma spun around toward Logan. "Hey!!"

Logan laughed. They both did. They started wandering through the cobblestoned plaza, slowly meandering in the direction of St. Peter's Basilica.

"So, what about you?" asked Emma as they strolled across the plaza.

"What about me?" replied Logan, unsure what she was asking him.

"Have you ever gone out of the country? I mean, you do have a passport, so I assume you must have gone somewhere..."

Logan chuckled. "Ah, yes, all the way to a place in a galaxy far far away called Toronto, a mind-blowing 475-miles northwest of Jersey City and a whopping 16 miles north of the US border. Went there with my mom a few years ago when she interviewed for a manager position at a fancy restaurant up there. Obviously, she didn't get it."

"That's it? Any other foreign countries?"

"Nope." He paused for a moment, then said, "You know, we've got several hours to kill before our appointment with your uncle's friend. Do you want to check out the Vatican Museum and St. Peter's Basilica? I mean, we *are* here."

"Definitely!" exclaimed Emma, thrilled that Logan was interested in doing so.

"Let's start at the Vatican Museum. I think I heard one of the tour guides say the lines are long, but they get longer the later it gets." Emma nodded agreeably.

They made their way to the Vatican Museum. There was still a wait, like the tour guide suggested there would be, but because it was early, the lines were manageable. Once they got in, due to their time constraints, they really only had time to quickly peruse the museum's extensive display of sculptures and Renaissance art on their way to the highlight of the Vatican Museum: the renowned Sistine Chapel. The long, rectangular Sistine Chapel contained dozens of breathtaking frescoes painted on its walls and vaulted ceiling by world-famous Renaissance artists such as Michelangelo, Botticelli, Rosselli and others.

"Here, follow me," said Emma, leading Logan to a rare open spot near the middle of the Sistine Chapel. With unabashed confidence, even among the Chapel's other guests, she lowered herself onto the ground to lay down on her back. "Come on," she said, urging Logan to do the same.

Following suit, he laid down beside her with their shoulders touching. Together, while laying on their backs side by side in the middle of the Sistine Chapel, they stared up at the extraordinary vaulted ceiling painted by Michelangelo depicting nine religious narrative scenes from the Book of Genesis. It was obvious to Logan why Emma had chosen the spot that she did. They laid directly beneath one of the most widely recognized paintings in the history of painting, Michelangelo's *The Creation of Adam,* portraying the hand of God reaching out with his index finger to touch the index finger on the hand of Adam and giving Adam life.

As they laid there, for an instant, to Logan, it felt like no one else was around, like it was just the two of them staring up at history. Emulating Michelangelo's masterpiece, Emma playfully moved her left index finger over to poke Logan's right index finger. Logan looked at her and she flashed back an amused smile. It wasn't long before a security guard approached and prompted them to stand up and move along. They both wished they could have spent more time in there, but they went to St. Peter's Basilica next.

"Maybe we'll be back someday," Logan intimated to Emma as they walked to the Basilica. Emma glanced at him, surprised by his comment, pleasantly so. She grinned slightly and kept walking into the cathedral's main entrance.

St. Peter's Basilica was a vast church constructed in the Renaissance-style, cruciform in shape with an elongated nave. The interior was lavishly decorated with marble, reliefs, architectural sculpture and gilding, and contained a number of fancifully-designed tombs of popes and other notable individuals built into the basilica's walls.

They strolled past the church's historic architecture, chapels, sculptures, and religious artifacts and, for a fleeting moment, Emma took Logan's hand. Maybe it was to lead him in the direction she wanted to go, or maybe because she was unconsciously reaching out to share the exciting experience with someone next to her. For the few seconds it lasted, Logan hardly had time to analyze it before it was over. He wasn't even sure Emma realized she had done it.

Just before 10:15 a.m., they headed over to the Vatican Secret Archives. Paulo was waiting for them right on schedule. Emma remembered him immediately. Handsome, dark-haired, and olive skinned, wearing thin-rimmed glasses and a fine Italian suit, he looked very much the part of curator.

"Welcome," said Paolo in a heavy Italian accent. "Immaculata, I am much pleased to see you again." He hugged her, kissed her on both cheeks, and shook Logan's hand. "And who might this be? A boyfriend?"

"Yep, he is," said Emma affectionately, playing along and hugging Logan's arm. "He's never been to Italy before, so my dad invited him to come."

Trying to keep up with Emma's flair for ad-libbing, and more than happy to embrace it, Logan added, "It's true, it's um, my first time."

"Thank you so much for doing this on such short notice," said Emma. "It's really a very kind favor."

"Anything for Enyo's Little M," Paolo replied. "And I was right, now that I see you, I wonder if Enyo has any idea how much you've grown. He will be most shocked tonight, I think. Where are your parents?"

Emma smiled. "They are enjoying the Vatican Museum."

"Ah, a much better choice than here, I think," replied Paolo.

"Again, thank you for taking us into the Archives," said Emma.

Paolo looked them over. "Dressed in blue jeans, so American teenager, but not proper attire for visitors of the Secret Archives. I will take you to my office in the basement, but you will still get to see some of it. We will walk through the North Corridor which houses some of the most notable scriptures and papal documents in all the Archives. We have treasures such as a handwritten transcript of the trial of Galileo, who stood accused of heresy for spreading blasphemy that the Earth was not the center of the universe. And a papal bull from Pope Alexander VI splitting the lands of the New World discovered by Columbus up amongst Portugal and Spain. The North Corridor is actually where I retrieved your document."

Paolo led the way and upon entering the North Corridor, it seemed like time stopped and transported them back to the 1500's. The corridor and its rows of books looked, felt, and smelled that old. Logan felt bad for thinking it, but the gentleman at the research table halfway down the corridor appeared that old, as well.

"Are the Archives actually *secret*?" whispered Logan to Paolo.

"Ah, a normal question, especially by Americans. The word 'secret' in 'Vatican Secret Archives,' translated to English from the VSA's proper Latin name, 'Archivum Secretum Apostolicum Vaticanum,' does not translate to secret or confidential the way you Americans mean it. It means, how shall I say it, eh, it means closer translation to 'private' because the Archives are technically the Pope's personal *private* property."

After a short staircase down, they reached Paolo's office. They went in and closed the door. Once they were alone in the ancient stone-enclosed office, Paolo posed a worrisome question.

"I must inquire, a document like this that you ask for, it goes many years without request. Some papal documents in these walls haven't been viewed for centuries. This one you ask for, you ask and then we receive another request for viewing the same document today at 13:00. More classmates of yours?"

Emma and Logan exchanged concerned looks.

Emma responded, *"No,"* and asked, "Do you know their names?"

"I don't know, I am sorry. The request was made through the Holy See to ready the document for viewing at 13:00 for a private audience. I don't ask questions when I get a request like that from the Sovereign. And this was before I announce any intention to view the journal excerpts."

Panicking, Emma asked, "Were you able to get the document?"

"Yes, fortunate for you, I was assigned preparation of the document today for the 13:00 viewing. I will go get it now. It is up in the Conservator's Office. Once I retrieve it, we will have it only for a few minutes before I must take the document up for Surface Examination and Cleaning. Please excuse me, I'll just be a minute." Paolo exited, leaving them alone in his office.

Logan immediately said what both were thinking. "Someone is following us, reading our texts and emails. There can be no other explanation. One or both of our email or phone accounts have been hacked."

Emma was irked. "That must've been who you saw taking photos of us at the airport. If someone thinks it's important enough to hack our phones, that tells me something big is going on here. I don't know who or what, but we've got a two-and-a-half-hour lead to see the document before they do."

"This is insane. I mean, if they're willing to hack our phones and follow us… could we be in danger?" Logan wondered.

"From a bunch of academic cheats? I hardly think so. And I don't care," Emma defiantly declared. She found herself ticked off. "Over my dead body will these jerks steal our work and take credit for what we've done when they've had five years to figure it out and discovered squat."

"Emma, whoever they are," said Logan, "they sure have gone to a lot of trouble. They seem like more than just academic cheats to me. There's more to this."

"Maybe you're right, but the fact that they've gone to all this trouble tells me that we're on to something huge and they know it. I'm not letting them win."

"Me neither," said Logan, a little unnerved by the turn of events but also, feeding off of Emma's stubborn bravery. "Let's turn off location services on our phones and set our settings to private to prevent tracking. Also, I think we should avoid sending any texts or emails until we figure out what's going on."

They took care of their phones, finishing just as Paolo returned with a folder in hand. He placed it down on his desk and said, "It is against VSA rule to make copies or photographs of VSA documents, so you must only take notes. Please, I hope you understand."

They both nodded their heads to indicate that they did.

Paolo put on a pair of thin gloves. He pulled an old worn-looking piece of parchment out of an acid-free polypropylene folder and carefully placed it down onto his desk on top of a thin metal sheet designed to prevent the document from touching potentially corrupt surfaces. Most of the text handwritten by Christopher Columbus himself was too faded to make out. The cursive lettering disappeared into the discolored parchment.

"This may be hard to read, but it's the only excerpt recovered," said Paolo.

"Hard to read? It's impossible," lamented Emma.

They had traveled a long way and at great expense to get a look at history, and now that they were here with only part of that history decipherable, Emma's stomach knotted up at the thought of running into a dead end.

"There are still some sections we can read," said a more optimistic Logan, hoping to make the most of the situation.

Paolo asked, "Are you working on this project, too?"

Emma quickly rectified Logan's minor slip up by telling Paolo something that was actually true for a change. "We go to the same school in Jersey City and are in the same class. It's a group project and we're in the same group."

"Ah," replied Paolo.

The legible passages were written in Spanish with a heavy overriding Portuguese influence; that was the language Columbus wrote in despite his Italian heritage. Although Logan was in the middle of his fourth year of Spanish in high school, the sentence structure matched nothing Logan had learned. Still, he knew enough to read and scan for words he recognized, and Emma was highly conversational in Spanish. Together they read, and Paolo assisted when they encountered difficulty with translation.

The passages generally appeared to describe Columbus' unexpected 4th voyage across the Atlantic Ocean, challenges his crew faced crossing the seas and encounters with infuriated colonists upon his return to the New World. It took more than a few minutes, but it was not long before Logan saw something.

"There!" he exclaimed. "What about this part?" Logan had spotted a word that caught his interest.

He eyed a section of degraded text referencing Copernicus, a famous European astronomer from the late 15th and early 16th centuries who believed the Earth was not the center of the universe more than 100 years before Galileo ever opined on the topic. Given the Copán Chamber's relationship to the stars, the Copernicus reference grabbed Logan's attention instantly.

"Mr. Baldassario, can you please help us read this part?" asked Logan, not wanting to mistake any words.

"Absolutely," Paolo willingly replied. He examined the text Logan was pointing at and translated it for them out-loud:

> "The freedom of the waves I did not expect to return to again. For my last voyage left me in chains. The blasphemous student of Novara spawned by Copernicus deceived me. For he sought safe passage to the New World aboard my Vaqueños on a lie. I return to the sea, my holy sanctuary, an indebted man,

for the sea hath wrest away my chains. My colonists have pointed me, I must now only find him, the Norwegian Albo, and return him to the sea. And no longer an indebted man shall I be; I will be whole with the sea."

"Interesting," said Logan. "So, he was looking for a Norwegian named Albo, who was a student of Novara?"

"Right," replied Emma, "and it sounds like the colonists told Columbus how to find him where it says, 'My colonists have pointed me.'"

"The Vaqueños is the name of the flagship from Columbus' third voyage in 1498," chimed in Paolo, not exactly sure what their project was about other than that it had to do with Christopher Columbus, but he was trying to help. "It appears whoever this Norwegian was, he was on that ship. Sounds like he talked his way onto the Vaqueños using a creative tongue."

"It also sounds like Columbus sailed back to the New World to find this Albo, but to return him back to the sea? That makes no sense," said Emma.

"Maybe it does," Logan replied. "Is he telling us something when he refers to the sea as his holy sanctuary? The other night when you were reading a passage from Columbus' chronicles about the end of his fourth voyage, Columbus referred to the Holy See as his holy sanctuary. Is it me or can you replace every reference to the word 'sea' in there with the words, 'Holy See,' and get a completely different meaning from the second half of that passage?"

After looking at it again and substituting the words 'Holy See' for the word 'sea,' Paolo read the second half of the revised passage to Logan and Emma: "I return to the HOLY SEE, my holy sanctuary, an indebted man, for the HOLY SEE hath wrest away my chains. My colonists have pointed me, I must now only find him, the Norwegian Albo and return him to the HOLY SEE. And no longer an indebted man shall I be; I will be whole with the HOLY SEE."

106

Emma, after listening carefully, shared her observations. "When you read it that way, it sounds like the Holy See freed Columbus from imprisonment by the Spanish Crown so he could go on a fourth voyage back to the New World to find this Norwegian Albo and bring him back *here*," said Emma. "Perhaps Columbus agreed to do this to repay his debt to the Holy See for securing his release from 'chains,' and to restore his standing with the Catholic Church."

Something Emma said caught Paolo's interest. He reached over and pulled another old-looking piece of parchment out of the same folder that Columbus' journal came from.

"This document was stored in the folder where I found Columbus' journal, separated by a sleeve. It is not part of his journal and was written by a different hand, in a different language, but maybe it relates. Based on what you're saying, I think perhaps that it does." He laid the parchment down next to Columbus' journal. It read:

> "In Norwegian nos effugit, ut rursus extendet falsa haeretica in mundum. Nos nescimus qualiter non. Ut possimus invenire debemus ei cum alius scriptor recens transitum Cristoforo Colombo. Locutus est die II Decembris, 1506. Papa Julius II."

"What language is that written in?" Logan asked Paolo.

"The language of the Popes, Latin. To English, it translates, 'The Norwegian has escaped us again to spread his heretical lies to the world. We know not how. We must find another to recapture him with Cristoforo Colombo's recent passing. Decreed this day, December 2, 1506. Pope Julius II.' Cristoforo Colombo refers to Christopher Columbus."

"Who was the Norwegian?" wondered Logan.

"Albo doesn't sound like a Norwegian name," added Emma.

"I have heard it," replied Paolo. "Albo is a popular name in many languages, Albo for male, Alba for female. It means 'white' in most languages, or a definition close to that."

"Oh, my god!" exclaimed Emma. She covered her mouth as if she had just uttered a foul word inside the Vatican. "I am sorry, Mr. Baldassario."

"Not to worry," said Paolo.

"Forgive me. It's just that Albo, albino, they derive from the same root etymology, 'alb', for the word 'white.' I didn't think about it until you said that."

Logan, putting it all together, wondered, "The Norwegian Albo, the Albino, the White-Eyed Star God, could they all refer to the same person?"

"We need to find out who this Novara is, and who Albo is," said Emma.

"Should I look it up on my computer?" asked Paolo.

"Yes!" stated Emma emphatically.

Paolo entered the words Novara, Copernicus, student, Norwegian, and Albo into the same search bar. The very first result which showed up was a link for the University of *Bologna*. They had come full circle back to the extra coordinate in the Copán star map.

"*Bologna?!?!*" Logan piped up. "Click on that one."

When Paolo clicked on the link, it took them to a description of a plaque found at a portico entrance for a building located at Via Galliera 65, Bologna, called the House of Domenico Maria *Novara*, commemorating one of the University's most famous students, *Copernicus*. After clicking on the image to pull up an oversized picture of the plaque, Paolo translated it for them:

"Here, where stood the house of Domenico Maria Novara, professor of the ancient Studium of Bologna, NICOLAUS COPERNICUS, the Polish mathematician and astronomer who would revolutionize concepts of the universe, conducted brilliant celestial observations with his teacher in 1496–1501. Placed on the 5th centenary of [Copernicus's] birth by the City, the University, the Academy of Sciences of the Institute of Bologna, the Polish Academy of Sciences. 1473 [—] 1973."

"So, Copernicus was a student of Novara's at the University of Bologna, too, from 1496 to 1501," said Logan. "That's probably how Copernicus met the Norwegian Albo."

Given what Emma suspected about the Norwegian Albo whom she also now believed might be the one the Mayans called the White-Eyed Star God, Emma added, "I wonder whether Copernicus came up with his theories about the universe on his own or whether the mysterious Mr. Albo had anything to do with it."

"Talk about changing the history books," commented Logan.

"Logan," said Emma, "you know what we have to do, right? We have to go… um… we have to see if my parents want to go to Bologna to visit the House of Domenico Maria Novara at Via Galliera 65."

"Such a fine idea. By train from Rome's Termini Railway Station, Bologna's only about two hours away," Paolo informed them. "It's beautiful."

Emma looked at Logan. She was ready to go.

"Mr. Baldassario, thank you for your time. This has been incredibly helpful," said Emma. Logan thanked him also.

"It has been my pleasure. May I have chance to meet your parents?"

Uh oh, Emma groaned to herself. When ad-libbing before, she had failed to anticipate that question. She needed to improvise fast and hope Paolo did not pick up on her sudden nervousness about having to produce her parents. "Can I go find them and bring them back here if there's time?" she asked.

"Perhaps they are still enjoying the Vatican Museum. Maybe I can go up with you and—"

Emma stopped him midsentence. "Who knows how long *that* lasted. When it comes to my dad, looking at art is like staring at the sun. He can only do it for a split second before he has to avert his eyes and move on to the next piece. They probably did the Vatican Museum in like 20 minutes and are probably somewhere else in Vatican City by now. If we have a chance later, can we take you for an espresso?"

"Of course, my pleasure it would be to meet them," replied Paolo.

Phew, Emma thought to herself.

Paolo escorted them up the stairs to a backdoor exit that was much closer to the Vatican Museum, thinking he was saving them valuable steps. Logan and Emma did not object; in fact, going out the backdoor might help them avoid the watchful eyes of anyone who saw them enter the VSA through the front entrance. He opened the door and said, "If you have a chance, call or text my cell phone."

"I most certainly will," stated Emma, feeling guiltier with each lie she uttered. "Thank you again. Please give my best to Gina and the twins."

"Of course," said Paolo, turning and closing the door.

Emma looked at Logan and said, "Alright, let's go. We don't have much of a head start."

Chapter 11 – History, Revisited

Emma and Logan caught the first available train from Rome Termini to Bologna, arriving at Bologna's Centrale Rail Station, in the early afternoon. Whereas Rome was a modern city built around its ancient ruins, architecture and history, Bologna's old-world charm had not quite given way to the charge of the 21st Century. With bumpy, narrow cobblestone streets and alleys, timeless churches, endless blocks of porticos, hidden canals and waterways, and even a leaning tower (Torre Garisenda) that would put Pisa to shame, Bologna still clung tight to its **3,000-year-old-**roots.

It was a 10-minute walk from the train station to Via Galliera 65 where the former House of Domenico Maria Novara was located. When they got there, they saw that the timeworn three-story building had been converted into a religious boarding school for middle and upper-grade students.

"We're here!" announced Emma.

"Even if our competition finished reading the journal and figured it all out by now, it's still going to be an hour or two before they can get here. The next train from Rome to Bologna doesn't leave for another hour," Logan said.

"Unless they fly," Emma responded. "Let's go in."

They approached the arched portico entrance to the Novara House. Right before going in, a loud alarm sounded, stopping them in their tracks. It came from the school and startled them both. Seconds later, boarding school students started rushing out of the building, followed by teachers trying to usher the students to safety in frenetic but organized fashion. All Logan and Emma could do was step aside and watch.

Before they figured out what was happening, yellow and green fire trucks with blaring sirens came screeching around the corner, racing up to Via Galliera 65. Several police cars followed. One fire engine stopped right in front of them.

As the firemen leapt down from their truck to the sidewalk, Emma shouted, "Cosa c'e'??"

"Perdita di gas," yelled one fireman before running into the school to deal with what was apparently being called, a 'gas leak'.

An officer shouted at Logan and Emma to back up. "*Indietro!! Indietro!!*" He also urged them to move through hand gestures. Emma and Logan stepped back.

"Per quanto?" asked Emma, trying to gauge how long the school closure might last for.

"Molte ore," replied the officer, only partially paying attention to her.

"Hours?? I can't believe this," said Emma, frustrated.

They stared at the building. Both had the distinct feeling the "gas leak" was a hoax.

"Whoever viewed the journal after us beat us to the punch," said Logan.

"Unbelievable," snapped Emma, now herself startled by the lengths the competition appeared willing to go to stop them.

"Come on," Logan urged, leading her away from the boarding school, "before someone sees us."

They slid deeper into the belly of central Bologna, ducking into an espresso cafe tucked away down a cobblestone alley several blocks from Via Galliera 65. They found a table in the corner and tried to blend in.

"How did they do that?!" griped Emma, dropping her backpack below the table. Logan followed.

"Obviously, they've got connections," responded Logan quietly.

"So, now what??" lamented Emma.

"Maybe what—"

"Mi scusi, posso aiutare voi due?" said a young, brunette waitress wearing an apron and standing over them.

Emma put up two fingers and responded, "Due espressi e due tramezzino per favore, grazie." The waitress walked away.

"I know you told me you were Italian, but I didn't realize you also spoke the language," said Logan, finding more reasons to fall for Emma every day.

"A little," she modestly replied. "You were saying…"

"What I was saying was… maybe what we are looking for isn't at the Domenico Maria Novara House."

"That building was our only lead."

"Positivity, remember?" Growing ever more comfortable in his role as Mr. Rogue Positive, Logan reassured Emma that things might still work out. "Columbus' journal entry didn't tell us to go to the House of Domenico Maria Novara, we just assumed it, right?"

"Okay, true."

"What if what we're looking for is somewhere else? All we really know is that the Norwegian Albo was a student with Copernicus under University of Bologna astronomy professor, Domenico Novara. So maybe that's where we should go... to the University of Bologna and check out the School of Astronomy and see what's there."

Their waitress returned with a tray holding food and drink. "Due espressi, prego," she said, gently placing two small shots of espresso in front of them, trying not to spill. "Due tramezzino," she added, lowering onto their table two bite-sized triangular sandwiches made of soft white bread and prosciutto.

"Grazie," replied Emma. "Dov'è Università di Bologna?"

The waitress responded, "Palazzo Poggi."

"Is it close?" Emma asked her. "Um, I mean, è vicino?"

"Sì, eh, dieci o quindici minuti, percorso."

"She says it's only a 10 or 15-minute walk to the University," said Emma, translating for Logan.

At this point, the waitress sat down in an empty chair beside Emma so she could be at eye level with them both. She smiled and, in Italian-accented English, explained, "To see Università Studium, outside go Via dell'Orso, a destra, eh, mi scusi... go right Via dell'Indipendenza, left Via Marsala, left Via Zamboni to Università."

"Mucho grazie," said Logan.

Emma laughed. So did the waitress. "Grazie mille," corrected Emma, saying *thank you very much* properly. The waitress stood up and walked away. Looking at Logan, Emma commented, "Your fusion Spanish-Italian needs some work."

They downed their espresso shots and took their tiny sandwiches to go. They dropped €10 on the table and took off for the University of Bologna under an early afternoon sky with shadows starting to creep in. They proceeded as inconspicuously as possible through Bologna's historic center, following their waitress' directions. They reached the University on the outskirts of the city center after about a ten-minute walk.

The building their waitress had sent them to, Palazzo Poggi, was a stunning centuries-old palace. It was also the headquarters of the University of Bologna and its conglomerate of five campuses educating more than 85,000 students. Palazzo Poggi had a large courtyard and a huge staircase leading up to a massive, palatial double-door entrance. Frescos and sculptures decorated the approach to the Palazzo, which housed museums, the university rector, libraries, an art gallery, working lecture halls, and administrative offices. Of course, Palazzo Poggi was not the only university building on the main campus. Surrounding the Palazzo was an entire compound of university buildings and museums, all the way up and down Via Zamboni.

They climbed the winding staircase to the grand double-door entrance. Over the door's threshold was a red and white circular logo with the words *"Alma Mater Studiorum A.D. 1088"* written in an outer ring, and the words *"Universita Di Bologna"* written in an inner ring, all wrapping around five narrative scenes depicting study and prayer.

Emma pushed open the door and, together, they stepped inside. There was an information desk right in front of them as they walked in.

"Scusami," said Emma to the young man staffing the desk. "Dove possiamo trovare la Scuola di Astronomia?

"What did you say to him?" Logan asked Emma.

Although Emma's accented-Italian sounded like she might be American, after hearing Logan speak, the desk attendant knew for sure that they were. He responded accordingly. "Department of

Physics and Astronomy at Viale Carlo Berti Pichat, 6/2, several minute walk from here on other side of SS9. Take Via Zamboni to Via Irnerio, cross over footbridge, follow walking path along Strada Statale N. 9 until you get there. Won't miss it. Magnificent, new four-story building, half-circle shaped, smooth beige exterior on west side, and glass scenic windows on crescent east face. Beautiful. Would you like map?"

Logan thought about it. Something did not seem right to him because the new Physics and Astronomy building was not a structure Copernicus would have ever set foot in unless parts of the old building remained intact. "How 'new' is the building?" he asked.

"Construction finished a year after the Department of Physics and Department of Astronomy merged five years ago."

"Where was the Department of Astronomy located before that?" asked Logan.

"Until a few years ago, it was here, and before that, it was at Palazzo Poggi's Old Observatory across the street. There is nothing here at the Palazzo anymore, but there is a museum in the Old Observatory where the astronomy school used to be that is open to visitors." The young attendant reached into a drawer full of museum brochures written in multiple languages and pulled out a version written in English. "Here, this brochure contains information about the University's fourteen museums, including one across the street called the *Musei di Palazzo Poggi,* which has exhibits where Astronomy Department used to be. Here you go." He handed it to them.

"Thank you," said Logan. Logan and Emma stepped off to the side to look at the brochure. Logan thumbed through the pages until he found a section discussing the *Musei di Palazzo Poggi* and a page about the Astronomical Observatory. They read it together:

The Bologna Astronomical Observatory

The Palazzo Poggi once housed the University of
Bologna's Department of Astronomy and

116

Astronomical Observatory. There is now a museum situated in the very rooms once used for astronomical observation and study in the Old Observatory. The rooms contain a remarkable collection of instruments used by renowned university astronomers over the years. In the Room of the Studiosi (Scholars) are original texts and writings from the University's most noteworthy astronomer, Nicolaus Copernicus, including Copernicus' seminal work, the *De Revolutionibus Orbium Coelestium*, relocated from its original home in the Archiginnasio of Bologna.

"Wait… Do you see the end of that last sentence??" exclaimed Emma. "What does 'relocated from its original home in the Archiginnasio' mean? Was the Astronomy Department somewhere else before Palazzo Poggi when Copernicus attended the University?"

Emma returned to the information desk and asked the attendant, "I am sorry for bothering you again, but can you please tell us what the 'Archiginnasio of Bologna' is?"

The young man replied, "It is no intrusion, at all. I would be happy to, but I think there is a page in the brochure I handed you that describes it much better than me. The Archiginnasio is one of the University of Bologna's earliest buildings." He pointed them to the page he was referring to:

The Archiginnasio of Bologna

The Archiginnasio of Bologna is one of the most important buildings in Bologna. Its construction dates back to the 15th century. For nearly four centuries, it served as the main building of the University. The Archiginnasio ceased being a University in 1803 when the University moved to Palazzo Poggi, where it remains today. The Archiginnasio still houses the Archiginnasio Municipal Library and an Anatomical Theatre, open for visitors to explore.

"Interesting," said Emma. "So, the Department of Astronomy was somewhere else before the Old Observatory at the *Musei di Palazzo Poggi?*"

The young man responded, "It has been in many places since the University was first founded in 1088, but from 15th to early 19th centuries, the Department of Astronomy was at the Archiginnasio until the University moved here."

"What's there to see at the Archiginnasio?" asked Logan.

"You mean, other than the library and theatre? Actually, it is one of my favorite places in city to go because of the history. Its upper hallways are decorated with more than 6,000 coats of arms dating back to 15th century, painted on the walls by students elected the honor from their *nationes*, means to you, eh, their *student organizations*. The coats always show year, student's nationes, hometown, name, and typically some personal words or art. Every year, students voted honor from their nationes did this. Is much fun. I highly recommend for you to see, if you have interest."

Intrigued, Logan asked, "Did the astronomy school participate in this coat of arms tradition?"

"Yes, I think all of the schools did, every year."

"Is it near here?" asked Emma.

"Ten minutes."

Logan looked at Emma and said, "It's worth a look, this Archiginnasio place. Coats of Arms preserved for hundreds of years seems like a place someone might put something if they wanted to ensure its survival."

"And the 15th to 19th centuries do overlap with when Copernicus attended the school," replied Emma. "I think we should start there and then visit the *Musei di Palazzo Poggi* after that."

Looking at the young man, Emma said, "Grazie."

Logan and Emma studied the brochure one last time. There was a tourist-friendly city map in there showing them exactly where they needed to go to find the Archiginnasio. Emma put the brochure in her backpack and off they went.

When they stepped back outside, the late afternoon sky seemed slightly darker, a bit less inviting. Although they wanted to keep an eye out for anyone following them, it was becoming harder to do so as the shadows grew longer.

"Let's stay off the main streets," said Emma. "The map in the brochure shows some side streets we can take."

Emma guided them along a more discreet route gleaned from the map. Ironically, they headed right back to where they started, Bologna's historic city center. They slipped through streets and alleys until reaching the Archiginnasio.

They entered the Archiginnasio's inviting 140-meter-long porch underneath thirty arches supported by sandstone columns. Inside, they found a central courtyard and two stairways leading to the upper floors where the halls of study awaited. Precisely as the info desk attendant described, thousands of coats of arms painted in the shape of a "shield" or "crest" lined the walls in both directions. Each shield was unique and personalized.

With the coats organized by year, following the signs, they headed down the hall dedicated to coats of arms from the 15th and 16th centuries. The coats got older the farther down the hall they went. They tracked the descending years until they found what they were looking for, shields dating back to the years 1496-1498.

1496 was the year Copernicus commenced his studies at the University of Bologna under Novara, and 1498 was when Columbus set sail on his third voyage aboard the Vaqueños carrying the Norwegian Albo. If there was something left behind by or about the Norwegian they now suspected was the White-Eyed Star God, they expected it to fall between the years, 1496-1498; that is, *if* the School of Astronomy participated in the tradition of painting a coat of arms on the wall every year.

They looked, and they were right! Each year, the designated honoree from the School of Astronomy painted a coat of arms on the wall, and in 1496, the designee was none other than Nicholas Copernicus.

A young 23-year old Copernicus outlined his shield with brilliant celestial designs on a four-pronged coat of arms with a symbol in each corner: the moon, a star-scope, the sun, and a winged angel borrowed from the coat of arms from his hometown of Toruń, Prussia.

"Look at that," said Logan. "Just like the guy at Palazzo Poggi said, the coat shows the year, 1496; name, Nicholas Copernicus; hometown, Toruń; and the name of his school, Astronomia. What are those words written below 'Astronomia?'"

Logan was referring to the words Copernicus wrote that read, "Il mio sogno è per contemplare le stelle, per un giorno, il mio paese di origine esse."

Emma studied them, and then, translated the words for Logan, "'My dream is to gaze upon the stars, for someday, my home shall be up there.' Interesting," she remarked.

"Hey, check this out," said Logan, pointing to a coat of arms two rows over from the year 1497.

"Is that…"

"I think we just hit the jackpot," proclaimed Logan. "It looks like the School of Astronomy's honoree in 1497 was someone by the name of 'Albo Nor.'"

"Albo?"

"Yep."

"Wow," said Emma.

"It says 1497, Albo Nor, Scuola di Astronomia, which I assume means School of Astronomy, and I don't know what those last words mean, 'città natale: sotto.'"

Emma did. She explained, "They mean, 'hometown: below.'"

Looking at what was 'below' on the shield, there was a significantly faded white brick castle with two towers flanking a larger tower in the middle. The whole castle sat on a dark hill against a red skyline. Presumably, the faded white brick castle represented Albo Nor's hometown in some way.

Painted over the coat of arms was a thin banner partially covering the castle, like a sash hanging from one's upper shoulder down to one's opposite waist. Set inside the banner were tiny letters they could not quite make out because the lettering had faded over time.

"We need to see what that says," said Emma.

"The brochure said the Archiginnasio still has a municipal library here today, right?"

"Yeah. I think I saw it on the first floor on our way in," replied Emma.

"Maybe the library has books about the shields on the walls," Logan suggested.

They went downstairs to the library. While it also cleverly incorporated gift shop elements into the aisles and walls between the shelves of books, it was, nonetheless, a still-functioning library. An elderly reference librarian wearing a long, white dress and long-sleeve gray sweater sat at the front desk, doubling as the gift shop clerk.

"Posso aiutarti?" the librarian asked.

Emma asked her in Italian whether the library had any books about the coats of arms on the 2nd floor.

"Sí," the librarian said. She led Logan and Emma to a middle aisle. After searching for a moment, she grabbed an older book called *Il Scudi di Tempo*, which Emma knew meant *The Shields of Time,* and handed it to them.

Logan flipped through the pages. It had photographs of the shields, although in black and white only, but it quickly became clear that *Il Scudi di Tempo* focused on coats of arms made by the University's more noteworthy alumni, including Pope Alexander VI, Pope Innocent IX, Pope Gregory XIII, Nicolaus Copernicus, and others of significance. Unfortunately, the book did not have Albo Nor's shield. Apparently, he was not 'notable' enough.

"Is this the only one that you have?" asked Logan.

"Mi dispiace, signore," replied the librarian. "I speak little English, but I did not hear entire question. Can you, eh, say again?"

"Do you have any more books about the Archiginnasio's coats of arms?" Logan asked again.

"For more stemmi, maybe, eh, try biblioteca's microfilm catalogare."

"What did she say?" asked Logan.

"She said, 'for more coats, maybe we can try the library's microfilm catalog."

"Yeah, that might work," agreed Logan.

Turning to the librarian, Emma said, "Per favore."

The librarian led them back to a cubicle near the front where the microfilm viewer was. She sat them down and returned to her desk to search the computer to see if she had what they were looking for. They were in luck. The coats were catalogued in film. Wanting to know which year they were interested in, the librarian asked, "Che anno?"

"1497," answered Emma, identifying the year that matched Albo Nor's coat of arms.

The librarian disappeared into the library's backroom to retrieve what they had asked for. After a couple of minutes, the librarian returned with a small box of flat film with the years, "1450-1600," written on it. She handed the box to them.

"Grazie," responded Emma.

Neither Logan nor Emma had used a microfilm reader before. Those had gone out of style when they were young, and computers took over libraries and archival systems around the world. Still, using the machine proved easy enough. They simply turned the machine on and fed the flat film strip into it, and on the screen in front of them, images of coats of arms appeared. Logan turned the knob in either direction, allowing him to move on to the next image or return to the previous image. He slowly turned the knob to the right until he found the coat they were looking for: a much clearer picture of Albo Nor's coat of arms depicting a white brick castle on a black hill, set against a red skyline, with a banner through the middle.

"Oh, wow. Those look like Roman numerals in the banner," said Emma, glad to now be able to better see what was written inside the banner. "Can we make them bigger?"

Logan rotated the knob on the right-hand side of the microfilm reader to enlarge the view. Indeed, they *were* Roman numerals − written in sets of two − for a total of four groups, as follows:

LXXMMCCLXVI - MMMCDLXVMMMCCCII

MMMCDLIVDCCCL - CXCVMMCMVIII

MMCMLXXXIXD - MMDCCXCIXDCCCXXXI

MMMDXXMMMCXXX - MMCCCXXVMMMCDLIII

Logan took out his phone to take a picture of the coat, but Emma immediately put her hand over his phone to stop him. "No. Let's write this down. Who knows what they did to our phones."

"Right." Logan went into his backpack, pulled out a pad and pencil and made a sketch of the coat, the castle, the banner, and the Roman numerals. He tore off the page and shoved it into his back pocket.

Logan removed the microfilm from the reader and put it back in the box. He handed the box back to the librarian and thanked her in Italian. Looking back at Emma, he said, "Okay, let's get out of here."

Chapter 12 – The Four Corners of a Triangle

When they left the Archiginnasio, dusk was falling rapidly.

"Let's find an internet cafe to look these Roman numerals up," suggested Emma. "There were several near the university we passed by earlier."

"It feels like we are walking in circles," said Logan as they made their way back towards Palazzo Poggi. As they did before, they stayed off the main roads, sticking to less-traveled cobblestone streets and alleys.

It took them only ten minutes to find an internet cafe in the student-dominated portion of the city with i-tablet stations set up for those looking to drink, eat, study, browse, and linger. They entered the café, which was bustling with University of Bologna students. The café had a strong espresso-bean aroma and, like the city itself, featured old-world charm, distressed stone-work and wood color tones interspersed with technology. They made themselves comfortable at a table in the back and got started.

First, they tracked down a website capable of converting Roman numerals into regular numbers. After converting them, they ended up with a list of four to seven-digit numbers:

72266 x 3468302

3454850 x 197908

2989500 x 2799831

3523130 x 2328453

"Are those more coordinates?" whispered Logan. "They look just like the numbers from the Copán Temple after being converted from hieroglyphics."

"Let's do what we did before," replied Emma excitedly while also trying to keep her voice down. "Insert decimals, treat the Copán Temple as absolute zero, and look these up."

Logan made the adjustments and plotted them out. Nothing unusual came up. In fact, three of the four plotted out in the middle of the ocean.

"Huh... that doesn't help us at all. These coordinates correlate with nothing," said Emma, sounding confused and a bit disappointed. She had expected, or at least, hoped, to see *something* interesting pop up. They both did.

Logan had a suggestion. "If the numbers in the Copán Chamber treated the Copán Temple as absolute zero, then maybe the numbers from the Archiginnasio do the same thing. So, what if we treat the Archiginnasio as absolute zero this time around, adjust all the numbers that way, and see what happens?"

"It's worth a shot," replied Emma.

They looked up the location of the Archiginnasio, found at +44.4922 N x +11.3436 E, and made the mathematical adjustments by subtracting or adding to the coordinates taken from the coat of arms. Once they recalibrated the numbers, they were ready to try again.

"Okay, *now* let's see where this first one plots out," said Logan. He typed in the adjusted numbers for the first set of coordinates and watched as the program pin-pointed the coordinate

126

on the global map. Their jaws dropped. It was a landmark on Mr. Jackson's class project list…

Stonehenge. The digital pin plotted out right in the middle of the infamous landmark and its outer circle of trilithons consisting of standing stone monoliths, some as tall as thirty feet and weighing as much as 25-tons, capped by equally large horizontal lintel stones that, when arranged together, looked like doorways. The circle of massive trilithons surrounded an inner ring of similarly stacked monoliths with an altar stone at the center, and smaller blue stones arranged in patterns on the ground. Believed constructed five to ten thousand years ago, answers to questions like its origins, who constructed it, how they did it, and why, have remained a mystery to this day.

"That's interesting," said Logan.

"Now, do you think *that* is a coincidence?" asked Emma, making her belief clear it was anything but.

Logan didn't either. "Let's try another one," he said, inputting the next set of numbers.

"Wow," he uttered. The second pin plotted out in the heart of one of the only archeological monuments in the world more famous than Stonehenge: *The Great Pyramid of Giza* in Egypt, another multi-thousand-year-old mystery of origin and purpose which was also included on Mr. Jackson's list.

Emma gasped. Putting her hand gently on Logan's shoulder, she urged, "Keep going!"

He typed in the third set of numbers and watched as the virtual globe on the screen rotated toward the Western Hemisphere. The program planted the digital pin right in the middle of yet *another* landmark selected by Mr. Jackson: The Gate of the Sun in Tiwanaku, Bolivia, the one with multiple 40-ton stone blocks moved from more than 50 miles away, lifted and fashioned into a free-standing, square-arched doorway without leaving behind even a single chisel or chain mark.

"Between Stonehenge and the Gate of the Sun, a lot of archeological monuments shaped like doors," said Logan.

"Just like the hieroglyphic doorway inside the Copán Chamber," added Emma, seeing a pattern. "And all of these coordinates, so far, seem plucked right from Mr. Jackson's list."

Logan eagerly punched in the last set of coordinates, excited to see what came next. The globe graphic on the screen rotated again toward the western half of the United States. This time, however, the virtual pin dropped in a place which was *not* on Mr. Jackson's project list... in southern Nevada in the middle of the desert 150 miles north of Las Vegas.

"That's odd, what's there?" asked Emma, expecting the pin to drop somewhere... *anywhere*... more interesting than that.

Logan zoomed in on the virtual map. Once he got closer, he realized what it was. "You're not going to believe this... it's a place called Homey Airport, a restricted air force base also known as... as *Area 51*."

"You mean, *the* Area 51?" asked Emma.

"Yep, the holy grail of UFO conspiracy theories. The U.S. government claims it is just an 'Air Force base,'" said Logan, air-quoting the words, 'Air Force Base.'

"Yeah, right," uttered Emma. "I wonder what's there that compares to all of these other landmarks. And how would the Norwegian Albo have even known about Area 51?"

"Well, it wouldn't have been called Area 51 back then, so—"

"I know that," snapped Emma, lightly backhanding him. "What I mean is, how would he have known about what's there?"

"There're plenty of stories about Vikings visiting North America long before the Europeans did, and many of them were *Norwegian*... maybe that's how," theorized Logan.

Emma looked at him, intrigued by his knowledge on the topic.

"History Channel," he replied nonchalantly.

"Still, I don't see how any of these coordinates fit together."

"The coat of arms did say Albo Nor's hometown was 'below,' referring to the White Castle... maybe we're focusing too much on the coordinates."

"Good point. Alright, let's try searching for coat of arms, white castle, red sky, black hill, and see what comes up," said Emma.

Logan typed in the search parameters. Pages of coats, crests and shields came up, hundreds of them. For more than a half hour, they scrolled down through the images, examining those that came close, but none matched. It took playing around with the search terms, but eventually, they found what they were looking for.

"*That's it,*" blurted Logan, pointing to a thumbnail image of a shield on the screen displaying a white brick castle with two towers on the sides and a larger tower in the center, built on top of a black hill and set against a red sky. He clicked on the image to make it larger.

"The shield and castle look just like the one painted on Albo Nor's coat of arms in the Archiginnasio," said Logan.

"Does the image identify who the coat of arms belongs to?" asked Emma.

Logan read the title at the bottom of the image. "It says, 'Château, Falaise, France.'" He clicked on the link and it took them to a Wikipedia page describing Falaise as a community of approximately 8,300 people in the Calvados region of *Normandy* in northwestern France. The page went on to explain how the coat of arms for Falaise celebrated the small town's dominant feature, the Château de Falaise.

"What's so interesting about that Château place?" asked Emma, unfamiliar with it.

Logan clicked on the image and a new window dedicated solely to the Château de Falaise opened.

"Listen to this," he said. "The Château de Falaise was the commanding Castle of the Dukes of Normandy, a long line of Norman Kings that included, amongst others, Duke William II, also known as *William the Conqueror*, who led the Norman Conquest of England and redefined the English monarchy."

"Maybe the Norwegian Albo wasn't Norwegian, at all. Maybe the 'Nor' stands for Normandy," said Emma. "Let's plot out the Château de Falaise," said Emma.

Logan went online and pulled up the Château's GPS location: +48.8932 N -0.2039 E. He wrote down the coordinates on the same piece of paper containing the other coordinates. He then typed the coordinates in to add them to the virtual map on the screen that already displayed pins for Stonehenge, the Great Pyramid of Giza, Tiwanaku, and Area 51.

Emma studied the map, which now contained *five* plot points: one in Nevada, another in Bolivia, and three across the Atlantic in England, France, and Egypt. How they all fit together was no more apparent now than it was before. "There's got to be something more to this," she said. Logan did not disagree. Then, it occurred to her...

"You know, on that first night when I realized the Copán numbers correlated to the stars and constellations, I carefully studied some of those constellations. Are you familiar with the Winter Triangle?"

Logan shook his head, so Emma leaned over him, opened a new window on the screen, and punched in the search terms 'winter triangle.' Logan leaned back to make room, taking in a whiff of the strands of her hair dangling in his face. Clicking on the image results, Emma selected the very first one to display the Winter Triangle constellation on the screen:

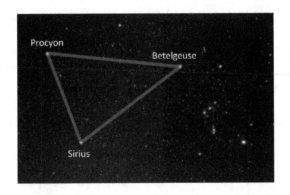

"Procyon, Betelgeuse, Sirius," she said, pointing to the constellation. "The stars, when connected by lines, form an elongated triangle that look like a piece of pizza pointing slightly up and to the right, like a clock-hand pointing at 2 o'clock." Using her finger to demonstrate, she explained, "Procyon's visible here at the top left of the Winter Triangle, Sirius is at the bottom left, and Betelgeuse is located all the way out to the upper-right tip of the pizza slice. Do you see it?"

"Yeah, I see it," said Logan.

"Great." Emma next clicked back to the GPS world map, which still had all five coordinate pins displayed. "Now, looking back at the world map, and specifically, at Area 51, the Gate of the Sun, and Stonehenge, do you see a similarity in the configuration of those landmarks?" she asked. She could tell he wasn't quite following, so she pointed to Area 51, then drew an imaginary line with her index finger down to the Gate of the Sun in Bolivia, then northeast over to Stonehenge in England, and lastly, back west again to Area 51. Her imaginary lines formed a triangle with Area 51 at the top left, the Gate of the Sun in Bolivia at the bottom left, and Stonehenge far out to the upper right. Just like the Winter Triangle, the three landmarks formed a pizza slice that pointed slightly up and to the right.

"The triangles match," said Logan.

"Right. Now, the Winter Triangle includes on its right side, the constellation Orion the Hunter, with Orion's back shoulder signified by Betelgeuse, the same star that marks the upper right tip of the Winter Triangle. And if you draw a line from Stonehenge south to the Great Pyramid of Giza, it resembles the line that one might draw from Betelgeuse down to the leftmost star in Orion's Belt, Alnitak." She drew an imaginary line with her index finger from Stonehenge down to the Great Pyramid of Giza in Egypt, and then toggled back and forth a few times between the screen displaying the Winter Triangle and the map so Logan could compare the two:

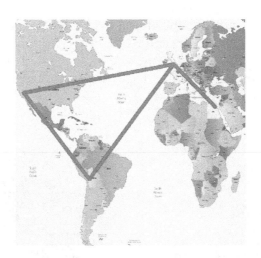

Emma continued. "And if you then draw a line from the Great Pyramid back over the Atlantic Ocean to the Gate of the Sun in Bolivia, it looks just like the line one might draw from Alnitak back to Sirius." Again, she toggled back and forth a few times between screens so he could compare.

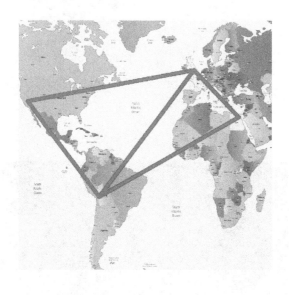

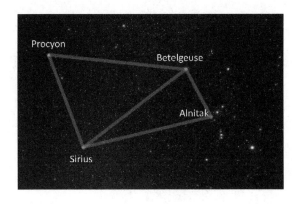

"Okay," said Logan.

"Now, do you see it? The quadrilateral that you get when you draw a line from Procyon to Betelgeuse, down to Alnitak, left to Sirius and back up to Procyon, looks just like the quadrilateral you get if you draw a line from Area 51 east to Stonehenge, south to the Great Pyramid, southwest to Tiwanaku and up again to Area 51. The quadrilaterals are identical."

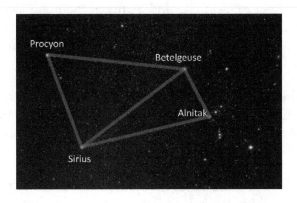

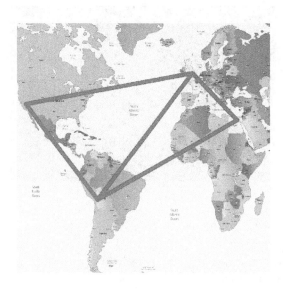

"I agree, I see it, but I'm still not sure what all this means," said Logan.

Emma clued him in. "With the configuration of these four archeological monuments on Earth mirroring the configuration of Procyon, Betelgeuse, Alnitak, and Sirius in the night sky, it's almost like they were put there thousands of years ago to provide humans with a geographic map on the Earth's surface of the portion of the galaxy Albo Nor wanted us to look at."

Speaking softly to avoid anyone overhearing, he replied, "So, you're saying these ancient monuments were put there by aliens thousands of years ago to create some kind of map to where they live in the universe?"

"A map with landmarks that would stand the test of time and tell us exactly where to look in the sky, a map sitting on the surface of our planet no one knew was there," Emma said.

"I can't believe I'm actually saying this, but assuming you're right, where does the Château de Falaise fit into this?"

"That's Albo Nor's 'home' according to his coat of arms, right?"

"Yeah."

"He's given us the quadrant of stars in the night sky he wants us to look at. Now, we just need to see if the Château de Falaise matches up with any stars in that quadrant of space that might just be his *home*."

She pulled up the online star map they had studied earlier in the week when looking for the extra Copán coordinate. When she found it, she clicked on the "Constellations" button and selected the Winter Triangle and Orion. The two constellations popped up on the screen, adjacent to each other, sharing the common star Betelgeuse.

After completing that step, she toggled back to the GPS world map showing all five coordinates on the screen for Area 51 in Nevada, Stonehenge in the UK, the Great Pyramid in Egypt, the Gate of the Sun in Bolivia, and the Château de Falaise in France. She right-click copied the screen.

Turning back to the online star map, she clicked a button called "Overlay" to transpose the copied portion of the GPS world map on top of the online star map. She clicked "Paste Overlay with Translucency," so they could still see the star map behind it. The GPS world map dropped right on top of the star map, with the star map still visible behind it like Emma wanted.

"It's a perfect match," said Logan, astonished, staring at plot points that synched up. Area 51 sat right on top of Procyon; Stonehenge sat right on top of Betelgeuse; the Great Pyramid of Giza covered Alnitak; and the Gate of the Sun in Bolivia mirrored the placement of the star, Sirius.

"Now, with the maps synched up, is there a star where the Château de Falaise is sitting?" wondered Emma.

They studied the star map and compared.

"Would you look at that," said Logan, "the Château de Falaise plots out right on top of a star in the Orion constellation called TYC 129-75-1. Again, it's a *perfect* match!"

Clicking on TYC 129-75-1, the star map offered very little information about it other than to say it was part of the Orion Constellation found at the star position 05 h, 54 m, 56.87 degrees by +07 degrees 15'59.6." Its distance from Earth was unknown.

"There's only one thing left to do before we tell the world what we've discovered," said Emma. "Go to the Château de Falaise in France to see what's there."

"You know, if we do that, we're going to miss our flight back home tomorrow morning."

"I know," said Emma, "but if we don't finish this, if we go home empty-handed, we'll never get back here before our competition solves this mystery and takes credit for our discovery as their own. I'm not letting that happen, are you?"

"No way," uttered Logan defiantly. He was no more willing to give the opportunity up than Emma was.

"My parents are probably freaking out right now," realized Emma. "Our phones have been off since we left the VSA this morning. It's almost 7:30 now, meaning back home, it's midday. I've probably got a half dozen missed calls and texts from them. And we can't call or email them because those jerks following us will track us down in seconds."

"Not if we borrow a phone and call a friend whose line they haven't thought to trace," suggested Logan. "Let's call Chad and have him call our parents."

"Yes! That's exactly what we should do!"

"We can have Chad call your parents and my mom and tell them that we lost our phones, but that we are fine, not to worry."

"Alright, I'll call him," said Emma, standing up.

"But you can't tell Chad where we are or where we are going," added Logan.

"I know. Wait here. And while I'm gone, take care of the tablet." Emma left to go talk to a girl she suspected was an American student studying abroad. They hit it off instantly and the girl let Emma borrow her cell phone. Emma went toward the restrooms for privacy, and while she was gone, Logan knew what to do.

First, he accessed the tablet's settings and deleted all prior history, web searches, and cached memory to prevent anyone from retracing their digital footprint. Then, he wiped the tablet clean by forcing a complete system manufacturer re-set. Finally, to remove the tablet from view altogether, Logan got up and handed it to the young Italian gentleman working behind the counter, telling him the device had crashed. When the young man tried to turn the tablet back on, he too stared at a system reboot screen.

"You're right, it … eh … non funziona correttamente … eh … not work correctly … mie scuse," said the young man. He walked back to the office and put the device in a drawer.

It took Emma only a few minutes to complete her call with Chad. On her way back, she gave the phone back to the friendly student and gave the girl some money to cover her meal. When Emma returned, she asked Logan, "Did you do it?"

"Yep. It's done. What did Chad say?"

"He said he'd call your mom and my parents. He got the sense something's wrong."

"You didn't tell him anything, did you?"

"No, and he wasn't too happy about it either. He just said to be careful. I told him we would explain everything just as soon as we could."

"You ready?" asked Logan. "It's 7:30 p.m. already. If we're going to do this, we need to go now."

"Yeah, let's go."

After paying, they left the cafe for the train station. The streets and alleys were now enveloped in darkness and packed with locals and tourists enjoying the nightlife of Bologna's city center.

A few minutes into their walk, Logan said, "We're going to make history together, you and I."

Emma blushed. His comment brought a huge smile to her face. "I like the sound of that," she replied. Like she did earlier that morning in St. Peter's Basilica, she reached out and took his hand, only now, there was no question what she meant by it. There were sparks between them.

In that moment, Logan honestly did not know whether he was more excited by their imminent historical breakthrough or by the lightning bolt of emotions shooting from his hand, up his arm, and into his heart. He had never been in love before, but right then, he was sure of it... he was completely in love with Emma James.

Unfortunately, the moment was short-lived. Off to the side, Logan noticed two men walking in their direction. The first man had dark hair and wore a black jacket with beige slacks. The second gentleman wore a dark brown leather jacket and blue jeans. He was burly with pale skin and short blond hair. He looked just like the man Logan saw earlier in the morning staring at them at the airport.

"Damn, we've got a problem," he whispered to Emma. "Two men walking toward us, one looks just like the guy I saw this morning."

Emma peeked. As soon as she locked eyes with one of them, they darted after the teenagers.

"Run!" yelled Logan.

They let go of each other's hands and bolted up the street. They raced by restaurants and tables with patrons and wove through crowded Saturday evening streets, but they couldn't shake their pursuers.

"Here, this way!" shouted Logan, cutting down a side street leading toward the university.

As they ran across the road, a car cut them off, screeching to a hard stop in front of them. To their astonishment, the driver pulled a gun and started firing at them. Emma screamed as they changed directions and kept running. The men on foot continued to pursue. The car followed, briefly cutting the two men off.

The sound of gunfire reverberated through the streets, sending pedestrians diving for cover. Parked car windows exploded as bullets flew by. This had gone *way too far*, thought Logan, angry and frightened.

The car gained on them. Emma yanked Logan's hand to pull him down a narrow alley, which let out onto a cobblestone street abutting a six-foot-tall brick wall. Although Emma had thought the alley was too narrow for the car to pursue, it did, making its way toward them rather rapidly. Right before it reached them, Emma and Logan climbed the wall and jumped over, dropping down onto a back-alley on the other side of the wall. The pursuing car came to an abrupt stop at the wall and reversed course, intent on finding another way around.

The two men on foot, meanwhile, scaled the brick wall and kept coming. They pulled their guns and started firing at Logan and Emma who ran up a path between two buildings that intersected with a more well-traveled street. Just before the men caught up to Logan and Emma in the street, another car intervened, smacking the two men out of the way while skidding sideways to a stop. More gunfire rang out, but this time, the shots came from a different direction and were not fired at Logan or Emma. Instead, someone was shooting at the two men who were chasing them.

"Get in," yelled the driver of the stopped car as the men on the ground rolled out of the way to avoid incoming bullets.

When Emma and Logan hesitated, another voice from the car's passenger seat, this time female, screamed, "Hurry up! Get in if you want to live!"

Emma grabbed Logan's hand and pulled him toward the car's rear driver-side door. One of the men on the ground lunged toward Emma, grabbing her leg. In a moment of pure instinct, Logan kicked him in the gut, knocking him over. The teenagers jumped into the car, which sped off even before the door was closed.

Shots fired again, shattering their escape vehicle's rear window. Everyone in the car flinched and ducked as they hurriedly drove away.

"You two, okay?" asked the fair-skinned red-headed female passenger with a refined British accent.

Neither Logan nor Emma responded at first, both still in shock from being shot at for the first time in their lives. Logan's pulse was racing a mile-a-minute, and he was out of breath. Emma seemed equally winded and her hands were shaking.

Their driver, who appeared to be in his late forties or early fifties with a scruffy face, light brown hair, and graying sideburns, accelerated down another alley and made a right onto a side street that ended in a tunnel. Although relieved to be leaving the bullets behind, Logan and Emma hardly felt safe. They had no idea whose car they had jumped into or whose side their rescuers were even on.

Finally, after gathering himself, Logan asked, "What's going on?!?"

"Who are you two?" screamed Emma.

"We're trying to help you," said the British woman.

"Help us? From who, from what?!" replied Emma.

142

No one answered them until they came out of the other end of the tunnel, their car merging onto the Italian Autostrada and accelerating to top dial speed. There was no longer any indication of pursuit. For now, it appeared they were safe.

"My name is Dr. Jonas Arenot," said the driver, "and this is my wife, Professor Jill Quimbey. I promise we'll explain everything in a few minutes, but first, we need to get you out of the city."

Chapter 13 – Finally, A Little Help

They sped away from central Bologna at a high rate of speed, leaving the firefight behind.

"Quick, you need to ditch your phones," urged Dr. Arenot.

Emma gulped, hoping there was another option. "Why can't we just shut off–"

"Because they're tracking you!" exclaimed Professor Quimbey.

Dr. Arenot pulled over at a roadside lagoon and yelled, "Throw them in!!"

Logan and Emma did as Dr. Arenot asked. They threw their phones into the lagoon. Instantly, a sickening feeling of isolation settled into the pit of their stomachs. They were officially cut off from the world.

Dr. Arenot resumed driving away from Bologna.

"Tell us who those men were!" demanded Emma.

"We don't know," said Professor Quimbey. "They could have been—"

"Anyone. They could have been anyone," interrupted Dr. Arenot. "Uptin will explain everything when we get back, but whoever they were, they wanted to know what you two were talking about back there."

"If they wanted to know, killing us wasn't going to help them find out," said Logan.

"So, what *were* you two talking about?" asked Dr. Arenot, peeking into the rear-view mirror at the teenagers while still endeavoring to pay attention to the road.

Emma immediately put her hand on Logan's knee to make sure he didn't say anything. It wasn't like either of them knew what Dr. Arenot and Professor Quimbey looked like. "Where are you taking us?" she asked, her trembling hand still resting on Logan's knee. Logan put his hand on top of hers to remind her that, like he promised before they left, they were in this together.

"Almost there... we're just outside of Bologna now," responded Dr. Arenot.

He pulled off the Autostrada onto a dark road somewhere outside of the city, the sketchy looks of which made Logan and Emma even more nervous. After multiple turns down dimly lit roads through a rundown neighborhood, Dr. Arenot pulled up to a dilapidated brown three-story apartment building with a post office on one side and a laundromat on the other. He drove into the apartment building's subterranean garage and parked.

"Alright, let's go," he announced, getting out of the car. Professor Quimbey followed.

"Yeah, but to where?" muttered Logan under his breath just loud enough for Emma to hear. Emma took a deep breath and opened her door. Logan did the same.

They got out of the car and followed the professors toward a parking garage elevator. Uneasy, Emma took Logan's hand, needing the comforting touch of a friend. They both did.

After entering the elevator, Dr. Arenot pressed the third-floor button and up they went. The creaky elevator rose without any urgency and had a funky scent that smelled like spoiled food. When they reached the third floor, the elevator doors opened to a drab hallway that smelled the same. Dr. Arenot led them all the way down the hallway to an apartment at the very end.

Rather than reach for a key, he stared up at a broken light fixture above the door for several seconds. Logan thought it odd until he heard a beep and the sound of an automated mechanism unlocking a secured door.

Dr. Arenot pushed the door inward, revealing a miniature command center with computers, oversized monitors, transparent glass panel maps, and other technology. Emma and Logan were amazed to see that inside this dilapidated apartment building, a state-of-the-art command center existed, filled with millions of dollars' worth of high-tech equipment. After they entered, Dr. Arenot closed the door behind, locking them inside.

A young man in his mid-thirties, with a clean-cut blond head of hair, wearing a crisp dark gray pinstriped suit and a white dress shirt, sat at a table in front of them. Seated beside him was a similarly-young, cheerful-looking red-headed woman with freckles, more casually dressed, staring at a computer screen. She gave them a huge smile when they walked in, one which suggested she had been looking forward to their arrival.

Dr. Arenot promptly inquired, "Any word from the team?"

"No, nothing yet," said the woman, who excitedly got up to introduce herself to Logan and Emma. "Hi, my name is Bailey. So nice to finally meet the both of you. Brilliant work, you're literally heroes at the—"

"Okay, that's enough, Bailey," said a gravelly voice from off to the side. A brown-haired gentleman with a bristled crew-cut and dressed in military fatigues, stepped into the room's center. "I think they've had enough surprises for one day."

Was that Uptin, Logan wondered?

"Commander Lewis," said Dr. Arenot, straightening up and saluting the hardened-looking commander.

"Why do you do that?" said Professor Quimbey to her husband. "You're a civilian, you know. He doesn't care."

"At ease, Professor Quimbey," responded Commander Lewis with a fleeting grin. Professor Quimbey rolled her eyes at him. He continued, "I just heard from Bryant and O'Neal. They got out of the city center safely and are on their way back here, now."

"Well, I should hope so. You nearly got us all killed!" snapped Professor Quimbey.

Commander Lewis did not share her concern. In fact, he appeared amused by it. "I inject a little spice into your boring academic life, and this is how you treat me? I would think a thank you is in order, but if you feel the need to blame someone, blame the teenagers over there," he said, pointing at Emma and Logan.

"Um, excuse me?" questioned Emma, throwing an offended look in the Commander's direction. "I'm sorry, but who are you?" she asked. "And is someone going to tell us what's going on, where we are, and who the hell those men were who tried to kill us?"

At this point, the finely dressed gentleman who was sitting next to Bailey when they first walked in, stood up and inserted himself into the conversation. "Emma, Logan, my name is Agent Uptin." Agent Uptin reached out to shake their hands, and then, he continued. "Those men back in the city were Khazanian Information Dealers... mercenary terrorists. Espionage for sale. The Khazanians sell state secrets to terrorist groups and hostile foreign governments."

Logan was confused. "What do they want with us? They'd kill us over the Copán star map Dr. Arenot discovered five years ago?"

"It's not just a star map," said Professor Quimbey. "There's more—"

"You're not authorized to share that information, Quimbey!" barked Commander Lewis, cutting her off.

Professor Quimbey did not agree. "And why not? It's not as if these kids don't know almost everything we do and in just two short weeks, they've figured out a heck of a lot more than any of us or your agencies were able to figure out in five years. So, I suggest if you want to make sense of this before it's too late, you'll upgrade their code word clearance or whatever stupid word it is your U.S. government uses when deciding who to let into your little club."

"I like her," whispered Emma to Logan.

Uptin thought about it. "The Khazanians don't make a move like they did with the two of you before unless they learned what they needed to know. Once they've got what they need, they eliminate their sources, making sure they alone can sell the information to the highest bidder. Whatever you two were talking about back in the city, the Khazanians obviously heard or saw what they wanted to know, and that prompted them to make a move."

"But how could they hear what we were talking about in the café? We whispered," said Logan.

Uptin shook his head dismissively, suggesting that their amateurish efforts did nothing to impede the Khazanians' surveillance. "Audio locational tracker, zoomed eye technology, who knows… these days, they can practically see and hear through anything. I apologize for being frank, but the Khazanians weren't the only ones spying on your conversation. There are a lot of interested eyes and ears on this. The clock is ticking. We need to know what you know and fast."

"Why?" said Emma. "Why does national security depend on whether the world finds out that Columbus was a bounty hunter, or that Copernicus plagiarized his theories, or that aliens might actually exist. No one will believe it anyway, just another far-fetched story on the back of the tabloids. And I sure as hell don't understand why the information is valuable enough to kill for. Interesting? Sure. But interesting enough for the U.S. government to set up a high-tech command center inside an apartment building thousands of miles from U.S. soil? Hardly. You're keeping something from us, and we're not saying a god damn word until you tell us what it is."

Emma stared down Agent Uptin, unwilling to break her gaze, intent on burning a hole in his soul, if necessary.

After the brief stare-down, Uptin blinked. "Okay, Commander Lewis, as of now, I'm granting them temporary NSA 51 Level clearance."

"Yes, sir," said the commander. Suddenly, it was clear to Logan and Emma who was in charge.

Uptin kept giving instructions. "Team, let's get them up to speed quickly. We may only have hours, maybe days, and we're certainly not getting the last several months back." Uptin paused, and then, looking at Logan and Emma, said, "We need your help, and you need ours. So please, let's work together. Dr. Arenot, Professor Quimbey, take them back to the 'Lab' and see what the four of you can come up with. And Bailey, standby for transport instructions. I have a feeling we're about to be told we need to go somewhere and fast."

The professors led Emma and Logan down a short hallway where the bedrooms were located. After all, despite having a living room set up like a command center, the apartment was still a functioning two-bedroom apartment. Before they reached the first of the two bedrooms, the door to the apartment opened.

In came Agents Bryant and O'Neal wearing civilian clothing, both fearless-looking soldier-types sturdily built for combat. Agent Bryant had a shaved head while Agent O'Neal had slightly more hair on top, sporting a tight buzz cut that left traces of his light-brown hair behind. Jointly, they saluted Commander Lewis.

"All clear back in the city?" asked the commander.

"Yes, sir," answered Agent Bryant, brushing himself off to remove some dirt from the skirmish in Bologna's city center. "Targets scattered just as soon as you got the kids out."

"He means just as soon as *we* got the kids out," mumbled Professor Quimbey to Dr. Arenot, refusing to let Commander Lewis have any credit.

"Good work," complimented Commander Lewis. "Dismissed." The two men retreated down the narrow hallway where Emma, Logan, and the professors were standing, squeezing past them and continuing on to the second bedroom at the very end. They went in and closed the door. Commander Lewis returned to the private conversation he was having with Agent Uptin and Bailey while Emma, Logan, and the professors turned into the first bedroom.

The inner wall to the right of the bedroom door was covered top to bottom by a giant world map with 9,097 pins stuck into it – it was a wall-sized Copán coordinates map. The side wall to the right had a makeshift desk in front of it stacked with books, notebooks, a laptop computer, pens and pencils. Underneath the window in the outer wall in front of them were boxes of books, supplies, and other random items. Finally, to the left of the door when they walked in was a couch, and in the bedroom's center, a card table with four metal folding chairs surrounding it.

"This is the Lab?" wondered Logan.

"Yep," replied Dr. Arenot. "That's Uptin's little nickname for it because this is where we've been working and researching."

The four of them sat down at the card table.

Emma looked at Professor Quimbey, who was sitting across from her at the table, and asked curiously, "Do you all live in here?"

"Please, call me Jill, and oh, god, no, of course not. We've got all the apartments on the third floor of this vacant apartment building rented for individual living quarters. Jonas and I have an apartment at the other end of the floor."

"What is all of this, anyway?" asked Logan.

"This," Dr. Arenot said, "is the dysfunctional collaboration of the National Security Administration, the Central Intelligence Agency, the Department of Defense, the National Space Agency, and that Uptin guy is a special appointee of the president, I think. Honestly, I'm not even sure which of those agencies he works for, but this is his show."

"How did you both end up here?" asked Logan.

"Good question," Dr. Arenot responded. "I suppose they needed someone intelligent in the room who knew what they were looking at. Because my team discovered the Copán Chamber in Honduras first, and made some progress sorting out the hieroglyphs, they thought my involvement made sense. And when my wife—"

"Uh-hem," Professor Quimbey piped in.

"I'm sorry... and when Professor Quimbey identified the atmospheric and gravitational anomalies in the hidden chamber, we started working together on this mystery. That's really how we got to know one another better, and the next thing I knew, she married me." Dr. Arenot paused, smiled, and kissed Professor Quimbey's hand. "A few months ago, Uptin called us and asked for our help. They lured us both away from Harvard for this top secret and extremely well-paying sabbatical, staffed us with a team of defense types, gave us some high-tech equipment, and brought us to Bologna, assuming we'd be able to solve this mystery by now. Only, we couldn't. It took you kids two weeks to do that, and all for a school project, too. Remarkable, I have to say."

"So, you *did* get my email?" asked Logan.

"I did, only I wish you hadn't sent it. That email put you in the Copán tracking database, and the U.S. government, the Khazanians and who knows who else on your trail. Apparently, someone hacked my email address, your phones and emails, too, putting them on your scent. With what's out there on the dark web, nothing's secure anymore."

"I don't get it though," said Emma. "Why the Department of Defense, the CIA, NSA? And why are these Khazanians involved? Over a map? What's this really about?"

"There's something very unusual going on inside the Copán Chamber," said Professor Quimbey. "The atmosphere is slightly different in there, maybe imperceptible to humans, but there is a skewing of gravity and movement of normal matter inside the chamber, and..." She paused. "Time passes differently in there."

"What do you mean time passes differently?" asked Logan.

Professor Quimbey explained, "I mean time moves at a rate inside the chamber that is .0134 tp faster than the rest of the planet."

"*How* is that possible?" asked Emma, shocked.

Dr. Arenot quickly confirmed, "It's not."

"Well, .0134 tp, or whatever that is, doesn't sound like a lot," said Logan.

Professor Quimbey concurred. "It means Planck time, and no, it isn't. You probably wouldn't notice it if you stood in the chamber for days or even years. But if you had to travel hundreds of light-years at the speed of light, the .0134 tp quotient would dramatically shorten the passage of time."

"Some believe the Copán Chamber is a transport or portal of some kind, a technology that can be exploited for military advantage," said Dr. Arenot. "Imagine if you could strike your enemies just by transporting onto their soil using portal technology, getting in and out instantly, undetected, and without anyone being able to stop you. I'm sure you can see how hostile governments and terrorist groups see this technology as an opportunity."

"And the U.S. doesn't?" countered Logan, finding it hard to believe the United States had purely innocent intentions.

Dr. Arenot said nothing. He knew Logan was right. "To us, this is a historic breakthrough, the academic and scientific discovery of a lifetime; but others see only the opportunity to weaponize the technology for military gain."

When Dr. Arenot finished, Professor Quimbey upped the stakes even further. "And because of the time distortion, there's also a concern—"

"More like paranoia," interjected Dr. Arenot.

Professor Quimbey kept talking, "… a concern there could be a time travel aspect to this technology. No one knows for sure if that's possible... but can you imagine someone with malevolent intent traveling back in time to change the past, wiping out entire civilizations or countries before they come into existence, eliminating world leaders or important historical figures before they ever rise to prominence or are even born? One small change to the continuity of events through history could destroy our world as we know it, eradicating billions of lives over thousands of years like they never existed, changing the course of human history."

"That's what the government is afraid of," said Dr. Arenot, "and why this initial academic mystery has turned into a matter of national, make that *international*, security—"

"That is valuable enough to kill for," said Logan, beginning to realize the magnitude of what was at stake.

"And if our enemies can't have the technology, they sure as hell aren't going to let us have it either," said Dr. Arenot. "They'll blow the whole thing up before that occurs, and who knows what happens if they do, destroying atmospheric and temporal anomalies no one understands. The results could be catastrophic."

Emma looked dazed. She was trying to process the significance of what they had gotten themselves into. It was more dangerous than she ever imagined.

"Maybe we would've figured this all out sooner," said Dr. Arenot, "had we not been walking around Bologna with our heads buried in the sand, relying more on technological gadgets searching for gravity, matter and time distortions, and chasing signals, rather than using our brains like you two. I've always told my students to think, to analyze, and not to rely on technology to do it for them. I should've taken my own advice."

Emma's stomach knotted up at the thought of all the information their conversation back in the cafe conveyed to the Khazanians. "We had no idea what was going on."

"It's not your fault," said Professor Quimbey.

"But it is," replied Emma. "We handed the info right over to the Khazanians and led them straight to it."

"Straight to what?" asked Professor Quimbey.

"Tell Commander Lewis we need to leave for northern France ASAP," Emma declared.

"Why? Where are we going?" asked Professor Quimbey.

"Falaise, France," announced Logan. "In the Archiginnasio, Albo Nor left behind a coat of arms with coordinates on it that plot out to Stonehenge, the Great Pyramid of Giza, the Gate of the Sun in Bolivia, Area 51, and the Château de Falaise, and a clue we think means the Château de Falaise was Albo Nor's home."

"Is this 'Albo Nor' the same individual Columbus referred to in his journal entry as... what did he call him... the 'Norwegian Albo'?" asked Dr. Arenot.

"We think so," answered Logan, now having a question of his own. "Were you the ones who viewed the journal after us?"

154

"We were," confirmed Dr. Arenot in a matter-of-fact, unapologetic tone.

"And the Novara house? Was that you, too?" asked Emma, slightly irritated.

More apologetically this time, Dr. Arenot responded, "I am sorry about that, too, but like Uptin said, you've had a lot of people listening to your calls, reading your emails and texts, some of them very dangerous. And as for the House of Domenico Novara, that was Uptin's call. Lucky for you, actually, because had we not returned to the city to check out the Novara House with Bryant and O'Neal, we wouldn't have been close by to help you when all hell broke loose."

"If it makes you feel any better, we found absolutely nothing in the House of Domenico Novara," said Professor Quimbey. "Although who knows if you kids would have found something we missed. You two make a great team."

Logan glanced at Emma, grinning. Emma's face turned a subtle shade of pink.

"So, what do you expect to find at the Château de Falaise, then?" asked Dr. Arenot.

"We don't know," conceded Emma. "When you plot out Stonehenge, the Great Pyramid, the Gate of the Sun, Area 51, and the Château de Falaise on a map, and then, overlay that map on top of a star map, those landmarks synch-up perfectly with stars in the night sky called Alnitak, Betelgeuse, Sirius, Procyon and TYC 129-75-1... and the Château de Falaise sits right on top of TYC 129-75-1. We think those landmarks were put there to tell us where in the night sky to look to find the Norwegian Albo's 'home,' and that leads us to the Château de Falaise, which matches-up with TYC 129-75-1. That's where we should go next to see what's there. I'm sure that's where the Khazanians are headed."

"Fascinating," said Professor Quimbey, "but perhaps there is still more to it, no?"

"What do you mean?" asked Emma.

"What I mean is, maybe you're right. If those landmarks really were put there to tell us where in the night sky to look to find this Albo Nor's home, maybe we should do just that, look at the stars and point the telescopes at TYC 129-75-1. We've got access to some of the most powerful deep space telescopes in the world and the backing of the United States government. That's got to count for something."

"Did I say how much I like her?" Emma asked Logan with an ear-to-ear grin.

"It's worth a shot," agreed Dr. Arenot. "And we do have time," he added, "especially with all of the logistics and planning Uptin's team has to take care of before we can go anywhere. We better hurry, though, before the Khazanians sell their information to a buyer capable of turning their own telescopes on TYC 129-75-1. If that star has a story to tell, we won't be the only ones to hear it for long."

Professor Quimbey got up from her folding chair and popped her head back out into the hallway. "Uptin, Lewis, we have some instructions for you," she said, loud enough for the two men in the living room to hear. The men hurried down the hall and into the bedroom. Professor Quimbey explained, "We need to get to France ASAP before the Khazanians."

"Bailey!" shouted Uptin.

"Yes, sir," replied Bailey from the other room, hurrying down the hallway to join the group in the Lab.

When she entered the bedroom, Uptin said to her, "Bailey, I need you to take down some instructions."

Bailey lifted her pad and pen, ready to take notes.

Chapter 14 – The PAPA

First Lieutenant Bryce Jameson grabbed a hot cup of coffee from the Pentagon Courtyard Cafe which, at 10:00 p.m. at night, served hot beverages loaded with caffeine from vending machines. It wasn't the best coffee in Washington, D.C., but it was good enough for the start of another long night below ground where Lt. Jameson worked the night shift in the Pentagon Array Deep Space Detection Unit, called the "PADS Unit" for short.

Suited up in his dark blue Air Force uniform, he made his way to the elevator bay doors found halfway down the hallway, being careful not to spill his lid-less coffee cup. He scanned his access card, pressed the down-button and waited for the elevator doors to open. When they did, he walked in and placed his handprint on the scanner above the keypad. Once the digital handprint screen turned green, he pressed "Sub-4" and down he went.

When the elevator shaft doors re-opened, 1st Lt. Jameson approached one final security checkpoint guarding the entrance to the PADS Unit, a retina screening machine resembling a water fountain. He leaned in to allow the device to scan his eye. After confirming his identity, a thick metal double door opened in front of him. The PADS Unit awaited.

The PADS Unit controlled and monitored a classified, high-orbit telescope array called the "PAPA" (short for Pentagon Astronomical Primary Array), which studied radio waves from deep space. The PAPA employed state of the art technology to expand and retract a spherical reflector dish more than 30 meters in diameter. Equipped with four extending radar transmitters, mirror refraction actuators, radiation sensors, and frequency enhancers, it was as powerful as some of the largest telescopes in the world, except the PAPA operated in outer space.

The Pentagon used the PAPA to explore deep space, as well as to detect inbound risks such as asteroids, meteors, and anything else that might pose a threat to Earth, from solar radiation bursts to electrical storms. As one might predict, the Pentagon also used the classified telescope array to spy on other countries from time to time. Of course, that was not its primary purpose, just one of the perks of putting such an advanced piece of equipment into orbit.

It took 1st Lt. Jameson thirteen years to get into the PADS Unit, including four years attending the Air Force Academy where he studied Astro-Physics, six years serving in the Air Force, and three years of post-graduate work at Cal-Tech. Although he was as smart and qualified as they come, that still barely landed him the job in the PADS Unit where the government spent significant tax dollars studying things it wanted to maintain plausible deniability over.

When he walked in, Captain Ainsley Lain said, "Long day?" Captain Lain, dressed in an Air Force-issued dark, navy-blue suit which complemented her collar-length brunette hair, was busy finishing up her shift operating a complex console of buttons, displays, and screens dedicated to the PAPA. "You look horrible."

"Nice... what, no hug or hello first?" 1st Lt. Jameson responded, taking her harassment in stride. "I got sucked into attending a spectrum analysis symposium with Davies this morning after I got off. I'm seriously working on less than 1 1/2 hours of sleep."

"You could have said *no*, you know," Captain Lain replied with a smirk.

"Davies got me into PADS. He's going to be running the thing someday. I always feel pressure when he asks me to go to one of those lectures with him."

"Well, just tell him the next time he asks that you lack the guts to say no, but that you really do need your beauty sleep because otherwise, you'll show up to work looking like total crap, completely embarrassing yourself in front of Captain Lain."

"Ains, I really miss working the night shift with you. Always fun. Like playing with nails and matches."

Captain Lain laughed, stood up, and made room for him. "Don't break anything while I'm gone. I don't want to show up tomorrow morning having to recalibrate the instruments because Bryce Jameson can't figure out the difference between an actuator and a reflector dish."

"You can stay if you like... otherwise, don't worry, I'll call you before that—"

The red phone on the center console rang, an indicator of incoming priority instructions. 1st Lt. Jameson sat down in a rolling chair and answered it.

"Jameson," he answered. Curious, Captain Lain stuck around to listen, wondering what was happening before she took off for the night.

1st Lt. Jameson repeated the instructions out loud. "Code-1 PAPA priority... copy... Captain Lain recalled... copy." He looked at Captain Lain, "Sorry, ma'am, you've got to stick around." Whatever informality existed between them before was now gone in light of the Code-1 call.

Captain Lain sat back down at the console in the rolling chair beside 1st Lt. Jameson. He continued speaking, relaying the orders received over the phone to Captain Lain, who wrote everything down.

"05 h, 54 m, 56.87 deg... +07 degrees 15'59.6," 1st Lt. Jameson announced.

Captain Lain wrote down the coordinates and punched the numbers into the computer. After doing so, she advised, "Access availability confirmed... two hours, eight minutes, and counting," referring to the PAPA's ability to receive signals from the coordinates while orbiting. During any given 24-hour day, the PAPA's ability to examine subjects on the other side of the globe was impaired by a lack of line of sight, but for now, the coordinates remained in range for at least another two hours and eight minutes.

"PAPA Protocol 5... copy," said 1st Lt. Jameson.

Captain Lain fired up the array and all of its component enhancements, including the four extending radar transmitters, mirror refraction actuators, the radiation sensors, *and* the frequency enhancers. It was not common to utilize the entire telescope array and all its parts simultaneously because of the stress that placed on the PAPA, so when the NSA Director called in Protocol-5, they knew something urgent was up.

It took a few minutes, but when the array was ready, Captain Lain proclaimed, "Target acquired and fixed. Tracking now."

1st Lt. Jameson hung up the phone. Captain Lain reminded him, "Remember, we have to provide updates at 15-minute intervals in all Code-1 priorities."

Captain Lain punched the coordinates into the database to see what they were looking at. Surprised, she said, "Why TYC 129-75-1? Based on these readings, TYC 129-75-1's been checked before... not by the PAPA, but that star has definitely been checked. Why a Code-1 priority for a re-check on a star?"

"Got me," replied 1st Lt. Jameson. They both knew only the NSA Director could call in a Code-1 priority, making the order that much more curious. Many times before, Code-1's had been called in, usually in response to hostile or aggressive military action, an inbound meteor threat, or other weather-atmosphere related risks requiring a high-level assessment, but in their combined 10 years of experience in the PADS Unit, a Code-1 had never been called in for a re-check on a star, rendering the order *extremely* unusual.

After a few minutes of suspense-filled silence, the first data points came back. *Static.* Zero deviations on all bandwidths with readings suggestive of standard intergalactic noise. No atypical radio waves. No radiation variances. All *zeroes.*

"Okay...," said Captain Lain, trying to think things through. "Lieutenant, let's have the frequency enhancers expand the range from 20 MHz to 5.0 GHz, parse out solar radiation bursts, remove sound waves from interstellar gas, planetary plasma waves, and increase the electromagnetic radiation wavelengths."

"Yes, ma'am," responded 1st Lt. Jameson, trying to keep up with his commanding officer's rapid-fire instructions. She was pulling out all the stops. He quickly keyed her commands into the computer.

"Also, might slow us down a bit, but let's up the radio spectrum bandwidth to 400 million simultaneous channels, see if anything pops."

Again, 1st Lt. Jameson complied, making the adjustments. They both waited. And waited. And waited...

"The 15-minute reporting benchmark's coming up, ma'am," said 1st Lt. Jameson.

"Lieutenant, let's prepare an initial Code-1 report of *data negative*," ordered Captain Lain.

"Yes, ma'am," replied 1st Lt. Jameson. He typed it in and reported back, "*Data negative* report entered and—"

"Wait!" blurted Captain Lain. "The PAPA's blinking. It's got something. Activate audio."

1st Lt. Jameson activated the audio and played the radio waves over the loudspeaker. They heard a sound resembling chirping birds and undulating low to high pitch sound-wave fluctuations . The real discovery by the PAPA, however, wasn't what they could hear, but rather, what they *couldn't*... the PAPA had also picked up on a series of intense "fast radio bursts" or "FRBs" hidden within the radio waves, each emission lasting no more than a millisecond, broadcasting at a radio frequency millions of times deeper than the lowest frequency discernible by the human ear.

"Ma'am, the PAPA's reporting a series of FRB transmissions," said 1st Lt. Jameson, "with non-randomized markers."

"Really??" questioned Captain Lain, shocked.

Naturally occurring radio waves were typically random. But in this instance, not only were the radio waves accompanied by FRBs, an extreme rarity in itself, but the FRBs were also generating something resembling a pattern. PAPA protocol required them to wait one minute based upon the theory that naturally occurring interstellar events might produce random radio waves that, when measured in short periods of time, might present like a pattern due to the small sample size.

"Ma'am?" asked 1st Lt. Jameson, wondering what to do about the 15-minute reporting period. Blowing it off was not an option; it was a breach of protocol.

"Lieutenant, revise and send a Code-1 report stating *possible positive detected*."

1st Lt. Jameson revised the report he had previously typed into the computer and hit send.

"Alright," said Captain Lain, "we've got 15 minutes to make sense of what the PAPA is trying to tell us. Let's run the pattern recognition software and set it for standard two-minute segments."

After several minutes, the initial two-minute segment report came in. 1st Lt. Jameson read the results out loud. "1 FRB... 3, 4, 3, 8, 8, 6, 7, 6, 1, 5."

The initial two-minute segment report focused solely on patterns lasting longer than one minute. Assuming one did, the second two-minute segment report checked to see if the pattern repeated and if so, the PAPA would perform a higher-level comparison.

After a short wait, 1st Lt. Jameson reported, "The second two-minute segment results are in. I'll be damned... the pattern's confirmed *again*. The PAPA's reporting thirteen instances of the identical pattern."

"Hmm, that's highly unusual," replied Captain Lain. "Before the next two-minute segment report comes in, can we rule out terrestrial interference? Satellites?"

"Yes, the PAPA's reporting no terrestrial sources. The PADS database has cross-referenced and confirmed... whatever it is, it's not originating from a satellite or terrestrial transmission."

"What about origin? Can we confirm this is coming from TYC 129-75-1?" Captain Lain wanted to make sure before sending in the report.

"Telemetry, angle, and source readings all confirm with a... with a .034% margin of error... the PAPA's convinced it's receiving from TYC 129-75-1, either that or the PAPA's a $3 billion-dollar waste of taxpayer money."

Just then, the third two-minute segment report came in...

"Repeating pattern confirmed, again," said 1st Lt. Jameson. "1, 3, 4, 3, 8, 8, 6, 7, 6, 1, 5."

"Such an oddly specific repetitive pattern, too," commented Captain Lain, trying to sort out the intergalactic puzzle. Intuitively, she knew there was no way the repeating FRBs with pattern markers could be the result of any natural phenomenon she was aware of.

"Ma'am?" asked 1st Lt. Jameson, awaiting orders.

"I'm thinking," replied Captain Lain, spying her own reflection in the computer screen staring back at her. "Let's do a quick system check, make sure everything's working properly."

1st Lt. Jameson ran the systems diagnostic and, after waiting for a few seconds for the results to come back, advised, "Everything checks out normally. No system or telescope malfunctions reported. Now what?"

Captain Lain pulled out a red notebook from a basket hanging beneath the computer console labeled the *"PAPA Procedures Manual."* Although she essentially had the procedures manual memorized, she rapidly thumbed through the pages anyway just to see if she was missing something. The last thing she wanted to do was send the pattern report upstairs until she was certain they had done everything they could to vet the results. Only, she could not think of any verification protocols they had failed to follow.

"I suppose there's only one thing left to do," said Captain Lain, ready to submit the data. Looking at 1st Lt. Jameson, she said, "Let's upload the pattern recognition reports and send them in. They obviously knew something was up, otherwise, they wouldn't have called in for a re-check on TYC 129-75-1."

1st Lt. Jameson uploaded the pattern recognition reports. "Uploaded and ready."

"Send," ordered Captain Lain.

"Yes, ma'am." He hit send. "Pattern recognition reports sent."

Now, all they could do was wait for further instructions and make sure the PAPA kept recording for the remainder of the observation window before TYC 129-75-1 went dark for the night.

"I guess you got your wish, Bryce. It looks like we'll be working together tonight after all," said Captain Lain. "You want to share that cup of coffee you brought down?"

"It's a little cold, but you're welcome to have some. So, is this like a coffee date?"

"In your dreams," she replied. "In your dreams..."

Chapter 15 – A Change of Plan

"Emma, it's time to get up," whispered Logan, gently rubbing her cheek to wake her. Although he knew it was time to go, he hoped she would sleep just a little bit longer so he could look at her peaceful face.

Emma stirred. "What time is it?" she mumbled with half a voice and a yawn. She sat up from the contorted position she had fallen into on the couch in the 'Lab,' her long hair still dangling over her face.

"I don't know, 2:30 a.m... maybe 3 a.m.," replied Logan.

Agent Uptin walked into the bedroom. "You kids, ready to go?" he asked.

"As ready as we'll ever be," answered Logan, stretching. Emma stood up and, together, they followed Agent Uptin back out to the living room command center.

When the teenagers came out to the living room, Bailey approached them holding two mugs. "Made you kids some cocoa," she said, handing one mug to each of them.

"Thank you," said Emma. "That was so nice of you."

"Thanks," added Logan.

"If you want coffee instead, just let me know, I've got a single cup machine over—"

"Bailey!" snapped Agent Uptin, abruptly interrupting her. "This isn't a bed and breakfast. What's the status?"

Bailey responded, "The charter jet is waiting for the team at the Bologna Guglielmo Airport to fly you all to Caen, France, just a half hour north of Falaise. Transport will be waiting for you when you get there."

"Good work," said Agent Uptin.

"Team, let's move out," announced Commander Lewis, who had changed into civilian clothing for the trip. "Bailey, keep us patched in at all times. Until we return, I have notified the Pentagon that you have Combat-5 clearance. Stay alert, but don't get power happy."

"Yes, sir," Bailey replied.

"What does Combat-5 clearance mean?" Logan asked Agent Bryant.

Agent Bryant, running his hand over his shaved head, replied, "It means he's granted her temporary mission control authority to call in backup military support for us, no questions asked or further clearance needed, for up to ten men and two helicopters. If she calls an emergency in, the Pentagon will immediately provide the support and ask questions later."

"Alright, let's go," said Agent Uptin.

"Wait, Agent Uptin, a call is coming in for you, sir," announced Bailey.

Agent Uptin put up his hand to stop the team and picked up the phone. "Right, yes, confirmed," he said into the phone. He hung up the line and went to his computer terminal. "An email's coming in that I need to read." Looking at Emma and Logan, he added, "Sounds like your little star had something to say, after all."

With nervous anticipation, they waited. The fifteen seconds it took for Agent Uptin to receive the message felt like an eternity. When the email finally came in, Agent Uptin opened it up and read it, taking his sweet time to process it.

"So, what does the email say?" asked Dr. Arenot impatiently.

Agent Uptin replied, "Radio waves from TYC 129-75-1 are sending back a repeating pattern... 1, 3, 4, 3, 8, 8, 6, 7, 6, 1, 5... that's it. That's all it says."

"What was that again?" asked Logan, reaching for a pen sitting on top of Uptin's desk.

Agent Uptin repeated the numbers, "1, 3, 4, 3, 8, 8, 6, 7, 6, 1, 5." Logan wrote them down on the palm of his left hand as Uptin spoke.

"What do those numbers mean?" asked Bailey.

Commander Lewis did not care. "If we're going to hit the window for Falaise, I suggest we move now before the enemy arrives," he said, thinking squarely inside the box. In fact, thinking inside the box was the *only* thing Commander Lewis knew how to do.

"Let's stand down for a minute, Commander," responded Agent Uptin. "Arenot, Quimbey, thoughts? Commander Lewis is not wrong, we only have a limited window of time before—"

"They're coordinates," blurted Logan, having already converted them in his head. He presumed like every other clue that, "They're coordinates telling us where to go, 13.4388 by 6.7615, or it could also be—"

Agent Uptin acted quickly. "Bailey, will you input the coordinates 13.4388 x 6.7615."

Emma interjected, "But those aren't the correct—"

"Bailey, input the coordinates," insisted Agent Uptin over Emma's objection.

Bailey did as instructed, entering the numbers into their global tracking database. When done, she said, "GPS marks that location in Central Africa, at the southern border of the country of Niger in the middle of the desert near the city of Maradi."

Bailey zoomed in using a satellite view of the Earth's surface. Although the imaging lacked perfect clarity, there was nothing there but dirt.

Agent Uptin looked confused.

"Like I was trying to say, the coordinates could also be 1.3438 x 86.7615 or 134.3886 x .7615," said Logan, looking at his hand and moving the decimal points around to come up with variations of the coordinates that still left four digits to the right of the decimal.

"Bailey," said Agent Uptin, "try those." She did and they plotted out in similarly uninteresting places in the middle of the ocean.

"And what *I* was going to say before Mr. Uptin cut me off is that 'absolute zero' is wrong," said Emma.

"Of course," realized Logan, kicking himself for having missed that crucial fact. "What if we use the Archiginnasio," he said, "or better yet, what about the Château de Falaise? All other times we've located coordinates, absolute zero changed to the current source. Wouldn't that now be the Château?"

"Ms. Bailey," Emma started to say, "if you treat the Château de Falaise, found at..." She paused. She reached over and pulled out the notes found in Logan's back pocket, and then continued, saying, "Found at +48.8932 N and -0.2039 E, and treat that as absolute zero from a coordinate standpoint, and go…" She grabbed Logan's left hand to look at the numbers he wrote down on his palm. "And go north 13.4388 degrees and east 6.7615 degrees, from the Château de Falaise, where does that put you?"

Bailey made the calculations. "If I did that, the coordinates 13.4388 x 6.7615 would fall in Møre og Romsdal, a county in western Norway. Specifically, it falls in a remote area of the Storfjorden fjord in the Sunnmøre region near Stranda, fed by the Norwegian Sea."

As soon as Emma and Logan heard the coordinates plotted out in Norway, they knew it was right. The name "the Norwegian Albo" made sense more now than ever.

Bailey zoomed in on the aerial view. It showed the glistening, icy blue waters of the Storfjorden fjord, surrounded on both sides by vertical, snow-powdered cliffs with cracks, crevices, and passageways weaving their way into the cliffs.

"That's it, there's gotta be something down there," said Logan.

"How can you be certain?" asked Agent Uptin. "Dr. Arenot, what do you think?"

"I tend to agree based on the Norwegian reference we saw yesterday in Columbus' journal entry *and* the teenagers have been right about everything else, so... I think we need to see what's in that fjord."

"I agree, too, but let's just be sure about this," replied Agent Uptin. "Bailey, can you try the remaining coordinate variations and move the decimal points around like the kid said, treating the Château de Falaise as absolute zero?"

"Yes, sir." She did as asked. "The other two coordinate variations both plot out in the ocean, as well, one in the northern Arctic Ocean and the other in the southern Indian Ocean."

"Neither sounds promising," said Agent Uptin. "I have an idea... Commander Lewis, you and I will take the transport to

170

France that Bailey's already arranged to check out the Château de Falaise and see what's there. Meanwhile, Bryant, O'Neal, you two will fly with Dr. Arenot, Professor Quimbey, Mr. West, and Ms. James to Norway to investigate the coordinates in that fjord and report back. We can check out the other coordinate options next if these leads are a dead end."

Everyone agreed Agent Uptin's plan sounded like the best option because it allowed them to investigate both locations at once before the Khazanians figured things out. Seeing no objection, Agent Uptin said, "Okay, it's settled. Bailey, let's get on the phone and start making things happen."

It took another 25 minutes for Bailey to make the new arrangements. When ready, Agent Uptin said, "Alright everybody, it's time. Good luck with your assignments. Stay in touch with Bailey."

Agent Uptin and Commander Lewis headed out the door and departed for the airport. A few minutes later, another car, an SUV, came to pick up the Norwegian-bound team made up of Emma, Logan, Dr. Arenot, Professor Quimbey, Agent Bryant and Agent O'Neal, to take them to Bologna's Borgo Panigale Airport, a private jet airport where Bailey had chartered a plane to take them to Ålesund, Norway. Ålesund was in the Sunnmøre region of Møre og Romsdal county at the mouth of the Storfjorden fjord on Norway's northwestern coastline. With a total flight time of around five hours, they would arrive in Norway at approximately 9:45 a.m. Sunday morning.

After the teams departed, Bailey continued monitoring their progress, proudly enjoying her logistical arrangements. She took great pride in putting together a perfect plan.

She walked over to make herself a cup of coffee from the single cup machine she had offered to Logan and Emma earlier. When it was done brewing, she took in a deep whiff of the coffee aroma hoping it would help wake her up; monitoring an operation at 4 a.m. in the morning was early even for her.

She settled back into her chair and used her cell phone to make a call. "Viktor, it's the Dealer," she said.

She listened to a male voice on the other end of the call speaking Russian. "У вас есть эти данные?" ["Do you have it?"]

"My team's got the targets secured, the information acquired and multiple coordinates to transfer," replied Bailey.

"Отправьте мне информацию чтобы я мог ее изучить." ["Send me the information so I can review."]

"No Viktor, that's not how it works. No games or I sell it elsewhere. I've got the North Koreans on hold, you jerk."

Over the phone, Viktor could be heard saying, *no, no.*

"$25 million wired to my account. You have the instructions. Once the money hits the account, then I send it."

"Американцы подозревают?" ["Do the Americans suspect?"]

"Of course, they don't," responded Bailey. "The kids have bought everything hook, line, and sinker. My team's put on a frickin' brilliant Academy Award-winning performance, and the professors have been clueless since the beginning... they still think they're working for the U.S. government. You better hurry though, the CIA is smarter than you. They probably eavesdropped on the same information we overheard the teenagers discussing in the cafe about TYC 129-75-1. It won't take them long to figure out what we now know and to point their own telescopes at the star if they haven't done so already. Now, do you want the information and the Americans delivered to you or not?"

"Я пошлю 10 миллионов долларов сейчас, а остальное после того, как получу информацию на американцев." ["I will send $10 million now, and the rest after I have the information and the Americans."]

"Tell you what, Viktor, because you've been such a good client in the past and let us borrow your country's telescope array for feedback on the star, I'm going to offer you a discount. If you want the information and an explanation as to what it all means, I'll sell it to you for $30 million."

Viktor angrily objected to the price increase.

"That's what you get for trying to change the deal, you jerk. Now do you want it or not?"

"*Da*," he said on his end of the telephone line, capitulating to Bailey's demand.

"Wire the money now, all of it. When it hits the account, I'll transmit."

Bailey waited for her screen to confirm receipt of the funds. When the notification popped up stating "WIRE COMPLETE," Bailey immediately transferred the money out of that account to an entirely different one, at another bank on another shore in another country.

"Что так долго?!" ["What's taking so long?! "]

"What, you don't trust me? What kind of person do you think I am?!?" shouted Bailey, offended that Viktor would question her integrity. "Standby for transmission of all coordinates, mission information, flight and travel details, and pictures of the Americans." She paused, waiting for the secure message to clear her outbox. "Okay, the files have been sent."

She waited a few seconds for Viktor to acknowledge receipt. "Viktor, some free advice because I like you so much: go heavily armed to the site in the Storfjorden fjord in case the CIA shows up, but I suggest you don't eliminate the Americans until they've found what they are looking for. They're quite smart, especially the teenagers. Let them do their thing, and then you can kill them or, at least, kill the professors and keep the kids. I was getting ready to eliminate the professors anyway because they were getting us nowhere, but those teenagers may continue to prove useful. My men will play along in the meantime, keeping the Americans in line until you're ready."

"Da," said Viktor.

"And one more thing, Viktor, don't kill my men. If you do, you know the price — $5 million per asset — so tell your men to aim their guns at the right targets this time. I don't want another incident like we had in Azerbaijan two years ago. Is that clear?"

"Da," he replied loudly through the phone.

"Nice doing business with you, Viktor." Bailey hung up the phone and said, "Jerk." She settled back into her chair and took a sip of her freshly brewed coffee. "Ahhh... that's a good cup of coffee."

Chapter 16 – The *Hvit Fuge Stranda*

The pre-dawn flight to Ålesund went faster than expected. Perhaps it was the unique comforts of flying on a private jet with seats that folded out into beds and personal tablet devices at each seat. If ever there was a selfie-worthy moment for a teenager, this was it. Unfortunately, neither Emma nor Logan had their phones, nor would the government ever in a million years allow them to post something like this!

Thanks to Norway's latitude in the northern hemisphere, this late in the year, the nights lasted far longer than the days did. Sunrise was close to 8:30 a.m., with only nine hours of daylight. As a result, it was not until the sun pulled its chin over the horizon that Logan could see, for the first time, what they were flying over… majestic mountains, white snow caps, glaciers, grass fields, and the splintered branches of Norway's deep coastal fjords.

"Have you ever seen anything so stunning?" asked Dr. Arenot, leaning over to talk to Logan as the teen peered out the window.

Logan stole a glance at Emma, who was sitting beside Professor Quimbey, and replied, "Nope."

Dr. Arenot sat down next to him. "Bet you never thought your school project would lead to something like this."

"Never thought *anything* would lead to something like this," replied Logan.

"Right," acknowledged Dr. Arenot. "I know I said it back in Bologna, but the way you two followed the history, the numbers and the clues like you did was really quite remarkable."

"Thanks."

"It's that type of critical thinking that makes for a great scientist, historian, archeologist, or really, *anything*. So, what are your plans after graduation?"

"Thought maybe I would take some computer science courses, then go into programming or something like that."

"Have you ever thought about going into archeology?"

"Never really thought about it, no."

"Well, you should. You've got a lot of potential."

Logan laughed. "And you think my potential's in archeology?"

"I'm just saying I think you'd be good at it. I see a lot of myself in you, young kid with a sharp mind, seeing details in history others don't."

"Does it pay anything?" wondered Logan, thinking ahead to the years of education and student loans that a career in archeology almost certainly required and the fastest way to get his mom out of her job.

"A little," replied Dr. Arenot, before conceding with a chuckle, "okay, not much. Still, you have a knack for problem-solving."

"Emma's the one with the knack... she sees things I miss. Sometimes, I feel like I'm just along for the ride."

"Don't sell yourself short, kid. The synergy that exists between you and Ms. James... trust me, it takes two." The professor winked. Logan smiled.

"So, why'd *you* go into archeology?" wondered Logan.

"Ever since I can remember, I've always been fascinated by the question of who we are, and the answer to that question always starts with where we came from. I've been looking for answers my entire life. When I was young, and the other kids were outside playing, I was the one inside reading history books, trying to see if there's something tying each of us together in the great fabric of humanity."

"And if there isn't?" challenged Logan.

"If there's one thing I've learned over the years, it's that we all fit into the puzzle somewhere."

Logan doubted that. He clearly did not fit into his father's puzzle. And what kind of master plan could possibly have his mother working fifteen hours a day just to scrape by? If anything, he felt like they were discarded puzzle pieces.

"*Everyone* fits in somewhere," said Dr. Arenot reassuringly, sensing the young man's doubt. "Sometimes, it just takes us a little while to figure out where."

Logan grinned ever so slightly. He liked the sentiment of hope embedded in Dr. Arenot's response.

The plane began a casual descent toward Ålesund Airport where they would land in about fifteen minutes. During the descent, Logan looked over and saw Agent Bryant open a silver case, double-checking to make sure he had all the weapons they would need. Agent Bryant said something to Agent O'Neal, who subsequently moved closer so they could divvy up the weapons between them. If Logan needed a reminder that this trip with Emma had taken on a life of its own, watching Bryant and O'Neal load up was it.

After touching down in Ålesund, they made their way to the airport's outer curb. Bailey had arranged for a car to take them to Stordal, an agricultural and fishing village just over an hour away. Once they got there, the plan was for them to charter a boat to take them out onto the frozen waters of the Storfjorden in search of the coordinates received from TYC 129-75-1.

The finely-timed arrangements were seamless and convenient; Bailey had taken care of everything like an expert travel agent. Logan figured she was probably looking on from her computer back in Bologna, proudly watching the logistics unfold precisely as she planned.

The long drive to Stordal around the Storfjorden fjord's winding perimeter evoked the teenagers' imaginations of the legendary Vikings who traveled these same waters more than a thousand years ago. At many points, the fjord branched off into smaller fjords, and every so often, they would see small villages or homes nestled into the gentle valleys squeezed in between the mountains and rocky cliffs.

The farther into the Storfjorden they traveled, the higher the mountains reached, starting at 1,600 feet near the mouth of the fjord and reaching 4,900 to 5,900 feet the closer to Stordal they got. Shorelines consisted of steep cliffs that plunged deep into the water and no beachfront. Not exactly ideal for sunbathers.

When they reached the fjord-side village of Stordal, Logan marveled at how much it embraced a more tranquil way of living from an earlier time. With a pace of life slower than the easy flow of the Storfjorden's waters, the few people walking around did so carrying baskets and pulling livestock behind them. There was one inn, one restaurant, and scattered homes around the village. And there was one boat dock, which was where they headed next.

A well-put-together shack guarded the dock with a sign that said, *Storfjorden Vann Utleie*, meaning Storfjorden Water Rentals. A simple, straightforward name that left no doubt as to what could be purchased there. Needing a boat with a guide, Agent Bryant approached the stalky, blond-haired man standing behind the counter while the rest of the group hung back.

"Hallo," said the friendly gentleman to Agent Bryant.

It only took a few minutes for Bryant to negotiate a full day rate with the business' proprietor named Svend who, for the significant money Bryant offered, agreed to personally guide their boat down the Storfjorden. The rocky stretch identified by Bryant spanned from Stordal to Stranda, although if the TYC 129-75-1 coordinates were accurate, they expected to be able to pinpoint the exact location in the fjord they were looking for within 1,000 feet of precision.

Svend excitedly readied his ferry boat for the six passengers, preparing to earn more money for this one trip than he had the entire preceding month. He thought it odd that the band of tourists only wanted to examine the cliffs on the side of a small segment of the fjord rather than tour the entire fjord for what they were paying him, but he wasn't going to ask any questions. Bryant told him they were conducting an ecological study, and that was good enough for him. If there was time later, he would make the offer again in case his passengers changed their minds, especially since he worked off rental fees and *tips*.

The boat shoved off and they floated south through the Stranda-pass portion of the Storfjorden. As he always did for unprepared tourists, Svend pulled out from a hidden compartment underneath the fishing harpoons, a stack of heavy wool coats to warm up his guests. He distributed them much to the delight of Logan and Emma who had been freezing since they stepped off the plane. It wasn't like either of them had brought clothing warm enough for the cold weather of Norway. They had packed for the more temperate conditions of Rome and Bologna, but when it came to sailing the Norwegian fjords in late October, they were several layers short of comfortable.

Bryant stayed with Svend to help guide him to the coordinates using a GPS app on his phone. Svend did his best to work with Agent Bryant but made it very clear through his animated voice and hand gestures that he strongly disliked using technology to navigate. It offended his Viking roots.

As for Logan, Emma, and the two professors, they marveled at the beauty of their surroundings, acting like awestruck tourists. Floating down the fjord's icy blue waters in between the snow-dusted cliffs and mountains had that effect.

While they admired the beauty, O'Neal kept a close eye on them. Logan caught a glimpse of O'Neal's eyes a few times and did not like it even though he knew O'Neal was just doing his job. Still, it made him uncomfortable.

It took nearly an hour to reach their destination, a portion of the fjord-side cliffs corresponding with the adjusted coordinates received from TYC 129-75-1. At first glance, the near vertical cliffs offered no obvious answers. Svend advised them that he had been this way a thousand times before and never noticed anything out of the ordinary although he did mention there were a few crevices in the cliffs adventure seekers liked to hike into.

He guided the boat close to the first of the two crevices. It was located high up the rock face and required a perilous rock climb to reach. It was an option, but none of them were prepared to scale the cliffs given their current gear and attire, not to mention their complete lack of climbing experience.

"Other one accessible more," said Svend in his best English.

"Take us there," ordered Agent Bryant.

Svend shimmied the boat down the fjord another 150 feet. It was not until they floated directly in front of the second crevice that it appeared in front of them, obscured by rocky outcroppings on both sides that concealed the entrance.

"Here," said Svend. "Yes? This?" he asked. The crevice was narrow and snow-packed at its base. Svend explained, "Hikers call it *Hvit Fuge Stranda*, in English it means the White Crack of Stranda because of all the snow that packs in there during the winter. Late in season, I sail by this crevice, sometimes it is filled white with snow from top to bottom."

Looking at the crevice, it appeared more accessible just like Svend had said it would be. Svend pulled the boat up to the side of the cliff where a series of large rocks allowed for a workable albeit icy climb. Proceeding cautiously, they could scale the rocks which got progressively taller all the way up to the mouth of the crevice about twenty feet above water level.

"Today good weather," said Svend. "Yes?"

Dr. Arenot blew a warm breath of air into his hands and said, "This is what we came for."

"Svend, can you anchor the boat down here so we can climb up?" asked Agent Bryant.

"I can," Svend answered. He maneuvered the boat as close to the rocks as possible and dropped an anchor. "If the water gets rough, I pull off and stay near. I don't want to slam rocks."

"Fine," said Agent Bryant, "but stay close."

Svend pulled out a wood plank, opened the starboard-side door panel, and laid the board down on the deck. He shoved the plank out until it reached the first rock, holding it tightly so his guests could walk onto it. "Not stable. Careful."

Agent Bryant went first. Despite walking cautiously, he still nearly fell into the water as the boat bobbed up and down, causing the plank to rise and fall.

"Careful, I say," reiterated Svend.

Professor Quimbey went next, heeding Svend's warning, extending her arms outward like she was walking a tightrope. She made it safely. After her, Emma darted across the board with confidence. Logan and Dr. Arenot took their turns next, navigating the plank without incident. Finally, O'Neal brought up the rear.

They climbed the rocks being extra careful not to slip. Some of the rocks required a hop or large step to reach, with each slightly taller than the next. In a way, the placement of the rocks seemed intentional, like someone had arranged them to allow a person to ascend from water level up to the crevice. They stepped off the last rock into the *Hvit Fuge Stranda*. Agent O'Neal was the last one in.

There was a layer of packed snow at the base of the crevice. Travel through the narrow passage was slow-going, although the crevice widened the farther in they walked. After 10 minutes, they came upon an entrance to a small cave, although the crevice kept going beyond the cave.

"It's a cave," commented Dr. Arenot. "There's a path leading inside."

"Okay, let's go in," said Agent Bryant, not hesitating for a second.

As the group started to walk in, Logan and Emma, while excited, suddenly got very nervous. After everything they had been through and discovered over the last few weeks, it had all come down to this: a cave called out by coordinates sent from another world! They anxiously followed the others in.

Inside, it was hollow with no outlet and plenty of trash left behind by disrespectful hikers. Professor Quimbey pulled out a small gravimetric device to take a reading of the gravity inside the cave, but nothing out of the ordinary registered. Additional examination of the cave with flashlights revealed nothing unusual in the small, empty cavern.

"Huh. There's nothing here," said Logan, surprised and noticeably disappointed. He had fully expected to find something more interesting than trash.

"Let's keep going," said Agent Bryant. "We can come back here if we need to."

The group exited the cave and walked five more minutes. They reached the end of the crevice where, lo and behold, there was another cave. As they did before, they went in and Bryant lit the way with a high-grade flashlight. Again, nerves overwhelmed Logan and Emma. This being the end of the crevice, they felt like this time, this *had* to be it. Logan and Emma were even more anxious than before.

The passage wove inward approximately thirty feet, emptying out into a round cavern with large boulders strewn about the floor. Enough light made its way in from outside of the cave to provide a dim level of visibility. As before, they poked around looking for clues. Logan studied the rough, uneven cave walls. Emma examined the rocks on the cavern floor. They found more plastic bags, wrappers and soda cans on the ground, confirming hikers visited this cavern, too.

Professor Quimbey pulled out her portable gravitometer to take more readings. "Look at this," she said to Dr. Arenot. "We've got a .004 dip in gravity."

"Interesting," he replied, removing a small barometric device from his bag to check the atmospheric pressure in the cave.

Bryant and O'Neal looked at each other. O'Neal began pulling his pistol out of his jacket, but Bryant shook him off. It was almost time to put an end to this charade, but not quite yet. Besides, it was only a matter of minutes before the Buyer's men arrived, so Bryant figured they might as well let the Americans solve as much of the puzzle as possible in the meantime. And truthfully, Bryant was interested in the outcome. In all his years as a mercenary, this was definitely his most interesting assignment.

Meanwhile, Emma walked around studying the boulders on the cavern floor. There were seven of them, which was, coincidentally, the same number as the number of landmarks that had come up during the Copán mystery: the Gate of the Sun in Tiwanaku, the Great Pyramid of Giza, the Copán Temple, Stonehenge, Area 51, the Château de Falaise and now, the Storfjorden. But was it a coincidence, she wondered? Studying the boulders a bit more, Emma noticed that, from a birds-eye perspective, the rocks rested in a pattern on the cave floor resembling the placement of Albo Nor's landmarks around the globe, that is, if the cavern floor was a map.

"Hey," she said, getting everyone's attention. "Don't think I'm crazy, but the seven boulders in here, if you look at them, they rest in a configuration on the ground that *kind of matches* the configuration of Albo Nor's seven landmarks around the globe."

Logan started walking around the boulders to see what she was talking about. It did not take long for him to see it, too. "That is wild. You're totally right. I wonder what it means."

Emma had a theory. "Maybe it's like a keypad to open a door, where you need to push the numbers in order, like a combination or something."

"Are you saying these rocks are buttons?" mocked Agent Bryant. "That's the stupidest—"

"Wait a minute," interrupted Dr. Arenot, "not so stupid. If you're right, then what order would you propose to push them in?" he asked Emma.

"Well, I'm not sure," Emma replied. It wasn't like she had worked everything out yet. "First, I assume Albo Nor came here to the Storfjorden." She walked over to the rock that most closely approximated Norway on a map and put her hand on it, slightly pressing down. It did not budge.

"I see what you're doing," said Logan, catching on. "Everyone, touch a boulder." Logan touched two at the same time.

"No," interjected Emma, "there has to be a pattern that allows one person to do it because the Norwegian Albo would have been alone." After considering the options, she proposed, "Let me do it." She walked around and touched each of the rocks, starting with the rock approximating the location of the Storfjorden, then Area 51, followed by the Château de Falaise, the Copán stone, Tiwanaku, the Giza stone, and lastly, she finished it off by pressing down on the stone representing the theoretical location of Stonehenge. Nothing happened.

"What about touching the stones based on the order of when the Norwegian Albo may have visited or built the sites," suggested Logan.

"Stonehenge is the oldest of these landmarks, I think," said Professor Quimbey. "That site is estimated by historians to date back as far as 5,000 to 8,000 years."

"Next oldest would probably be the Pyramid at Giza," said Dr. Arenot, "and then, the nearly 2,000-year-old Gate of the Sun."

"And the Copán Temple is 1,500 years old, based on articles I read, including yours, Dr. Arenot," said Logan.

"That's right," remarked Dr. Arenot, impressed.

"But based on what we know," remarked Emma, "the Copán Temple is not a place the Norwegian Albo visited until after leaving Italy with Columbus in 1497. And it's anyone's guess when he visited Area 51 since we have no idea what's even there."

"And where does the Château de Falaise fit in?" wondered Logan.

"Well, if TYC 129-75-1 is the Norwegian Albo's home, maybe we should assume he started there, and press Falaise first," replied Emma.

"That makes sense," agreed Logan. "But what about here? Did he come here after leaving TYC 129-75-1? Perhaps we press Falaise first, Storfjorden second, and see what happens."

"It's worth a shot," said Emma. So, she tried again, walking around and pressing the rocks in order, one at a time: Falaise first, then Storfjorden, Stonehenge, Giza, the Gate of the Sun, Copán and for now, she pressed Area 51 last. The result was the same. Nothing happened.

Agent O'Neal was totally unimpressed. "This is a complete waste of time," he muttered. "You kids have no idea... you're just guessing, and we're running out of time. The Khazanians could be here any minute."

Professor Quimbey had another idea. "Perhaps it has nothing to do with the order, at all. Maybe it's simpler than that. If you're going to assume Falaise goes at the beginning because it's Albo Nor's home and he would have started there, shouldn't you assume he went home at the end, too? And that means Falaise also needs to go last. Maybe the order of where he went in between doesn't matter."

"Okay, let's try that," said Emma. She walked over and pressed the boulder representing the theoretical location of Falaise. Next, she marched around and touched each of the other stones in no particular order before returning to press Falaise one more time. It was the only rock she touched twice. This time, something happened...

After pressing "Falaise," all of the boulders started glowing a blue luminescent color, and a loud pulsating hum engulfed the room. It startled everyone.

"What's happening?" asked Agent Bryant, uncomfortable with things he could not control with a gun.

Next, portions of the cave walls lit up the same shimmering color of blue, forming what looked like six doorways or portals in the cave walls. After a few moments, the portals stopped shimmering blue and began showing in crystal-clear detail what waited on the other side.

Dr. Arenot could see straight into the portal beside him. He recognized it immediately: it was the Chamber of the White-Eyed Star God. "That is remarkable," uttered Dr. Arenot in awe.

To Professor Quimbey's right, she could see the unmistakable sight of Stonehenge's massive stones stacked on top of one another. Stonehenge's monoliths appeared close enough for her to touch but just on the other side of the portal.

186

Another portal revealed a dark space that was harder to make out than the others, but through it in the shadows, they thought they saw a sphere resting on the ground. Area 51, perhaps?

Next to that one was an image of a dim chamber with limestone walls baring faint imagery that looked like Egyptian hieroglyphs, likely a hidden room inside or beneath the Great Pyramid at Giza.

To the right of that portal was a stone doorway that looked like Tiwanaku based on the outdoor setting.

And lastly, located to the right of that one was a beaming white portal of light projecting a glare almost too bright to look at. While no one knew what was on the other side, it did not look like the Château de Falaise. One could make the educated assumption Albo Nor's home-world awaited.

"You know," Dr. Arenot said, his voice quivering, "Nordic mythology talks about beings called the Ljósálfar, which means Light Elves, who were said to live in a place called Álfheimr. They were described as 'fairer than the sun to look at' in Snorri Sturluson's Prose Edda."

"Elves?" asked Emma.

"Yeah, you know, like in the Hobbit, Lord of the Rings," said Logan.

"I know what they are," remarked Emma. "Just not sure why we're talking about them now."

"Well," said Dr. Arenot, "I'm not saying we're going to find elves. I'm just saying we're standing in a cave looking for the home-world of an albino extraterrestrial nicknamed the White-Eyed Star God by the Mayans, staring at a doorway of white light. Maybe elvish mythology started right here."

"I guess there's only one way to find out," responded Emma, taking a step closer toward the light portal. Logan, Professor Quimbey, and Dr. Arenot followed her, prepared to examine it with her.

Meanwhile, Agents Bryant and O'Neal had seen enough. They pulled their guns. It was time for them to secure their targets.

Chapter 17 – The Enemy Among Us

Emma, Logan, and the professors stepped in the direction of the shining doorway of light they presumed led to Albo Nor's home-world, preparing to study it closer. Professor Quimbey broke out another device ready to take readings from the portal, while Dr. Arenot picked up a small stone that he planned to toss in as a test.

The faint sound of gunshots echoed from somewhere outside the cavern.

"Um, did anyone hear that?" asked Emma, startled.

"Yeah… that sounded like gunshots," replied Logan, all of the sudden feeling very uneasy.

"*Svend!?*" gasped Emma.

Pop!!! Pop!!! The sound of gunfire, much closer this time around, penetrated the cavern followed by the unmistakable buzz of an automatic weapon.... *t-t-t-t-t-t-chk-chk.* Vibrations triggered by explosions shook ice, rock, and dirt from the cavern ceiling.

"What's happening??" shouted Professor Quimbey.

"Damn," Bryant quietly whispered to O'Neal, sliding his gun back into his jacket pocket before anyone else could see it. He signaled for O'Neal to do the same. "We've got company," he mumbled to O'Neal.

"Oh, my god!" screamed Emma, dropping to one knee and covering her head after another blast. An eardrum-crushing boom rocked the cave drawing a shriek from Professor Quimbey.

"Who is it, the Khazanians?!" yelled Dr. Arenot.

"Probably," Bryant shouted back, perpetuating the lie about the Khazanians first concocted by Bailey. He looked at O'Neal hoping to quickly reach a consensus on an escape plan by eye contact alone. The Buyer was under heavy fire. The CIA maybe, perhaps the North Koreans, but whoever it was, Bryant knew it wasn't good. There was no way out of there. Their fate depended entirely on who won the battle outside and on the number of bullets left in their guns and extra cartridges hidden inside their jackets.

Another ear-shattering explosion caused Professor Quimbey to cover her ears and shout, "Bloody hell!!"

"Now what do we do??" yelled Emma.

Before either Bryant or O'Neal could answer, gunfire bounced off the outer rock and at least one bullet entered the cavern.

"Quick, over here," hollered Logan, leading the group to a safer location deeper in the cave. It was not much better.

O'Neal and Bryant pulled out their weapons and ducked behind the boulders, preparing to defend themselves. Logan watched the agents get ready, naively thinking they were preparing to defend the four of them.

The first armed intruders entered the cave in a frenzy, screaming in Russian, "Встать!!!" ["Stand up!!!"]

Having expected the Russians' arrival based on Bailey's information about the Buyer, O'Neal did just that... he stood up, tired of the charade, and ready to fight alongside his new business partners. But in the blink of an eye, O'Neal's life ended. One of the Buyer's three panicking men gunned him down with an automatic weapon right where he stood. The round of bullets fired into O'Neal's chest blew him back several feet where he lay motionless on the ground, his eyes still open from the instantaneous shock of death.

Emma covered her mouth to prevent a scream from leaking out. Her horrified, tearing eyes had never witnessed death like that before. And worse, she knew if they moved an inch, they were next.

Infuriated, Bryant hollered, "Мы на вашей стороне!!! Нас послал Дилер!!!" ["We're on your side!!! The Dealer sent us!!"]

His words caused the Buyer's men to hesitate. Taking advantage, Bryant sprang to his feet with his gun pointed at the head of the man closest to him, knowing full well the automatic weapons held by the others could kill him in a second if this did not work.

"Нас послал Дилер!!! Нас послал Дилер!!!" Bryant kept shouting. ["The Dealer sent us!! The Dealer sent us!!"]

Before the standoff resolved itself, more troops plowed into the cavern. The Russians fired in the direction of the intruders to stop them, but the incoming targets protected themselves with large bullet-resistant square shields. At least one of them threw a smoke bomb into the cavern to impair visibility.

Logan and Emma looked at each other. Neither had any idea who was shooting at who nor could they see Bryant anymore through the spreading smoke. They could hear gunshots and see sparks from gunfire, but not much else.

"There's no way out of here!" exclaimed Logan.

Just then, a bullet ricocheted off the cavern wall and struck Dr. Arenot in the back. He collapsed to the ground. Professor Quimbey screamed and fell on top of him.

"Jonas!! Jonas!!" she cried.

Lying face down, Dr. Arenot weakly uttered, "Go!"

"Go where?" said a devastated Emma, flinching and ducking at the pop of more gunshots.

"To the portal...," Dr. Arenot whispered in agony before passing out.

The light portal was the only one they could see through the smoke. It also happened to be the closest one to them. Meanwhile, Bryant took a bullet and went down, not that any of them could see him fall. The chaotic battle continued to rage on.

Professor Quimbey wasn't going anywhere. "You kids, go... I'm staying here with Jonas," she said. Professor Quimbey laid Dr. Arenot's unconscious head in her lap. Neither Emma nor Logan moved, so Professor Quimbey shouted at them, "Go!!"

Logan grabbed Emma's hand, pulled her up from the ground and ran toward the light portal. He intended to lead her to safety no matter what, even if it meant his own life.

Just a step or two short of the portal, a bullet ripped through the smoke and struck Logan in his right calf. "*Aaahhh,*" he cried, stumbling to the ground. As he fell forward, using his forward-falling momentum, he pushed Emma into the portal. Emma disappeared into the light. She was gone.

With a fleeting smile of satisfaction, Logan tried to crawl toward the portal, but before he could get there, a blue explosion erupted. Bullets had struck the base of one of the rocks causing a discharge of blue-electricity to splinter outward toward each of the other surrounding rocks. Everyone caught inside the dancing ribbons of blue light, including the two remaining Russians, one of the intruders, and Logan, collapsed from the electrical shock, unconscious. Then, like someone had blown a fuse, everything went dark; all went quiet. The portals disappeared. The battle was over. And Emma was somewhere up in the stars.

Chapter 18 - Too Many Cooks in the Kitchen

When Logan awoke, highly trained soldiers were pouring into the cavern, securing the cave, disarming and handcuffing the remaining men. Logan crawled along the cavern floor to the wall where Emma disappeared. He could not believe she was gone. It had all happened so fast. In the heat of the battle, all he could think about was getting her to safety. Now that it was over, all he could think about was getting her back.

Using the wall for leverage, Logan propped himself up, grimacing from the searing pain emanating from the bullet wound in his right calf. He placed his hands on the stone where the light portal once glowed, running his fingertips over the rock, feeling for Emma. It felt hard. It felt cold. With his calf throbbing and feeling woozy and light-headed, Logan lowered himself back down onto the ground. Moments later, a male soldier approached him. He had an American flag sewn into his uniform at the shoulder.

"You… you're American," said Logan, surprised and relieved.

The soldier, seeing the bloodied jeans at Logan's right calf, asked, "Can you walk?"

"A little," replied Logan, trying to stand up but struggling to put weight on his leg.

"Here, take my arm," offered the solider. Once Logan did, the soldier helped him hop out of the cave.

On the way out, Logan asked, "Did you find Emma?" Logan had watched her disappear into the portal. He knew what he saw. Still, a small part of him hoped. The soldier did not respond. He had no idea who Logan was talking about and other things to focus on.

Outside, U.S. soldiers were busy dropping long cables into the crevice from a flat plateau high up above. One by one, they lifted the Americans out of the *Hvit Fuge Stranda*, including an unconscious but alive Dr. Arenot whose body the soldiers pulled up in a basket.

They boarded one of two Boeing CH-47F Chinook multi-rotor, multi-blade helicopters waiting atop the Stranda plateau. The CH-47F's and their complement of soldiers had traveled to the Storfjorden from over the North Sea where they were stationed at Lakenheath Air Force Base in the United Kingdom, just ninety minutes southwest of Norway on the UK's eastern coastline. Once they were in the air, back to Lakenheath was where they headed next.

A team of doctors at Lakenheath's first-rate military hospital awaited Dr. Arenot's arrival, prepared to take him into emergency surgery. Until then, two medics aboard the helicopter, one male, one female, worked to keep him alive while a third male medic triaged Logan's bullet wound. The medic cut Logan's jeans at the calf to access his injury.

"You doing okay?" asked the medic to Logan, yelling loudly over the noise of the helicopter engine and spinning blades.

Logan, grimacing from the blunt force being used to stop the bleeding, replied unconvincingly, "Uh, yeah, okay." Logan bit his upper lip to hide his discomfort.

"You have an exit wound," shouted the medic.

Logan, in quite a bit of pain and not hearing the medic clearly over the deafening helicopter noise, asked, "What?"

Louder this time, the medic shouted, "The bullet... it went in one side of your calf and out the other."

Logan nodded. No wonder his entire calf felt like it was on fire.

Once the medic stopped the bleeding, he wrapped Logan's calf in a temporary bandage, shot him up with a stiff antibiotic booster, and injected him with a strong painkilling serum.

"Ah, that hurts," Logan groaned, wincing as the medic pulled a huge needle out of his calf.

Somewhat sympathetically, the medic responded, "Yeah, I bet. My advice to you is, next time, don't get shot. The docs at Lakenheath will check you out further once we get there. Hang tight for a few minutes... pain meds will kick in soon."

"Thanks," replied Logan, but by the time he did, the medic had already turned around to join the team assisting Dr. Arenot.

Professor Quimbey moved over to sit with Logan, fighting the urge to help her husband, trying to stay out of the way like the medics had instructed her to do. She put her arm around Logan.

"He's going to be okay," Logan reassured her, looking over at her distressed face.

With tears in her eyes, she replied, "I hope so." She wiped one back, and then, looking at Logan's leg, asked in a tear-infused voice, "How are you feeling?"

"I'm alright," he answered. "Everything's going to be fine, I promise," he said again, trying to comfort Professor Quimbey, and perhaps, even himself a little as his thoughts drifted to Emma.

Together, they sat back, watching, hoping and praying. Like the medic told him would happen, once the meds kicked in, the pain in Logan's calf subsided to a tolerable throb, making the remaining hour-plus helicopter flight back to Lakenheath tolerable. They reached the air force base, which was part of the UK's Royal Air Force base in the Forest Heath district of Suffolk, England, at around 3:30 p.m.

As soon as the CH-47F's landing skids touched the tarmac, medical personnel took Dr. Arenot by stretcher into surgery. Professor Quimbey frantically followed. Logan, meanwhile, limped off the helicopter with the assistance of the medical staff who took him indoors for a re-check on his wound.

Logan sat on a treatment table while a female nurse carefully examined the bullet's entry and exit points in his calf.

"Looks to me like a clean through-shot," said Lt. Anney, poking, prodding, and treating the wound. Eventually, she yanked on the bandage to make sure it was tight.

"Ouch!" he yelped.

"Sorry," she apologized. "I thought you were tough."

"Why do you say that?" asked Logan, cringing as Lt. Anney kept adjusting his bandages.

"We don't get many soldiers in here who've tried to stop a bullet with their leg like you."

The comment drew a smile from Logan. "Right..."

"There... all done," she said, much to Logan's relief. "You should be almost as good as new, in... *4-6 weeks.*"

"Thanks."

Logan stood up from the treatment table and limped to the door. Because of the aching yet confusingly numb sensation in his calf, he momentarily lost his balance and fell to the side. Lt. Anney caught him.

"Whoa, careful there. You alright?" she asked.

"Yeah," said Logan, embarrassed, holding Lt. Anney's right forearm.

"You sure? Do you need some crutches?"

Logan steadied himself and re-tested his calf. "Yeah, I'm sure."

Logan tried again, this time making his way to the door without incident. A young soldier was waiting for him just outside the exam room on the other side of the door.

"Mr. West, this way," instructed the solider.

He escorted Logan out of the medical wing and down what, of course, just happened to be the longest hallway possible, to a small drab room at the very end. Logan limped all the way there. The room had two chairs and a small square wooden table in the middle that appeared set up for a military grade interrogation. There was a rectangular black window panel in the wall. Logan could only imagine how many people were on the other side watching him.

Logan's imagination started running wild with thoughts of all the unpleasant interrogations he had seen on TV over the years. Even though they were not on American soil, the U.S. Constitution still applied in here, right? He kept reminding himself that he had done nothing wrong, but since when did *that* matter.

Like the long wait one had to endure in the small patient room at the doctor's office after being summoned from the larger waiting room, Logan sat on an uncomfortable plastic chair waiting for his turn for an eternity. He badly wanted to get out of there so he could focus on finding Emma but unfortunately, he knew that was not happening any time soon. If only he could reach Bailey and Uptin, they could explain everything and help, but he also wondered, why weren't they already helping?

Just as Logan expected would be the case, a stiff-looking military officer barged into the room predictably employing every intimidation technique in the book. He slammed the door. He cursed. He stared Logan down with an evil eye and no words except for an irritated grunt. He threw a stack of papers onto the table. It was all enough to make Logan laugh.

"You know, I haven't done anything wrong, so you can drop your act," said a defiant Logan.

"You sure about that?" replied the officer, ready to test Logan's resolve.

"Pretty damn."

"You think now's the time to be funny, Mr. West? We've got four dead bodies in Norway including a Norwegian national, a Harvard professor fighting for his life on an operating table, and four Americans working with world-class espionage mercenaries."

When he put it that way, Logan realized it didn't sound so good, although the reference to "espionage mercenaries" confused him. Who was he referring to? More cautiously, Logan asked, "And who are you?"

"I'm Captain Ross."

"Captain Ross, sir, I don't know who you are or what you think I did wrong, but I'd appreciate it if you'd start by telling me—"

"Where is Ms. James?" blurted Captain Ross.

Logan hesitated. He did not know how to answer him. "I... I don't know."

"Is that what you're going to tell Immaculata James' parents who are already struggling to understand why their daughter secretly got on a plane with you Friday and flew to Europe without their knowledge? Imagine how they are going to feel when I tell them that she's now missing after last being seen in Bologna with *you*. So rather than asking me what *I* think you did wrong, why don't *you* start by telling me what *you* think you did wrong."

"Are you accusing me of something?"

"Good question... should I be?"

Suddenly, Logan was scared. Did he need a lawyer? He did not know any other than Emma's dad, and he already knew how that conversation was going to go. He wanted more than anything to get Emma back, but if Captain Ross locked him up, how was that ever going to happen? He was in more trouble than he thought. Almost desperately, he urged, "Call Agent Uptin, Bailey, or Commander Lewis."

Captain Ross ignored him and asked, "If you can't tell me where she is now, then can you at least tell me when the last time was that you saw Ms. James?"

"During the fight in the cave, she..." Logan paused. How was he going to explain it? There was no way Captain Ross was going to believe him. Still, he had to try. "She disappeared into a portal that appeared in the rock when we activated—"

"Mr. West, stop screwing with me. I'm serious. Where is Ms. James, and don't give me anymore B.S. about how she disappeared into a magic portal." Captain Ross paced back and forth.

"But it's true. Professor Quimbey was there," said Logan. He could think of no other way to prove his version of events than to identify witnesses who could corroborate his story. "Ask her."

200

"Maybe I will after her husband gets off the operating table, *if* he gets off the operating table."

"Ignoring what I have to say won't help you. I'm telling the truth."

Aggravated, Captain Ross sat down in the chair on the opposite side of the wood table from Logan. He leaned forward with his arms crossed and said, "Fine, then tell me, is Ms. James alive?"

Logan answered with a less than convincing, "Yes."

Captain Ross followed up with the obvious question, "How do you know she's alive if you don't know where she is?"

"I don't know how I know... I mean, I assume she's alive... I think she is."

"And you don't know because she disappeared into a... a portal?"

"Of light..."

"She disappeared into a portal of light??"

"To another world."

"Okay," grumbled Captain Ross, jumping up in frustration. "West, if you don't start telling me the truth—"

"I am telling you the truth! Agent Bryant was there, too. He saw it, ask him." Logan was not yet aware of Bryant's fate in the cave.

Although it pained him, Captain Ross felt compelled to ask, "And who is Agent Bryant?"

"He was one of the CIA agents in the cave protecting us."

"I'm sorry to tell you this, but there were no CIA agents in that cave."

Logan was confused. "But I don't understand… perhaps they were undercover, and you just don't know it."

"Mr. West, I know more than you think I do and trust me when I tell you, there were no U.S. operatives in the cave. Now, who were you working with?"

Logan felt sick to his stomach. He had no idea what was going on, no idea who he could trust, and no idea what the truth was anymore. "They said the CIA, the DOD, the NSA… that's who they told me they were working for."

"And you believed them?"

"Well, yeah."

"Last evening, you were spotted in downtown Bologna running through the streets with Ms. James fleeing from gunfire. Who were you running from?

"The Khazanians."

"The what?"

"The Khazanian Information Dealers."

Captain Ross looked puzzled. "Never heard of them. Is there anything you're going to tell me that's true?"

"Yeah, that this is a waste of time. Emma's out there and we aren't going to find her sitting in here."

"Until I get some real answers, Mr. West, you'll sit right here. And if Ms. James' life depends on it, I suggest you start cooperating or I will hold you personally responsible. Whose getaway car did you jump into last night in Bologna with Ms. James?"

"Getaway car?"

"When you were being shot at, our agents saw you jump into a car. Whose car?"

"If your agents were so concerned about our safety, perhaps they could've stepped in to help us. Sounds like they didn't give a sh—"

"I'll ask again, whose car?"

"Dr. Arenot was driving with Professor Quimbey in the passenger seat."

"Where'd they take you?"

"Honestly, I don't know. I think we headed north, maybe east. I was so friggin' turned around at that point... I remember going through a tunnel that led to the Autostrada. It seemed like ten minutes or so before we got off on a remote road and parked in a subterranean parking garage below an apartment building in between a post office and a laundromat."

"You see, Mr. West, it's not so hard to cooperate if you try."

Logan gave him an irritated look.

"How long have Dr. Arenot and Professor Quimbey been working with the mercenary group?"

"What are you talking about? What mercenary group? Agents Uptin, Bailey, Bryant, O'Neal and Commander Lewis were all working for the CIA, DOD, and NSA. Dr. Arenot and Professor Quimbey thought the same thing."

"All lies, Mr. West. You were played for a fool, and right now, I'm just trying to figure out who was in on it."

"I find that hard to believe. Dr. Arenot and Professor Quimbey would have said something."

"Unless they were in on it, too," suggested Captain Ross, insinuating something Logan refused to believe.

"There's no way. They thought they were working for the same defense types we did. They're not spies. They were only interested in solving the mystery, in—"

A door opened, and in walked a high-priced suit worn by a tall, light-haired gentleman, with a scruffy face, puffy bags under menacing dark brown eyes and a worn-down appearance that looked like he had been doing his job for far too long. The gentleman was carrying Logan's backpack.

"That'll be all," said the man to Captain Ross, who half-heartedly agreed to suspend his interrogation after the new gentleman pulled rank on him.

The man waited for Captain Ross to close the door. After the Captain exited, the man said, "Here you go, Mr. West. You dropped your backpack in the cave."

"Thanks," said Logan, taking it from him.

"Some interesting notes in there," commented the gentleman.

Logan quickly, almost desperately asked, "Is everything still in there?"

"Sure, kid, except for what we confiscated in the interests of national security."

"Wait, what—"

"Mr. West, my name is Russell Karpyn, CIA Director - European Command. May I call you Logan?"

Logan shrugged his shoulders indifferently. "Nearly everyone since Emma and I got off the plane in Italy has claimed to work for the CIA, DOD, or NSA. I mean, seriously, I'm not sure we've met anyone who didn't. And now, Ross is telling me it was all a load of crap... so why should I believe you?"

"Fair enough," Karpyn conceded. He pulled out a laminated badge with his picture, name, and rank, "Russell Karpyn, CIA Director – European Command – CIA # 385-583."

"It's a palindrome," said Logan, nervously making small-talk.

"What?" asked Karpyn, thrown off by the comment.

"Your badge number, 385-583, it's a palindrome, you know, spelled the same forward and backward..."

"Got it," replied Karpyn, completely uninterested in Logan's observation.

Logan had to admit, Karpyn's badge looked legit and he *was,* after all, sitting in a U.S. military base, lending credibility to Karpyn's claim. "I suppose you're not going to let me call the president to confirm?"

"That's correct."

"So, what happens now? Are you going to ask me a bunch of questions like the last guy did?"

"The Dealer. She goes by the name, the Dealer. She buys and steals state secrets and information of high-value to sell on the open market. That's who scooped you up off the streets in Bologna and who you were unwittingly working for. And I doubt, or should I say, I'm certain the professors knew nothing either. That's how the Dealer works, she goes undercover, secures the confidence and cooperation of the individuals she needs information from, and then sells the information to the highest bidder."

"So now you believe me that we didn't know?" asked a surprised Logan. If Karpyn was trying to gain Logan's trust, it was working.

"I do."

"Then what was Ross doing before, grilling me?"

"I've read the emails, the texts, the transcript, and details of your journey. Ross doesn't know what I know although he may bluster more. What do you remember about her... the Dealer?"

Logan thought about it. Bailey was the only female in the room back in Bologna other than Professor Quimbey. Karpyn had to be referring to Bailey, right? "Are you saying Bailey is the Dealer?"

"I don't know what name she gave you. What did she look like?"

"Redheaded, freckles, like 5' 4", she reminded me of my Aunt Cathy. She seemed so nice."

"Yeah, that's her, and trust me, she isn't. She's vicious. Would've killed you in a second if it benefited her. She probably instructed her men to finish you off when they were done with you in the cave or at least, to hand you over to her buyer."

"And Uptin? Lewis? Bryant? O'Neal?"

"All of them worked for the Dealer, all extremely well-paid mercenaries using aliases, I'm afraid."

Logan's head spun. He couldn't believe it; he didn't want to believe it. He and Emma had been played, and now, Emma was missing because of it. "I need to get out of here! Emma's still out there and none of this is helping her."

"I appreciate your desire to help Ms. James, I really do. And I promise we're going to do everything possible to get her back."

"I doubt that. Your agencies have had how many years to figure all of this out? You guys got nowhere. It took us two weeks."

"No doubt, impressive, Mr. West, but we've got it from here, and I need your cooperation to let us do our job. Frankly, I'm counting on it."

"But I need to get back to Norway, to the cave."

"That won't be happening," Karpyn informed him. "That cave's crawling with the Norwegian investigation team operating in conjunction with our men. There's no more room in the kitchen for you."

"You need me if you're going to figure this out," insisted Logan.

"You may be right, and we won't hesitate to call on you if that turns out to be the case. The work you've done is tremendous, but you are seventeen and this is a matter of national security above your pay grade, one you and Ms. James, unfortunately, got mixed up with. I'm sending you home before you get into more trouble or worse, get yourself killed."

"But—"

"This is not a negotiation," declared Karpyn.

"The Dealer, she's still out there, you know. What makes you think I'll be safe once I leave here? Once I get home? Are you going to provide me with security? I've seen her face, her entire team, and I've seen how her operation works… if this was a movie, wouldn't I be the first person she took out?"

"Well, this *isn't* a movie, but if it will make you feel better, we can provide you with a security detail for the time being until we clear this all up."

"Do I have a choice?"

"No. Sorry kid. Thanks to your sloppy, unsecured conversation back in Bologna, the whole world's lining up to get a look at the technology inside that cave in Norway. We can't afford any more amateur mistakes."

"Mr. Karpyn, please—"

"Mr. West, we'll find her. You have my word. I've got a plane ticket waiting for you at London's Heathrow International Airport, an hour and a half from here. The plane takes off tonight, and with the time difference, you'll be home before midnight. We'll have a security detail waiting for you when you land."

"Alright," said a downtrodden Logan, now resigned to his fate.

"Oh, I almost forgot… here's a new cell phone for you, at least until you get home and buy yourself a new one. Thought you might need it in the meantime." Karpyn handed Logan a phone.

"How'd you know?"

"Like you probably guessed, we were tracking your phones until you dumped them in a lagoon. Another reason I'm giving you this phone is that my number is programmed in there. So, if you think of anything you want to tell me, anything that might help, or if you have any concerns at all, please don't hesitate to call or text me. I mean it. The phone's TLS encrypted, totally secure."

"Would it be possible for me to see Professor Quimbey before I head to the airport so I can check in on how Dr. Arenot is doing?"

"That can be arranged."

Just then, Karpyn got a message on his phone. He pulled his cell phone out of his pocket, opened up the message and read it. His face went pale.

"What is it?" asked Logan.

Karpyn looked like he had just seen a ghost. "The *Hvit Fuge Stranda* at the Stranda plateau's been attacked. The cavern's been blown up. The crevice has totally collapsed over the cave opening. Four Norwegian soldiers and four American servicemen are missing."

Logan's heart sunk. "But how?"

Karpyn no longer appeared concerned with Logan's questions. He signaled with a mid-air whirl of his finger that it was time for Logan to go, prompting whoever was watching them from behind the black window panel to come retrieve him. Two soldiers walked in to escort Logan to Heathrow.

"Get him out of here," ordered Karpyn.

"Yes, sir," said the men.

"I want him taken straight to the airport. Lt. Edwards has the details, is that understood?"

"Yes, sir," said the men again in unison.

Logan put his head down. He was leaving, there was no way around it now. He followed the soldiers to a black SUV, preparing for what was going to be the longest drive of his life followed by an even longer flight home.

After Logan exited the room, Captain Ross came back in.

"Did the nurse do her job?" asked Karpyn.

Captain Ross responded, "Yes, Lt. Anney placed the tracking chip inside the bandages around his calf. She said it's thinner than the tape used to wrap his leg, totally undetectable by airport scanners, practically invisible. Between the phone you gave him and the tracking chip, we should have plenty of eyes on him until he returns to the States. And I'll have the additional security ready for him when he gets there."

"I hope this works. The kid knows more about this phenomenon than the rest of us, and with the girl dead and the Russians blowing up the cave, we need his intelligence now more than ever. We're taking a big risk letting him go."

"Do you really think the girl's dead?"

"Do you really think she went through a magic doorway of light?" replied Karpyn.

Captain Ross shook his head. "We just need to give him some space. If he runs, he'll lead us right to where we need to go next. And if he doesn't, there's no better way to catch the Dealer. She'll figure out quickly that we sent him home and that West is still the most valuable intelligence asset on this Copán mystery. She'll track him down the moment he lands in New York and when she moves on him, he'll lead us right to her."

"Better be right," said Karpyn. "If anything happens to the kid, his mother's gonna sue half the armed services and probably the president himself."

"Do you need anything else, sir?"

"A little luck. And get me the NSA Director on the phone. We've got another problem."

Chapter 19 – The Wisdom of Courage

The drive from Lakenheath AFB south to London's Heathrow Airport was a lonely one for Logan, even with two servicemen in the car. He was in too much pain from the throbbing of his injury to talk, and too disheartened to make small talk. He couldn't even listen to his own thoughts, doing everything possible to ignore the heated debate taking place inside his head about what he could have or should have done differently.

Fifteen hours ago, Logan was certain this was the best weekend of his life. Now, after everything that had happened, he was quite sure it was the worst. How could he have been so naive? The unyielding momentum of excitement, his desperate desire to help his mom, and his feelings for Emma, had all commandeered his judgment, leading to this impulsive adventure gone wrong, something he might regret forever.

Captain Ross was right: what was he going to say to Emma's parents? What could he say? The last thing they were going to want to hear from Logan was that he had no idea where she was or that all of this had been Emma's idea. Talk about pouring salt on the wound. And his mother, how was he going to explain this to her? Logan doubted the upcoming seven-plus hour flight back home was enough time for him to come up with the right words to convey adequate apologies to any of them.

And then there was Emma. Where was she? He looked out the window at the emerging stars in the night sky, wondering whether she was up there. How could he find her? How could he help her? The only thought that comforted him was the idea that maybe she did not need his or anyone's help up there, wherever she was. Emma was tough and smart. Perhaps the adventure of a lifetime, even the adventure of humanity's lifetime, simply continued when she went through the portal. Logan smiled when he thought about it that way, allowing the idea to consume his imagination for ten or fifteen seconds until the overwhelming feelings of guilt and remorse forced their way back into his consciousness.

When the SUV pulled up to Air London's Flight Terminal 3, Heathrow Airport Security Officers were standing on the curb waiting for Logan. His military escorts handed him off to the Heathrow Airport Security Officers and went over the instructions. When everyone was on the same page, the officers took Logan into the airport, walked him to the ticket counter to retrieve his boarding documents, and then walked him to Gate-31.

Logan plopped himself down in a seat a few rows over from the gate. The Airport Security Officers stood off to the side, giving Logan space but still keeping an eye on him.

Logan sat there and waited. As he did so, other travelers waiting for their flights to board started gathering around a nearby TV screen airing a local station's news coverage. The growing interest of those around him sucked Logan over to the big screen, too. He was just in time to see and hear the station's repeat of the news cycle featuring a finely groomed male newscaster with a British accent:

212

"This just in... We are getting unconfirmed reports this evening that early this morning, Russia deployed troops from its occupation on the west coast of Syria, south on the Mediterranean Sea to Egypt's Port Fouad, and in cooperation with Egyptian Armed Forces has militarized the area in and around the Great Pyramids of Giza. All civilians in the area have been expelled. The purpose of this military action remains unclear. However, in a joint statement issued by Russian Foreign Affairs Minister Viktor Menputyn and Egyptian General Amam Al-Darith, Russia and Egypt claim that 'While many may view the development as unexpected, the Joint Exercise between Russian and Egyptian forces has been planned for quite some time and reflects the long-standing history of goodwill and cooperation between the two countries. Russia's troops will return to Syria upon completion of the joint exercises.' The United Nations has not yet issued an official comment, but tensions in the region are high, and the British Ambassador to the UN was not shy when he spoke to the media today..."

The TV screen switched to a news conference held by British Ambassador Broon who said into the cameras:

"Great Britain objects to the overtly provocative military incursion by Russia and questions why any military exercise, if that is truly what this is, needed to be carried out covertly and involved one of the world's most notable landmarks. Clearly, the Russian and Egyptian governments selected the high-profile Pyramid Complex in Giza to capture the international community's attention, and they have succeeded, although to what end remains unknown."

The TV view switched back to the news reporter behind his station desk:

"The British Ambassador went on to warn Russia to stand down and outwardly questioned why Egypt, one of the United Nation's closest allies and advocates for peace in the region, has opened its arms to Russia's renewed thirst for expansion of its military presence throughout the Middle East and Europe. Israel, Jordan, Libya, Saudi Arabia, and Iraq have all reportedly deployed combat forces to secure their countries' respective borders adjacent to Egypt and the United States has mobilized its Atlantic fleet. An emergency session of the United Nation's Security Council has been called. Going now over to our Foreign Correspondent in Egypt, Becky Rainen — Becky, what can you tell us about the latest developments?"

Logan walked away from the TV, oblivious to the concerned looks spreading across people's faces after hearing the news. He fell back into a chair.

Reporters claimed that the purpose of the Russian incursion remained unclear, but Logan knew what its purpose was... the Russians blew up the cave in Norway to eliminate the site as competition and, using the intelligence the Dealer had sold them, struck a deal with Egypt to secure exclusive access to the Great Pyramids in exchange for sharing their findings from the alien technology hidden inside. And in so doing, the two countries had pushed the world to the brink of war.

"Air London's 8:15 flight to New York, AL-2378, is now boarding," announced a voice over the loudspeaker. "At this time, we are pleased to invite passengers in Group A to the gate."

Logan looked at his ticket and saw that he was in Group C. No surprise, as Group A was reserved for first class tickets. The evening flight was not full. Within minutes, the airline attendant announced boarding for the leftovers in Group C.

Logan got up and headed for the gate, but as soon as he saw the mad dash of anxious passengers rushing to the front of the line worried their pre-paid, reserved seats were somehow going to disappear if they did not hurry, he waited rather than fight for position. When the line dissipated, Logan calmly approached the gate, handed over his boarding pass to the gate attendant, and walked down the jetway to the 747 transatlantic jet. The frenzied rush to the gate made even less sense once Logan reached the bottom of the jetway where he found himself standing in another line behind slow-boarding passengers.

After he boarded the plane, the excruciating wait continued. Passengers in front of him desperately searched for available overhead compartments to stuff their belongings into, stressing that there would not be any remaining toward the back of the plane where their seats were actually located despite that the flight was only half-full. With nothing else to do but wait, Logan's thoughts started wrestling with one another once again:

"How can you do this when Emma is still out there?" screamed his courage. *"Get off this plane right now and go rescue her, you fool. If you don't, and they keep blowing up landmarks, you'll never have a chance. No one will. The cave in Norway is gone. The Great Pyramid's cut off. You'll never gain access to whatever is in Area 51. If you want to help her before it's too late and prevent a war, there are only a few options left: The Copán Temple and Tiwanaku, both more than 5,000 miles away. And how are you going to get there? Those are both impossible. Your only choice is Stonehenge, 70 miles west of here, and you can be there in just over an hour. And it is only a matter of time before they destroy all of those, too."*

Just when Logan felt the urge to bolt back up the jetway, his common sense weighed in. *"This is crazy. Haven't you caused enough problems? And if you leave now, that Karpyn guy is tracking the phone he gave you. You won't get 500 feet out of the airport, and that's assuming the Airport Security Officers aren't still waiting at the gate."*

Logan reached his seat, 37D, on the aisle. No one was sitting next to him, yet. He sat down, and his courage had only one more word for him: *love*.

That last word resonated with Logan. He couldn't just sit here. He had to help her. He took out the phone Karpyn had given him. He accessed the 'Contact List' to find Karpyn's cell phone number, *202-833-1999.* He studied Karpyn's number to memorize it just in case he needed it again. "202-833-1999," he said to himself. "Okay, a Washington, D.C. area code, that's easy... 833, and 1999, the year I was born." He said it a few more times to himself, "D.C., 833, the year I was born... D.C., 833, the year I was born... D.C., 833, the year I was born." After the last time, Logan hid the cell phone behind the magazines in the back of the seat in front of him and stood up.

He started making his way to the front of the plane. Like a salmon swimming upstream, he pushed his way forward through all of the passengers going the opposite direction. It was not easy, and a few passengers muttered curse words directed at him.

When Logan got to the front of the plane, a female flight attendant stopped him. "I'm sorry young man, but you can't get off the plane," she said.

"Have all of the passengers checked in yet?" asked Logan

The flight attendant responded, "Well, no, not yet, but still..."

"Can I please jump off, I'll be right back, I promise."

"No, I am sorry, but—"

"I forgot my insulin," blurted Logan, pulling a page out of Emma's book of tricks. "I left it in the bathroom...please, I need to go get it."

She looked at Logan skeptically. Her instincts told her Logan was lying, but what if he wasn't? Then again, what did she care if he missed his flight? "Alright, fine. Can I please see your boarding pass?" Logan showed it to her. She wrote down his name, seat and ticket number. "Alright, Mr. West, be fast. We're closing the doors in less than ten minutes."

"Thank you." Logan exited the plane and ran back up the ramp.

When he reached the gate doors, he peeked out into the terminal to see if the Airport Security Officers were still waiting for him. He looked right and then left, spotting them standing amongst other travelers over at Gate-33, watching an overhead television's ongoing report of Russia's stunning infiltration of the Giza Pyramid Complex in Egypt. Once Logan disappeared down the jetway, and after the officers waited fifteen minutes to make sure he did not come back up, the officers momentarily let their guard down, allowing themselves to become distracted by the unexpected turn of world events. While the officers were preoccupied, Logan slyly ducked right over to Gate-29. He quickly sat down in Gate-29's seating area alongside other passengers waiting to board, keeping his back to Gate-31. Paying close attention to make sure the officers weren't looking his way, one by one he slipped to the next gate and sat down, stealthily repeating the same approach a number of times.

As Logan turned the corner at Gate-23, over the loudspeaker, he heard the airline announce, "*Final Boarding Call for Air London's 8:15 flight AL-2378 to New York.*" Almost in the clear, he thought to himself. Unfortunately, the next announcement over the loudspeaker presented a problem: "*Passenger Logan West, please report to Gate 31 for boarding immediately.*" Logan cringed and mumbled an inaudible foul word, but the loudspeaker wasn't done: "*I repeat, Passenger Logan West, please report to Gate 31 for boarding immediately.*"

Logan had no choice now; he had to exit the airport and fast because the Airport Security Officers who escorted him to the gate were going to start scouring the terminal for him following that announcement. He walked toward Baggage Claim, watching for incoming airport personnel. Seeing no one, he picked up his pace.

Up ahead, he saw some Airport Security Officers heading his way. Logan ducked into an airport magazine shop and hid behind a robust display of tourist paraphernalia, which included snow globes and figurines of Big Ben and *Stonehenge*. How ironic, Logan thought to himself. After the officers passed by, Logan snuck out of the store and resumed his escape to the outside. Logan guardedly made his way through baggage claim, pretending to look for his luggage on the baggage carousel each time an officer or claim-check attendant looked his way. Eventually, he reached Heathrow's outer doors.

When Logan got to the airport's outer curb, he quickly slipped into a taxicab. He broke out all remaining money in his wallet and, at 8:34 p.m. on a Sunday night, made a desperate "last-ride-of-the-evening" proposition to the taxicab driver: €135 for a 70-mile one-way trip to Stonehenge. If this did not work, Logan didn't have enough money left to get home, although he suspected that wasn't going to be a problem. Somehow, he knew Karpyn's men would be on their way to find him once they figured out what happened.

Chapter 20 – What Would Emma Do?

Logan headed southwest on England's A303 toward Stonehenge in Amesbury. His driver Maurice, an elderly-looking cabbie complete with white hair, long sideburns, and a chauffeur's cap, was on his last fare of the evening. Because Maurice's home was out in North Waltham in the same general direction as Stonehenge, he agreed to take Logan to the ancient landmark.

Until they got outside of London, Logan kept his head down and Maurice kept to himself. Eventually, however, the cabbie's urge to chat kicked in.

"So, young man, why do you want to go out to Stonehenge after hours, anyway?" asked Maurice in a thick British accent, eyeing Logan in the back seat. "It's dark out there and closed, you know."

"For a girl," replied Logan vaguely. He looked over his shoulder for any sign of pursuit. So far so good.

"Ah, I see, so this is about a girl. That makes more sense. Most senseless late-night drives are," said Maurice.

"Not this one," replied Logan. "Not senseless, I mean."

"When it comes to men and women, it's always senseless. That's just how it is."

"Thank you, I'll try to remember that," chuckled Logan, amused by Maurice's unsolicited advice.

"So, what's her name?"

"Emma."

"She sure sounds pretty. Does she live in Amesbury?"

"No."

Maurice was thoroughly perplexed. "Then, why in the Queen's Kingdom did you offer to pay me €135 to drive you to Stonehenge at night when the girl doesn't even live there?"

"She doesn't live there, but I'm hoping to find her."

"Young man, I may be just a cabbie, but you sure sound confused... which is good. If you were thinking straight, I'd say she wasn't worth the trouble."

"She's definitely worth it," replied Logan. "You ever make one of these crazy late-night drives for a woman?"

"More than once," said Maurice with a reminiscing smile.

"Are you married?"

"I sure am, to the one that made the least sense of all."

"That figures," Logan responded.

After a few minutes of awkward silence, Maurice continued the chatter. "It's beautiful out here, some of the nicest country you'd ever want to see."

Logan looked outside the window into the dark. *It was pitch black out there*. He could not see anything. Logan waited for a moment and then asked, "Are we almost there?"

"Soon. Another half hour. Running out of patience for the ramblings of old Maurice, are you?"

"Of course not," replied Logan, concerned he may have offended Maurice. "I was just curious, is all."

"Do you want me to drop you off or to wait for you when we get there?"

"Why would you wait for me?"

"Just in case your friend doesn't show up," Maurice replied. He was worried Logan's journey to Stonehenge was going to be a wasted trip. He had seen it many times before. "If you want, I can take you back as far as North Waltham. I'll be heading back in that direction anyway. It's no trouble."

Logan thought about it. He didn't want to endanger Maurice any more than he already had, but more than that, he didn't have any idea what he was looking for or how long he would be when he got there. "That won't be necessary but thank you."

When they reached Amesbury, all was quiet. Stonehenge had been closed for hours. Those who wanted to stay in town for dinner had already eaten and left and the town's shops were closed.

The A303 continued right through the center of town. Maurice eased through Amesbury without attracting too much attention to his cab. Stonehenge was just up the road and it took only a few more minutes to get there.

As they approached Stonehenge, Logan could see its behemoth stone monuments from the road. Set in the middle of an enormous open grass field, it looked just like it did in pictures only taller. Even at night, Stonehenge was a remarkable sight with the bright moon lighting the crevices, cracks, and contours of the trilithons, bringing Stonehenge to life. Seeing it under moonlight like this, Logan wondered why Stonehenge ever closed at all.

Maurice drove the car up to the site, but the view from the A303 was as good as he could do for Logan. After hours, a concrete barricade prevented entry into the parking lot and security guards walked the premises. Maurice pulled over at the side of the road next to the barricade.

"All right kid, this is as close as I can get you. Are you sure this is what you want?"

Logan was sure even though he didn't know what to do next. He only knew that he had to do *something*. "I know it doesn't make any sense, but I've got to try."

"I guess you learned something from your old cabbie, after all," said Maurice.

"I most certainly did."

Logan paid Maurice and got out of the car. As he closed the door, Maurice said, "Take care of yourself, young man."

Logan replied, "Thanks, you, too." He shut the door and Maurice drove off.

With the Visitor Centre closed for the evening, Logan walked up to an information kiosk inside the parking lot to check out what he could find there. A security guard approached him.

"I'm sorry, son, but Stonehenge is closed for the night. Come back tomorrow," said the burly British National Monument guard.

"Yes, sir," responded Logan politely.

Logan spotted a discarded pamphlet on the ground dropped by a visitor earlier in the day. He bent down to pick the pamphlet up and quickly looked through it. It contained a narrative history of Stonehenge, as well as pictures and diagrams depicting the landmark's various standing and fallen stones.

"Thank you. I will be on my way," said Logan. "Good evening to you."

Logan put the pamphlet in his coat pocket and shoved off. When he reached the main road, he walked until out of the guard's view. He found a small access road to duck into for privacy.

Logan parked himself underneath a street lamp on the access road to study the pamphlet closer. Although the pamphlet offered a rich history of the ancient landmark including theories as to its construction, function, and purpose, Logan skipped past the academic pieces to look at the diagrams for clues as to what the Norwegian Albo might have left behind. There had to be something there.

Logan examined an overhead aerial photograph of Stonehenge and an illustration depicting the exact shape, dimensions, and placement of all of the stones at the site.

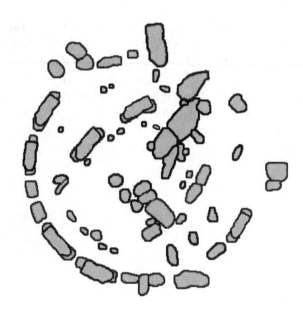

From the illustration, he could see the outer ring of doorway-shaped trilithons, made up of two large, vertical standing sarsens supporting a third sarsen laid horizontally across the top (the "lintel stone"), although in some cases, the sarsens or lintel stones had fallen over. Inside the outer circle was an inner ring of trilithons. Set in the ground between the two rings of trilithons was a circle of bluestones, with an oval-shaped arrangement of bluestones surrounding an Altar Stone in the center. While some of Stonehenge's sarsens and bluestones had gone missing over time, there remained ninety-three visible stones in all, and Logan had to figure out what to do with them.

He turned the illustration sideways, upside down, three quarters clockwise, and every conceivable angle in between, looking for a clue in the placement of the stones. If only Emma were here, seeing clues in the chaos was her specialty. What would Emma do? What would she look for? Logan pondered this for a moment and then it came to him... *constellations*. She would look for constellations.

With that in mind, Logan looked at the illustration again. He only knew a few constellations, so he started with the ones that had come up over the last twenty-four hours: The Winter Triangle and Orion. As soon as he imagined the constellation Orion in his mind, something stood out to him smack in the middle of the Stonehenge diagram... there were three stones on the ground in a straight line inside the inner oval of bluestones, set at the foot of the area arranged for worship in front of the Altar Stone:

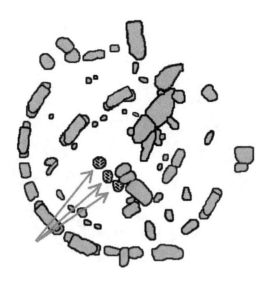

The three stones immediately reminded Logan of the stars in Orion that formed Orion's Belt. After studying the stones for a few more seconds, Logan realized something even more astonishing… the stones of Stonehenge did not just include Orion's Belt, the footprint of stones at Stonehenge incorporated the *entire* Orion constellation.

"That can't be," Logan said to himself. He visualized the constellation and it was all there: Orion's sixteen main stars were replicated on the ground by sixteen of Stonehenge's ninety-three visible stones. The sixteen stones depicted a hunter standing in ready position, with a bow held in his outstretched left arm, and his right arm cocked back and up.

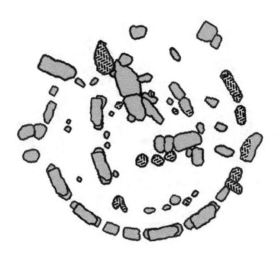

To make sure he wasn't seeing things, Logan pulled a red pen out of his backpack and drew a line from stone to stone to draw out the Orion constellation. After doing that, it was even clearer than before: sixteen of Stonehenge's stones undeniably formed the shape of Orion…

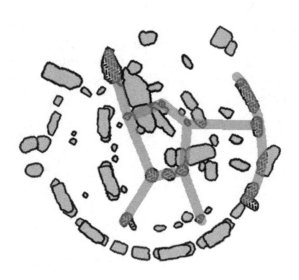

"This is incredible," he muttered. The proportions weren't exact, but there was no question about it in his mind: Orion the Hunter lived inside the stones of Stonehenge and that could not be a coincidence. Nothing in this entire Copán adventure had turned out to be *just* a coincidence. For hundreds of years, historians and archeologists have speculated about why the ancients built Stonehenge. Now, Logan believed it fair to wonder if they built it and placed the stones where they did to conceal the Norwegian Albo's secret. Was Stonehenge an ancient ritual site or a doorway to another world? Logan knew there was only one way to find out.

He returned to the main road, walked back toward Stonehenge and disappeared into the long-grass field surrounding the ancient monument. Guards patrolled the area, so Logan stayed low to the ground, repeatedly dropping to his stomach to avoid detection. Steadily, he moved closer to the stones.

When Logan got within sprinting distance of Stonehenge, he laid flat on the ground and pulled out the pamphlet again. He needed to orient himself to which side of the monument he was coming up on and where the stones he needed to touch would be located. Feeling like he might only get one shot at this, he needed to get it right the first time.

In Norway, to activate the portals, Emma first touched the rock corresponding with the Norwegian Albo's home, TYC 129-75-1, then she touched all the other stones in random order, before finishing by touching TYC 129-75-1 one more time. Assuming it was the same here, all he had to do was figure out which rock in the Stonehenge diagram was the equivalent of TYC 129-75-1, a star in the Orion constellation found just below and slightly to the left of Betelgeuse in the night sky.

Logan looked at the Stonehenge illustration in the brochure, and sure enough, there was a small bluestone just below and slightly to the left of the stone that matched Orion's right shoulder, or Betelgeuse. That small bluestone corresponded almost perfectly with the location of TYC 129-75-1:

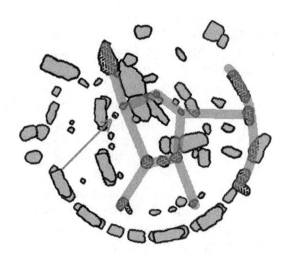

All Logan had to do now, presumably, was touch the small bluestone, then touch all sixteen stones forming the Orion constellation inside of Stonehenge and return to touch the stone representing TYC 129-75-1 one last time. He hoped that would work. If it did not, assuming the guards hadn't arrested him already for trespassing on a national monument (a big *if*), he would try other combinations.

Logan resumed his approach. After a few steps, just when he thought his window of opportunity to do this could not get any smaller, it did.

A car pulled up to the Stonehenge parking lot. Logan could not see it because he was coming up from the opposite end of Stonehenge, but he heard two doors open, two doors close, and two voices talking to the guards who intercepted them. Logan gulped. He recognized the voices. They belonged to the international criminals who he once called Agent Uptin and Commander Lewis. *Damn it.*

With Uptin and Lewis or whatever their real names were trying to talk their way onto the Stonehenge site, no doubt with fake credentials, the National Monument Guards were all temporarily distracted. Logan decided to make a break for it. He made a labored sprint toward Stonehenge's center, grimacing from the sharp sting of the bullet wound in his calf.

Before he reached the stone he believed represented TYC 129-75-1, Logan heard sirens off in the distance. In this sleepy town where crime rarely occurred, Logan knew those sirens were coming for him; what he did not know was how Karpyn's team had found him so fast and coordinated with British authorities. Then again, it was the CIA. *Double damn it*, Logan muttered.

Now, he really did have only one shot at this and he had to do it quickly. Logan touched the first stone and then promptly rushed to touch each of the subsequent stones. After half a minute, several guards who were busy dealing with Lewis and Uptin saw Logan and shouted, "Hey you!!! Stop right now!! Down on the ground!!!" A couple guards started heading for Logan.

The commotion directed at Logan drew Uptin and Lewis' attention. They spotted Logan and started running toward Stonehenge also. When the guards protested and told Bailey's henchmen to stay back, Uptin and Lewis simply shot them. Cold-blooded and cruel.

"Oh no!! Oh no!!" mumbled Logan, worrying he wasn't going to make it.

As soon as Uptin and Lewis started shooting, the guards heading for Logan scattered for cover, ironically affording Logan additional time to complete the sequence.

Logan kept running and touching stones. He had only three more to go when the patrol cars arrived. Authorities jumped out of their vehicles, communicating instructions to one another. Lewis provided cover for Uptin who entered Stonehenge's center theatre.

Logan had made all the rounds, and now, he just needed to get back to the center to touch TYC 129-75-1 one more time. He was only a few feet from the stone, but Uptin stood in the way.

Uptin fired at Logan who darted behind one of the tall standing sandstones.

"You can't hide back there forever, West," uttered Uptin.

"Sure, I can... you're about to be surrounded by officers itching to shoot you after what you just did to one of their own. Does Bailey pay you enough to die for her?"

Uptin did not respond. As Logan predicted, British cops started swarming around the perimeter.

"The game's up," said Logan who, while hiding on the other side of the stone, kept his hands high in the air so the police would not shoot him.

Rather than surrender, Lewis started firing back. Seeking cover from the guards and officers returning fire, Lewis hid behind one of the outer standing sarsen stones on the opposite side from where Logan was hiding. Lewis kept leaking out around the edge of the stone to shoot, sending officers ducking for cover. One officer attempted to sneak up on Lewis from the side, but Lewis picked him off. As the officers closed in, Lewis peeked around the stone's edge to fire, but this time, he took a bullet in the back. He never saw the Monument Guard creeping up from behind. Lewis slumped to the ground. Uptin knew he was trapped.

"No matter what Bailey's paying you, you can't take it with you if you're dead," said Logan.

"Drop your gun! Hands up!" the officers ordered Uptin.

Uptin didn't listen. After all of the things he had done over the last decade, there was nothing but a lifetime of prison, or worse, waiting for him if he gave himself up. He was not about to let that happen.

"Drop the gun now!" yelled the authorities one last time, but Uptin had other plans. Instead, as soon as Logan peeked out from behind the stone, Uptin pulled his trigger and leaped behind a fallen sarsen to avoid fire. Logan snapped his head back just in time.

Uptin, meanwhile, darted for the north side of Stonehenge. Officers shot at him, but Uptin dove and rolled to avoid the bullets. He fired back, taking out several guards and officers while making a desperate run to avoid capture. He managed to get all the way into the fields behind Stonehenge, disappearing in the darkness.

At night, and blocked by several trilithons, Logan could not see what was happening, but he could hear confused officers shouting at one another, searching for Uptin. While the officers struggled to figure out what to do, Uptin kept firing at them from a concealed hiding place behind a chunk of broken stone in the outer field. The sparks from his gun after his last round tipped authorities off to his location. The officers dropped low to the ground and steadily surrounded Uptin. Unwilling to surrender, Uptin fired his remaining bullets and scurried toward a road at the back of the field. Although he managed to avoid a few bullets, several shots struck him in the back. Uptin dropped to the field to die.

Meanwhile, back inside Stonehenge's inner circle of trilithons, two officers commanded Logan to move out into the open with his hands up. With his hands held high, Logan walked out into Stonehenge's center from behind the sarsen stone where he had been hiding, very close to the TYC 129-75-1 stone he needed to touch.

"Down on the ground, now!" the officers shouted. No longer having a choice, Logan dropped face first onto the ground right next to the TYC 129-75-1 stone.

Logan reached out barely an inch farther, and with the slightest touch of his finger, touched TYC 129-75-1. The portals activated. Three of the trilithons within Stonehenge's inner circle erupted in blue light and hummed. After a few seconds, just like they did inside the Norwegian cave, the portals crystallized to reveal other destinations behind them. The officers each stopped what they were doing, stunned by the standing trilithons' mysterious transformation.

The one to Logan's right projected a white light reminiscent of the doorway Emma had disappeared into earlier in the day. It was only a few steps from his position.

With the authorities' eyes momentarily fixated on the portals, Logan jumped up and ran to the light portal. Despite hearing the officers demanding that he stop, Logan dove into the portal before any of them could shoot. By the time the British officers realized what happened, Logan was gone, and the portal doorways disappeared.

Chapter 21 – Déjà Vu

The instant Logan went through the Stonehenge portal, he emerged somewhere else. He found himself standing inside a large white pyramid on top of an oval-shaped platform. Below the platform, he did not see a floor but rather multi-colored clouds swirling about, obscuring the ground beneath the pyramid, if there even was ground down below. Was he floating up in the sky? Up in the clouds? In the heavens? Wherever he was, there was no wind or noise. It was perfectly still inside the pyramid.

When Logan re-oriented himself, he saw ethereal beings of light, humanoid in shape but without any visible features behind their blinding illumination, gathering around him, moving silently and effortlessly. Logan counted a dozen or so, maybe more. They spoke to him, but he did not understand what they were saying, at least, not at first. Then, someone or something commandeered the thoughts inside his head, reading his mind and manipulating his words to form sentences he could understand, only he was not controlling what they were saying...

You will find the truth in her eyes, his thoughts said, although the thoughts were not his own.

"The truth about what," he asked.

Everything.

"I don't understand."

It is time.

"Time for what?"

To help her.

"Help her how?"

Find the star that rises before the brightest of them all.

"But, I don't underst—"

It is time to go back to the beginning...

Before Logan could ask another question, the platform beneath his feet disappeared, everything got blurry, everything faded and...

Δ ΔΔΔΔΔΔΔΔΔΔ

Click. The alarm went off and out blasted MegaWave's 'Jagged Edge of the Sun' smack in the middle of its chorus. Logan woke up, groaned, and opened his eyes. Only eight months and thirty-four Mondays to go until graduation. Wait a second... where was he?

He sat up. He looked around. He was back in his own bed. Logan instinctively reached for the side table where he normally kept his cell phone. He grabbed it and pulled it close; it was his phone alright, not the one Karpyn had given him. And the date on the screen read Monday, *October 17,* the same day he first received the Copán Temple project from Mr. Jackson. What was going on? Was it all a dream?

"That can't be," mumbled a confused Logan, feeling like Dorothy waking up from her long dream at the end of the Wizard of Oz.

He reached down to feel his calf. No bullet wound. He searched his cell phone for emails to see if today was any day other than October 17th, but the slew of incoming texts and emails confirmed the same thing: it *was* October 17th. He opened his text messages and perhaps most distressing of all, there were no texts from Emma James.

Logan sat there in disbelief as a disappointing realization came over him: his connection to Emma James and everything they had experienced together over the last two weeks was nothing more than a figment of his imagination. The doors he was hoping to open for himself and his mom, had been slammed shut. Perhaps it was for the best, he told himself, because what else could he do, he had to tell himself *something*. If it was only a dream, think of all the people who lost their lives in his Copán Temple fantasy who survived in reality. Yet it all seemed so real. The heartbreak of losing Emma *felt* so real and it hurt.

"Wait a second, why don't you just text her," he said out loud. He considered the possibility that if none of it really happened, Emma would not understand why he was texting. After all, prior to two weeks ago, which was now suddenly today, or so it seemed, they hadn't texted in years. Still, he had to try.

Logan went into his phone to pull up her contact info. It was not until just then that he realized he did not have her telephone number in his 'Contacts,' nor did he have it memorized. Even in his dying fantasy, when Emma programmed her number into his phone after class on the first day when they received the Copán assignment, he never looked at it. He just touched her name in 'Contacts,' 'recent calls' or 'recent texts' to call or text her. He had no idea what her number was.

Maybe he could talk to her at school instead which, if that was his plan, he had to get ready for and fast. Logan threw some clothes on and rushed out the door. When he got to Jersey North High, he went looking for Emma in the courtyard where she typically hung out before class, but she was nowhere to be found. And she did not show up for 1st-period.

Increasingly desperate and refusing to let go of his delusional fantasy that he had traveled back in time, Logan decided to ditch school and go directly to Emma's house. Yet when he got there and knocked on the door, no one answered. He left more confused than before.

By the time Logan got back to Jersey North again, 3rd-period had already started. Entering full stalker mode at this point, Logan waited outside Emma's 3rd-period class, but when the lunch bell rang, she did not come out with the rest of the students. Logan next headed out to the lunch courtyard to see if she might be out there. Unfortunately, Emma wasn't in the courtyard either, but David and Patrick were, and they walked up behind him.

"Bro, you look lost," said Patrick, catching up to Logan who was oddly meandering along.

Logan snapped out of it and looked at his friends who were now walking beside him. "Um..."

"Dude, you okay?" joked David, mocking Logan's uncertainty.

"Yeah, totally," feigned Logan while continuing to look for Emma. They stopped at a lunch table and the three friends sat down.

David pulled a sealed plastic bag filled with cold pizza out of his backpack, while Patrick retrieved a peanut butter and jelly sandwich from his bag.

"You bring anything today?" David asked Logan. "No rich person's leftovers from your mom's restaurant?"

Distracted, Logan replied, "Uh, no... forgot."

"You want in on this?" offered David, lifting up a piece of pizza for him.

Logan shook his head and kept looking for Emma.

"Who are you looking for?" wondered Patrick, noticing Logan's eyes scanning the courtyard.

"I'm, um, looking for Emma," replied Logan.

"James??" questioned David.

"Yeah."

"Why?" asked David.

"'Cause he's had a thing for her since elementary school, that's why," answered Patrick.

"It's for the proje…" Logan stopped before finishing the sentence. They hadn't been given their history project yet from Mr. Jackson. Saying that he was looking for Emma 'for the project' would have made no sense to them.

"For the what?" asked Patrick. "You hit your head or something?"

"Obviously he did, if he's planning to make a move on Emma James," said David. "Chad's going to squash you."

"Chad's not going to squash me," replied Logan.

"Hope you're right," responded David, "'cause the guy bench presses like three hundred pounds, and you, not so much…"

"I'll be fine," said Logan.

"Well, if you're wrong, I'm calling dibs on your Xbox," announced David.

"Like hell you do," snapped Patrick. "I practically broke that thing in with Logan, taught him everything he knows."

"No wonder he sucks," replied David.

"Hate to break the fun up, but I'll see you guys later," announced Logan, abruptly standing up and walking off without saying another word.

"Umm... okay... see you later," said a confused Patrick as Logan uncharacteristically walked away.

Logan felt bad for ditching his friends like that, but he was too anxious to just sit there and shoot the breeze with them. He needed to do something. He needed to keep looking for Emma and, for the remainder of the lunch period, he did just that, walking the entire school campus. Still, he couldn't find her anywhere. Where could she be?

When the end of lunch bell rang, the moment of truth had arrived... 4th-period with Mr. Jackson. If there was one place Logan remembered Emma being on October 17th, it was Mr. Jackson's history class when they first got the Copán assignment...

Logan entered Mr. Jackson's classroom with his fellow students, anxious to see her. He found his seat and waited. And he waited. Her seat across the classroom remained empty. When David and Patrick got to class, they immediately approached Logan.

"Hey man, sorry about before," said David. "You know I was only kidding, right?"

"Yeah, I know, sorry. I'm just having a weird day," explained Logan, although they couldn't possibly know *how* weird.

"Seriously, are you okay?" asked Patrick.

"Yeah. Thanks, guys, but really, I'm fine—"

The class bell rang. Patrick and David quickly found their seats. Logan looked back, and still, no Emma. Where was she? Had she not made it back? The alien beings had told him he needed to "help her." Was that because she was in trouble? Now, Logan was worried.

After his usual pleasantries, Mr. Jackson started talking, saying, "As we so often talk about, history, not me, is the greatest teacher. It provides civilized society with a rich compendium of information about the past, guiding us to learn from our mistakes and enabling us to make better choices in the future than our ancestors made. A great historian once said, 'our past actions define our future plans, so we better pay attention to our history.' Who said that?"

Experiencing an extreme case of déjà vu, Logan recalled those exact words coming out of Mr. Jackson's mouth previously. When Beck Raymer raised his hand to answer Mr. Jackson's question, the feeling of familiarity grew even stronger. However, after Beck answered the question, something Logan did *not* recall occurred... the classroom door quietly opened and in slipped Emma James. Her hair was pulled back in a ponytail, and she was wearing the same dark navy-blue pants and long-sleeve white blouse Logan remembered her wearing the first time around.

Maybe Logan had missed her late arrival the last time, but today was different; Logan was paying attention to every detail. When Emma walked in, while almost no one else noticed, Logan was completely transfixed.

As inconspicuously as possible, she slipped into her seat. Logan kept looking back but she stared ahead. Logan was not sure. Perhaps she wasn't sure either. At one point, for a moment anyway, Logan thought Emma had tears in her eyes.

Logan listened to Mr. Jackson's lecture, trying to read Emma's body language. Finally, when Mr. Jackson passed out the class project list, he eagerly searched for his name alongside Emma's under the topic, "The Secret Chamber of the White-Eyed Star God found inside the Copán Temple in Honduras." *Bingo!! There it was again!* While he did not understand how he had traveled back in time, there was no longer any doubt that he had, and that all of his memories were real. He knew it now for sure.

What he did not know was whether Emma shared those memories or his feelings. What if it was just him? What if she remembered none of it? When class ended, there was only one way to find out...

Logan got up from his chair to walk over to Emma. Emma stood up and started walking toward him. She picked up her pace and when they met, Logan started with, "Emma, I have to know if–"

Emma covered his mouth and kissed him. No hesitation. No concern for the stunned looks on the faces of others in the classroom. Not even the "get a room" comments from some of their classmates detracted from the moment. Chad put an end to the juvenile commentary by back-handing a few of the more immature commentators. Meanwhile, David and Patrick gave each other a proud fist pump.

When Emma kissed Logan, his heart exploded with happiness. He had spent the last few hours worrying that he had lost her, or at least, the version of their relationship that, until now, existed only in his mind. The mere thought that it wasn't real was unthinkable to him. It was depressing. But with one kiss, Emma had saved him from the unthinkable. It was the happiest moment of his entire life, and he wasn't alone in his euphoria.

Emma embraced Logan tightly with joyful tears welling up in her eyes. The last time she had seen him was during the gunfight inside the cave when he pushed her to safety after being shot. This time, Emma wasn't letting go.

"We need to get out of here," she whispered. She took Logan's hand, and together, they high-tailed it out of class.

They snuck out of school by heading to the south gate on the opposite side of Jersey North's football field. Located far away from the school's main buildings, school officials rarely paid attention to that exit. After leaving campus, they found a nearby park and a bench to sit on.

"Was it all real?" Emma asked, "Rome, Bologna, Norway, everything?"

"Yeah, I think so. I mean, if you remember everything, and I remember everything, it had to be real, right?"

"Oh, my god, I can't believe it," she said, laughing. "When I woke up this morning, I swear, I had no idea what was happening. I thought it was all a dream."

"I know. I thought I imagined the whole thing, that maybe it was all in my head. I was even more confused when I couldn't find you at school this morning, and when Mr. Jackson's class started, and you weren't there, I got worried something had happened to you."

"Sorry. I had my, um, an early admissions interview at Princeton this morning."

Surprised, Logan replied, "Princeton interview?"

"Yeah, my dad pulled some major strings to set it up for me."

"You never said anything about it."

"I know, I know. I'm sorry, it just never came up." In truth, she had kept it to herself because she felt bad mentioning it to Logan considering he couldn't even afford to go to a four-year college.

Logan did not seem offended though. Rather, he was excited for her. "So, how did it go??"

"Well, since I had already done the interview and answered all of the same questions once before, it should have gone well. But honestly, I think I did worse this time around because of how weird it felt doing today all over again, you know what I mean?"

He did. It was completely disorienting. "It's like a déjà-vu that won't stop. I wonder how they did it, how they brought us back in time?"

Emma could see the answers in her mind. They had put them there for her to see, to bring back to Earth to teach others. She tried to explain. "There are these particles called zeutyrons that go faster than the speed of light, and when they do, somehow, they can bend the space-time continuum around them so much that they can literally pull two distant points in space-time closer together until they are right next to each other, allowing a person to move between the two points like stepping through a door. Somehow, the Vaniryans, that's what they call themselves, have found a way to control it all."

It was suddenly obvious to Logan that Emma's experience when she went through the portal differed from his own. "Emma, what happened to you when you went through the portal?"

Emma started explaining, beginning with their last moments together in the cave...

ΔΔΔΔΔΔΔΔΔΔΔ

"Go!!" shouted Professor Quimbey over the deafening sound of gunfire in the cave.

Logan grabbed Emma's hand and yanked her up from the ground. He led her toward the light portal, leaving Professor Quimbey and Dr. Arenot behind, Emma's unassuming childhood friend, a hero.

A few steps short of the portal, Emma heard what she most dreaded... a gun firing and Logan crying out. He had been hit. She wanted to turn to help him, but as Logan fell forward, he put two hands on her lower back and pushed her into the light. Emma stumbled headfirst, falling onto her hands and knees, only, when she looked up, she realized she wasn't in the cave anymore. She was somewhere new, quiet, and peaceful.

Emma spun around to help Logan. She had no intention of leaving him behind in the cave to die, no matter where she was now or what was waiting for her when she got back there. But when she turned around, the portal was gone.

"Where is it?" she whispered to herself. There was no way back.

Emma stood up, now focusing on her surroundings. She was standing on top of an oval-shaped platform inside an ivory pyramid with no visible bottom, hovering high above swirling pastel-colored clouds. The four slanted walls of the pyramid rose to a peak hundreds of feet above her head. Gazing over the edge of the platform, there were minuscule openings in the clouds enabling her to see glimpses of the planet's surface far below and a complex grid of lights. The openings disappeared just as quickly as they appeared, erased by fast-moving clouds.

When she looked back up, dozens of humanoid beings were gathering around her, each enveloped by a bright-white, radiant light. She should have been afraid of them, but she wasn't. Instead, she felt welcomed, like an invited guest.

The humanoids started closing in. She stayed calm, not wanting to alarm them, or herself, any more than necessary. The aliens, taller than Emma, although not by much, put their glowing hands on her body, some touching her head or arms, others touching her waist or shoulders, revering her and behaving as if they had never seen her kind before. When done, they stepped back and started talking to her.

Emma did not understand what they were saying initially, but then, the thoughts inside her head began forming sentences she could understand, saying, *Hear us*. The intrusion into her thoughts startled her. She could not tell which alien was talking to her, but one of them stepped forward and telepathically repeated the same words again using her own thoughts, *Hear us*.

"I can hear you," responded Emma. The alien effortlessly moved up into Emma's personal space.

"Where am I?"

Vanirya.

"Where is Vanirya?"

Beyond your hunter.

"How did I get here?"

We will show you.

"Why did you leave behind what you did for us to find?"

Because it is time.

"Time for what?"

For tens of millions of years, we have traveled the stars, living on many worlds and leaving in search of a new home each time it became necessary to do so. That time is coming for humanity.

"What is coming for humanity?"

It is time for mankind to travel the stars.

"I don't understand. Why?"

It is a choice all worlds must face, whether to leave or stay. It is the path of creation, wonder, chaos, and destruction in the universe.

"Do you know what is coming for our world?"

No. Only that the future is inevitable for all. It always has been. It always will be.

"How long do we have??"

You have time.

"Is our planet in danger??"

The path of creation, wonder, chaos, and destruction in the universe is inevitable for all.

"Is there anything we can do to save our world? To protect it?"

Yes.

"What?"

Explore. Perhaps you will find the technology to save your world in the stars, or perhaps a new home, but it can take thousands of years to find a suitable planet among the hundreds of billions of stars in the galaxy and billions of galaxies in the universe.

"Is that how you discovered Earth, exploring planets in search of your next home?"

Yes.

"How do we do it?"

You must go to the star that rises before the brightest of them all.

Emma was confused. "Why? What's there?"

There you will find all that you seek, all that you need.

Before Emma could ask another question, dozens of voices entered her mind, flooding it with words, images, diagrams, and equations. The Vaniryans hijacked her mind, sharing information directly into her head like they were uploading data into a computer. Emma was overwhelmed as the Vaniryans took over her entire state of being. The avalanche of information pouring into her consciousness pushed her into that place between consciousness and unconsciousness, where one is no longer awake but not asleep either…

ΔΔΔΔΔΔΔΔΔΔΔ

"Emma, are you okay?" asked Logan. Emma's mind had drifted far away from him, and she had stopped talking. "Emma?" he repeated.

Emma snapped out of it, returning from wherever her mind had gone. She was back on the park bench with Logan. "What happened?"

"I don't know. One minute you were talking to me, and then, you kind of just faded."

"What was I saying?"

"It was pretty dark. Something about the inevitable end of the world, leaving our planet, saving it..."

Sparked by his response, Emma blurted out, "*Logan*… they told me what we have to do! We have to go to the star that rises before the brightest of them all."

Logan remembered the Vaniryans saying that to him, too. He thought about it and proposed a possibility. "Maybe 'the brightest of them all' refers to the brightest star in the night sky." He looked it up on his phone. Up popped an astronomy website saying, "The brightest star in Earth's night sky is a star called Sirius, often referred to as the 'Dog Star' because it's found in the *Canis Major* constellation. It rises immediately after a star called *Antecanis*, which is Latin for 'Before the Dog.' The non-Latin reference for

246

Antecanis translates to the ancient Greek word, Προκύων or Prokyon, which translates in English to *Procyon*."

"*That's it*," shouted Emma, picturing the Winter Triangle constellation in her mind. Thinking back to when they realized Albo Nor's landmarks mirrored the configuration of the Winter Triangle and portions of Orion, she remembered that Procyon corresponded on the map with Area 51. "Area 51! That's where we must go. We need to get in there."

"How are we supposed to do that?" wondered Logan. "It's got to be like one of the most secure places on Earth."

Emma had an idea. "What about calling Agent Uptin? Commander Lewis?"

Logan's whole face clenched up. Emma could tell there was a problem.

"What's wrong?"

"We can't do that."

"Why not?"

"Because Agent Uptin, Commander Lewis, Bailey, Bryant, and O'Neal weren't who we thought they were. They don't work for the U.S. government. They were lying to us the whole time. They betrayed us and sold all the information we gave them to the highest bidder. Bailey's the ring-leader, she goes by the name, the Dealer, and whoever she sold us out to, that's who came hunting us in the cave before U.S. soldiers intervened and saved our lives."

"That can't be!" exclaimed Emma in disbelief.

"It's true. The whole set up in Bologna was a hoax to get information out of us, and the joke was on us."

"But what about Professor Quimbey? Dr. Arenot? Them, too?"

"They were pawns in Bailey's game just like us."

Ugh, groaned Emma, who reminded him, "You mean, they still *are* pawns in Bailey's game…"

"Damn," Logan cursed, "you're right. Dr. Arenot and Professor Quimbey are still with Bailey in Bologna right now. They're in trouble."

"We have to help them. We've got to tell someone," said Emma.

"No one is going to believe a word we say, especially after we start explaining how we came across the information about Bailey and the professors and start talking about visiting aliens and traveling back in time."

Logan and Emma wondered who else, if anyone, they could reach out to.

After several moments of silence, Emma had a gleam in her eye. "I know this sounds crazy, but I have an idea that might just solve both of our problems at the same time. What about the President of the United States?"

"President Barrett?" asked Logan. "You can't be serious. Everyone we've run into since this all started has wanted to exploit the Vaniryan technology. And now, you want to just feed it to the person at the top of the government food chain?"

"Just hear me out… Did you watch the presidential debates when President Barrett ran a few years ago?" Emma asked.

"I mean, a little… maybe I caught a few minutes here and there, but since I wasn't old enough to vote, I didn't really watch much."

"Well, thanks to my dad, I didn't miss a minute of any of them. During Barrett's campaign, do you remember how he ran on a platform of globalism?"

"Yeah, I kind of remember that," said Logan.

"And do you remember that famous moment at the debate when the president's opponent mocked him for his globalism platform and how the president responded?" Emma quickly located the video of the presidential debate she was referring to on her cellphone. More specifically, she tracked down the popular one-minute snippet showing the two candidates sparring on stage from their respective podiums. She played the video for both to watch...

ΔΔΔΔΔΔΔΔΔΔΔ

CANDIDATE BARRETT: "If we are ever to overcome the hatred that divides our great nation, and the animosity that divides countries and tears the world apart, then we have to start thinking about ourselves as a united planet and look out for each other, not just for our own interests."

CANDIDATE JACKSON: "Senator, it sounds like you are running for President of the United Federation of Planets, not for President of the United States."

CANDIDATE BARRETT: "Well, Mike, the universe is a big place, far larger than we can comprehend, and given the way science has advanced the last two hundred years, anything is possible. What I do know is that we have to start thinking of ourselves not just as the greatest country on Earth — which I firmly believe — but also, as part of a global family, because whatever the future holds for our great planet, we are all in this together."

CANDIDATE JACKSON: "Andrew, are you saying you believe in aliens?"

CANDIDATE BARRETT: "Mike, what I'm saying is that it is time for our planet to get its act together before it's too late. Based on your environmental agenda and list of campaign donors, I don't think that is anything you care about."

CANDIDATE JACKSON: "But, senator, you did not answer my question. Do you believe in aliens?"

CANDIDATE BARRETT: "Congressman, I believe in protecting the future of our planet for the generations that come after us."

MODERATOR WAXLER: "I'm sorry, gentlemen, but we have to move on to the next topic if we're going to stay on schedule for the American people. Congressman Jackson, this next question is for you…"

ΔΔΔΔΔΔΔΔΔΔ

"Logan, President Barrett cares about the future of our planet. And from his comments at the debate about how the universe is a big place and how anything is possible, I think he'll be receptive to what we have to say. I think he's someone we can trust, and if there's anyone who can get us into Area 51, it's the president. And he can help Professor Quimbey and Dr. Arenot, too."

"Okay, just playing devil's advocate here, but how are we supposed to tell him? It's not like we can just walk up to the White House and knock on the door. Before we ever get a chance to talk to the president, the FBI, CIA, and NSA will interview us and scrutinize our story. And even if they believe us, which they won't, they're still not going to let two high school students from Jersey City talk to the President of the United States, *alone*. We have a better chance of getting struck by lightning."

Who was she kidding? No one was ever going to let two teenagers sit down with the President of the United States alone to talk about the end of the world, and their goal of keeping the Copán information secret from those who would seek to exploit it would go up in flames, putting them right back where they started… with governments and agencies falling all over themselves to exploit the alien technology.

"You're right," conceded Emma. "It's not like we can just call the president's cell phone direct."

"Wait a second. That's a great idea," replied Logan excitedly.

"What is?" asked Emma, not following along.

"Calling the president's cell phone direct. I have an idea. We need to go back to Philadelphia."

"Philadelphia? Why, to see Bryan Callister again?"

"Exactly."

Chapter 22 – An Old Friend

When Emma and Logan walked into Dewey's Comic Books & Hobby Shop in the early afternoon, it looked just like they remembered, or rather, like it was going to look tomorrow… that is, a colorful wall-to-wall masterpiece of comic books, pop culture, subcultures, hobbies, and art. A few patrons browsed the store's shelves and bins while watchdog Zack handled the counter just like he did the last time they visited Dewey's. Since new faces were a rarity in Dewey's, Zack asked, "Can I help you?"

"We're looking for Bryan," replied Logan. They kept walking toward Callister's back-store office without slowing down.

"You can't go back there," said Zack, taken aback by the sight of the teenagers marching toward his boss' office without permission. He urgently reached for the phone to give his boss a heads up.

"I'm his girlfriend," announced Emma, causing Zack to pause.

"That is so cool," Zack blurted out.

Emma and Logan walked right into the "Employees Only" door, which was already partially ajar.

"I don't have a girlfriend that I know of," said Bryan, swiveling around in his chair when they entered. He did not recognize either of them. "Thanks for barging in here unexpectedly though... usually it's my mom who does that, but now that you're here, what can I do for you?"

"We need your help," replied Logan.

"What, you guys need an out of print comic book or something like that?"

"No, nothing like that," responded Logan.

Emma piped in. "We need to get a look at your archives."

Bryan looked up at her. "I don't operate the archives anymo—"

"We know you still have them," interrupted Emma, "They're sitting in a box on a shelf above your head."

Her response caught Bryan off-guard. How could she know that? No one knew that he had kept a copy except for Zack and maybe one or two other close friends. "I could get in trouble, I'm sorry."

"If you're talking about that stupid letter you got from the U.S. Department of Justice, I'm telling you, it's all fake," said Emma.

Bryan jumped up and closed his office door. "Okay, how do you know about that?"

Logan started to say, "It's a long story, and you—"

"Well, you better tell me because I'm not paying a $100,000 fine."

"You won't believe us," said Logan.

"Then try me or let me know when you guys are serious about getting a look at my archives."

"We know why your 'L to Z' server doesn't work," said Emma. "Because your watchdog Zack back there spilled soda all over it last year during a marathon Dungeons & Dragons weekend."

"Zack or Cody could've told you that—"

"Ask them, we've never seen them before in our lives. We're from Jersey," countered Emma.

"Then how did you know that?"

Neither of them answered Bryan's question. Instead, Emma gave Bryan the same smile that usually got her way with Dad, and said, "We need your help to save the world. Now who works in a comic books store and doesn't dream of that?" Emma definitely had him thinking. About *what* was anyone's guess. Bryan continued staring at her without speaking.

After waiting a few more seconds, Emma said, "Bryan?"

"How about $50 and we won't tell a soul?" proposed Logan.

Bryan snapped out of it. "Okay… *deal.*"

Logan winked at Emma. She rolled her eyes.

"Okay, so, what do you guys need?"

"We need to gain access to the dark web," answered Logan.

"Um, why would you want to do that?" Bryan was already re-thinking the wisdom of his $50 deal.

"We need to find an app to hack into a cell phone to get a phone number," revealed Logan. "Pretty sure the dark web is where you find stuff like that."

"We're trying to help someone," added Emma, thinking some additional justification couldn't hurt.

Bryan, appearing very uneasy, responded, "What makes you think I have access to the dark web?"

Emma took this one. "Because, before you shut your archive site down, your little robots were archiving gateway sites to the dark web, and we think you know *exactly* which sites those are."

"Who *are* you guys??" Bryan could not figure out how they knew so much about him. He looked puzzled and unsure. He did not know what to do. Digging up harmless archived websites for $50 was one thing... cracking into the dark web where every site was more illegal or disturbing than the next was quite another.

"Bryan," said Emma, locking eyes with him to make sure she had his complete attention.

"Uh-huh," he responded, looking directly at her.

"Please, it's really important," she urged. She could tell she almost had him, but he was not yet persuaded. Looking at the black t-shirt Bryan was wearing, Emma recognized the illustrated comic-book image of a snow-boarder fighting off a villain while throwing a trick in midair. "Bryan, help us save the world, that's what Master X would do."

Bryan was stunned and impressed. "You know Master X?"

"Uh, yeah, who doesn't know about the 'extreme games' superstar who's also secretly a superhero?"

"I don't," conceded Logan. "You read the Master X comic?"

"There's a lot you don't know about me," Emma suggested to Logan with a grin. Looking back at Bryan, she said, "And if there's one thing I know, it's that Master X would not say '*No*' to someone in need just because he was afraid of getting caught."

Emma was totally right! Bryan now knew exactly what he had to do... he had to help them. "Okay, I'll do it," he said.

Logan said, "You rock."

Bryan got up and grabbed the box holding his server for websites starting with the letters A to K. He pulled the server out of the box, plugged it in, and booted up his archive. It did not take him long to navigate to the archived webpage he was looking for, a dark web search website called "DarknIyT."

"Is this site accessible on the internet?" wondered Emma.

"Nope," replied Bryan. "In fact, it never really was, which was one of its secrets."

"What do you mean?" asked Logan.

"Internet rumors say the creators of the website left it up for three days only to allow a few archive sites to capture it. Once that happened, DarknIyT's operators pulled the site down so anyone searching for it on the web would be unable to find it. The only way to access the page is to go to one of the archive sites that captured it. Basically, DarknIyT's operators used the archive sites to cache and hide their webpage."

"And yours was one of them?" asked Emma.

"Yep." Bryan pulled up DarknIyT's archived webpage. Clicking on it, the landing page dumped him onto a blank black screen. He saved the DarknIyT archive file to his desktop.

"There's nothing there. The screen's blank," said Emma. "Is it working correctly?"

"That's because you need special software to access the dark web," Bryan responded. He unplugged the archive server, put it away, and took out another external hard drive from the same box where he found his archive server. He hooked up the new device. "You need encryption software called TOR."

"TOR?" said Emma.

"Yeah, it's an acronym that stands for 'The Onion Routing project.' It was developed by the U.S. Navy in the 1990s to create a secret web for the government. But at some point, in the early 2000's, it went open source and the whole thing went public."

"Wow, I had no idea. I've never heard that before," said Emma. "What does the TOR thing do?" she asked Bryan.

"It's like a browser for the dark web that keeps users' identities anonymous by hiding their IP addresses through a series of re-routing relays."

"Of course, it does," said Emma sarcastically. "The things our government creates. So, do you have it?"

"Yep." Bryan booted up the TOR software on his computer. That piece of the puzzle was hiding on the second external drive that he had just plugged in. "Alright, here we go. Prepare to be disturbed."

The TOR browser opened on his screen. Bryan moved his cursor up to the browser's control menu and clicked on the Open File tab to open the DarknIyT file saved on his desktop. This time around, after opening it, the DarknIyT landing page looked different.

Still a black screen, the no-frills webpage now had a search bar and a series of red links on it. The red links consisted of a clickable list of the dark web's more popular categories curated and maintained by the site's operators for the convenience of users looking to apply a categorical filter to narrow-down their searches more quickly. The clickable list included some normal looking categories, a few intriguing ones, several obviously illegal choices, and a few incredibly alarming links:

Gambling
Guns
Chat
Abuse
Books

Directory
Blog
Hosting
Hacking
Anonymity
Forum
Counterfeit
Whistleblower
Wiki
Mail
Fraud
Market
Drugs
Violence
Arms
Social
Extremism
Finance
Trafficking
Identity
Government
Unknown
Other Illicit

Emma gasped. She was horrified by what she was looking at. A cold chill came over her as she read the dark web categories on the screen.

Logan also found the categories unsettling. He was staring at something he had no business looking at, dipping his toe into a cesspool of filth, criminal, and deviant behavior.

"You guys, okay??" asked Bryan. "I know, it's totally disgusting, but you came to me for a reason, because you need my help to hack into a phone to help someone. So, if that's what you want to do, then…"

"You're right," said Emma, pulling herself back together. "Thanks. Click on the 'Hacking' category."

Bryan did and it took them to a page displaying hundreds of links to hacking websites, too many to look at. Fortunately, there was a search bar at the top of the page that allowed users to narrow-down the results even more, within the category of hacking.

Bryan asked, "Do you guys want to look at all of these, or—"

"No. Let's try narrowing it down," interrupted Logan. "Type in 'cell phone.'"

Bryan entered the words 'cell phone' in the hacking-category search bar and a shorter list of cell phone-hacking results came up identifying websites with bizarre names, sites that sounded untrustworthy, and links that sounded like trouble. Logan, Emma, and Bryan scanned the results. They clicked on a few links discussing hacking, but none provided the solution they were looking for. It took a couple of minutes, but eventually, Logan saw one that he wanted to take a closer look at called "Hacking into a Transport Layer Security Encrypted Phone." When Logan saw that, he recalled his conversation with Karpyn when the CIA Director had handed him a temporary phone and told him the phone was "TLS encrypted, totally secure."

"Click on the Transport Layer Security one," instructed Logan.

Bryan did, and it took them to a website with the unnerving name of "CyberSatan."

"This is probably where a person's identity and financial information go to burn and churn for eternity," remarked Emma.

The site's visual platform consisted of a series of orange and red color schemes, satanic lettering and symbols, illustrated pictures of a twisted Satan pitch-forking computer screens, and fiery animations. The site oozed criminal intent.

"Here, read this recent CyberSatan post," said Bryan.

"Transport Layer Security (TLS) is a cryptographic protocol that provides communications security via embedding into all electronic communications modalities, military-grade 256-bit key encryption technology.

But now, bow down, CyberSatan's faithful followers and rejoice...

The new CyberSatanTLS app, using stolen NSA technology, disables TLS-encryption protection by employing a 256-bit counter-decryption algorithm, allowing access to the phone's apps and data.

*To get the app and sell your soul to CyberSatan, **click here**.*"

"Well, that sounds creepy," said Emma.

Less put-off by the thought of selling his soul to CyberSatan than Emma, Logan responded, "It should work though, right? I mean, all we need to do is access Karpyn's 'Contacts.'"

"I guess so," said Emma, although she really didn't know. She had never hacked into anything before. She was way outside her element. They all were.

"Bryan, what do you think?" asked Logan.

"I think the app's designed to hack into contacts, personal data, passwords, financial info, and stuff for identity theft and financial fraud. Sounds like what you need."

"Can you grab the app and put it on my phone?" asked Logan.

"Yeah, I can pull that down for you. Just so you know, and I know you don't need me to tell you this, but none of the stuff on this CyberSatan site is secure or vetted. You might as well just hand over your personal information to the dark web once you start using this app on your phone."

Emma was worried for Logan. "Do you really want to do this?"

Logan thought about it. "Let them steal my identity! I'm 17. I don't have a credit card and I've got less than $250 in the bank. Who's going to want to be me?"

"Logan, are you sure?" probed Emma, one more time.

"Yeah, it's cool. My mom's got one of those protection things you see on TV. If I do get hacked, I'm sure it'll be fine. And if not, I can always change my identity. I think I saw that option on the DarknIyT page, too."

"Alright then, here it goes." Bryan connected Logan's phone directly to the server and installed the CyberSatanTLS app.

"Alright, let's test this thing," said Logan. "Bryan, what's your cell number?"

"No freakin' way am I letting that app sniff my phone." He scrambled around his desk looking for something. He came up with another cell phone. "Here, let's use this one. It's a work cell phone that my old boss used to use for work calls. I keep it active for vendors so they don't call my personal cell phone."

"We were sorry to hear about Dewey," said Emma. "We know how much he meant to you."

"Yeah, man, really sorry," said Logan.

Bryan had no more energy to question how they knew so much about him and, in this instance, he didn't care. He simply appreciated their kind words. "Thanks," he replied. "Any personal information on here about Dewey is gonna be pretty useless now anyway. Rest in peace, buddy," Bryan said, looking upward.

"What's Dewey's number?" asked Logan, ready to try the app. Bryan gave him the number. Logan entered it into the CyberSatanTLS app on his phone and hit enter.

It took a few seconds, but as soon as the app made contact with Dewey's phone, Logan shouted...

"I'm in!! I'm looking at a replica mirror image of Dewey's phone on my own screen. And I can navigate through the phone's 'Contacts.'"

"Wait," Bryan blurted out, "a notification is popping up saying an unverified app is accessing the phone's data and giving me the option to allow, deny, or change permission settings."

"What kind of hacking app is this?" questioned Emma. "I'm no hacker, but shouldn't it be all covert without the conspicuous banner notification?"

"This is going to be a problem," said Logan. "The second Karpyn sees that notification pop up he's going to deny access or turn his phone off."

"We could try doing it in the middle of the night when he sleeps," proposed Emma.

"That's assuming the guy ever sleeps and even if he does, who knows when," replied Logan. "I mean, the guy's the Director of the CIA - European Command. He probably closes his eyes about once every two days."

"Wow, you guys are bad-ass. Are you like spies or something?" Bryan asked.

"Dude, seriously, of course not. We're in high school," Logan responded.

Either way, Bryan was impressed. He offered a suggestion. "You know, if you keep the guy on the phone talking while the Satan app does its thing, it will delay the notification pop-up until after he hangs up."

"Are you sure about that?" Logan asked.

"Yeah, I think so. Let's test it. I'll make a call from Dewey's cell phone, and while I'm on the phone, you can try hacking in again to see what happens."

Bryan dialed his personal cell phone using Dewey's. Seconds after doing so, his personal cell started vibrating on his desk. He let it ring through to voicemail. "It's recording a voicemail. Try it now."

Logan did. He punched Dewey's number back into the CyberSatanTLS app. "I'm in again. Still able to access 'Contacts.' Anything on your end?"

"Nope," said Bryan. "So far, so good. Give it a minute, keep browsing."

Logan kept scrolling through the 'Contacts' tab in Dewey's phone while it was still connected to Bryan's, opening and closing contacts.

After the minute was up, Bryan announced, "Okay… now I'm going to hang up both phones and see what happens." He disconnected both lines, and immediately after doing so, a notification popped up on Dewey's phone informing him that an unverified app was attempting to access the phone's data and giving him the option to allow, deny, or change permission settings. "There you have it," said Bryan. "It looks like you guys just need to keep that Karpyn guy on the phone while your app does its thing to delay the notification pop-up."

"So, we just need to keep him talking?" asked Emma.

Logan was confident they could do it. "That won't be a problem once we have him on the phone talking about how to find the Dealer and how he can save the lives of two Harvard professors."

"That's *awesome*," said Bryan. "You guys are waaayyyy cool. Anything else, then?"

"Nope," replied Logan. "I think this does it. Dude, you totally rock. Can I Venmo the $50 to you?"

"No need, man. This one's on me."

Just like she did the first time around, Emma walked around the desk and gave Bryan a thank you hug, a reward he more than appreciated. Once again, he blushed.

"Hey, let me know how it turns out, okay?" said Bryan.

"Will do," replied Logan, giving Bryan a fist pump. "Thanks again." It was time to go.

Logan and Emma left Dewey's. They made their way back to Philly's 30th Street Station, discussing what they needed to do next along the way. They had a solid plan in place, but before they could put it into action, there was one more person who they needed to talk to. Turning to Emma as they reached the train station, Logan said, "It's time to call Chad."

Chapter 23 – 1600 Pennsylvania Avenue

The next morning, Logan and Emma skipped school and headed to the place that was quickly becoming their favorite spot, Journal Square Station, to take Easterner Express 2167 south to Washington D.C. The commute to D.C.'s 17th Street Metro-Stop took a little over 4 hours, leaving only a 10-minute walk to 1600 Pennsylvania Avenue N.W.: The White House.

A few blocks north of the White House, just after 1 p.m., they stopped in a public park called Lafayette Square. They found a bench to sit on to call Chad like they had discussed with him the night before when they stopped by his house. When Logan and Emma asked Chad for his assistance, he was more than willing to help them and ready to play his part in their game of espionage.

As planned, Chad also found himself a park bench in Jersey City for their call. And just to be safe, he wore a sweatshirt with a hood to cover his head and partially obscure his face, in addition to a pair of dark sunglasses and latex gloves to cover his fingerprints.

The plan was for Chad to send a text message to Karpyn using a pre-paid cell phone that Logan and Emma had purchased for him from Walmart the night before. After sending the text at 1:15 p.m., Chad would follow it up with a phone call to Karpyn two minutes later. With Lakenheath AFB only five hours ahead, they expected Karpyn to answer his phone, especially after receiving the text message Chad was about to send him.

Emma, meanwhile, planned to listen in to see if Karpyn picked up by using her cell phone to call Chad's personal phone. Chad would then place his personal cell phone down in his lap and put the prepaid phone on speaker so Emma could overhear Chad's conversation with Karpyn. At the same time, Logan would have the CyberSatanTLS app queued up and ready to go on his own phone. If Karpyn picked up, Chad would try to keep him talking for as long as possible while Logan used the app to hack into Karpyn's 'Contacts' and hopefully, find a direct cell phone number for the President of the United States. After all, that was a number Logan expected the CIA Director to have.

As soon as the call ended, the plan was for Chad to take off before authorities tracked him down, and once he was safe, to smash the prepaid cell phone into smithereens and dispose of the bits in a couple of different trash bins. If everything went smoothly, Karpyn would have what he needed to capture the Dealer and rescue Dr. Arenot and Professor Quimbey, while Logan and Emma would have what they needed, the president's personal cell phone number so they could make the most important phone call of their lives.

From the Lafayette Square park bench, Emma called Chad, ready to go over the plan one more time.

"Let's go over it again," Emma said to Chad.

"Em, I've got it. I'm good," declared Chad. He was ready to rock and roll.

"Logan, you ready?" she asked.

"Yeah, the CyberSatanTLS app is queued up and ready to go. I've already punched in Karpyn's number. All I need to do is hit enter."

"Guys, are we sure we want to do this?" asked Emma, having second thoughts about hacking into the CIA Director's cell phone and just wanting to make sure everyone was on board.

"Rogue positive," declared Logan. "There's no other way."

"And Chad, you're cool with this?"

"Girl, I'm all in."

"You know, we are probably going to break like ten laws doing what we're about to do," Emma reminded them.

"Then, it's probably a good thing for us that your dad is a lawyer," responded Chad.

"Might mess up your dad's law school plans for you, but I'm good with that," said Logan.

Emma smiled. "I think I'm good with that, too. Alright then, let's do it."

At 1:15 p.m., Chad entered Karpyn's number 202-833-1999, which Logan remembered – DC, 833, the year he was born – from committing it to memory on the plane at Heathrow. Next, Chad typed in the text Emma and Logan had drafted for him to send:

> "I know where you can catch the Dealer and rescue the two missing Harvard professors who she's kidnapped. I am calling you in two minutes. Pick up."

It took some work last night, but with the help of the overhead map and street-view features of the Planet Earth app on the computer, Logan and Emma were able to retrace their steps back in Bologna to find the apartment building where Bailey's team was hiding with the professors. They started by searching for all post offices within a 20-mile radius of Bologna. That search generated a list of thirty-three post offices. From there, they narrowed it down by identifying all post offices located on the same block as a laundromat, shortening the list to three. And of those three, there was only one where there was an apartment building sandwiched in between. Chad had the address written down on a small yellow sticky note.

"Alright, hit send," said Emma.

Chad hit send and just like that, their foray back into the world of espionage had begun. About thirty seconds into what promised to be the longest two-minute wait of their lives, Chad's prepaid cell phone rang… the wait was over. Karpyn was calling *him*.

"Um, guys… he's calling *me*," screamed Chad. "It's on!! Get ready in three, two, one…"

Chad answered the phone. "Um… Hello."

"Who is this?" Karpyn tersely demanded.

"I can't tell you that, but I know where you can catch the Dealer," replied Chad.

Emma, listening carefully, signaled to Logan with a hand gesture, "Now!!!"

Logan hit "enter" on the CyberSatanTLS app to connect with Karpyn's phone. Logan held his breath while the app sent its signals through the satellites.

Meanwhile, Chad kept talking, slowly reading from the notes he made after talking to Emma and Logan the previous night. "You must be very careful. They are heavily armed, five of them. They have kidnapped two Harvard professors named Dr. Jonas Arenot and Professor Jill Quimbey, and the Dealer is using them to research, monetize, and sell the Copán Temple technology to the highest bidder."

Logan started to sweat. The app was not working as fast as he hoped. Just as he began worrying, a mirror image of Karpyn's cell phone appeared on his screen. "*Phew*," he sighed. He gave Emma a thumb's up. But his relief lasted for only a split second because the app next unexpectedly displayed the following message: "Enter Code: ++++++." The app had hit a roadblock.

"Oh no… oh no," Logan whispered.

Emma looked over and saw the notification on the screen. Together, they shared a look of panic. As if the stress level was not high enough, Emma next heard Chad say to Karpyn, "They are hiding on the third floor of an apartment building outside of Bologna…" With more hand gestures, Emma indicated to Logan that he needed to pick up his pace.

Logan racked his brain and he could come up with only one guess… the 6-digit number on the front of Karpyn's laminated CIA badge, the palindrome that was spelled the same forward and backward. But what was it? Logan closed his eyes to visualize the badge Karpyn showed him at Lakenheath: "Russell Karpyn, CIA Director – European Command – CIA # 583-385."

Logan kept mouthing the palindrome to himself, "CIA # 583-385… 583-385," so he would not forget it. He typed in "583-385" where the app prompted him to do so and was about to hit enter when something in his gut told him to stop. It was wrong.

"What is it??" he muttered to himself. He deleted the digits and re-entered a new sequence of numbers: "385-583."

"Logan, hurry," urged Emma, putting her hand on his leg.

He had no choice. Still not 100% certain, he closed his eyes and hit enter. It worked!!! He was back in.

At that moment, Karpyn asked Chad for the address, and Chad replied, "The address? You want the address?" Chad was out of time.

"Logan, he's asking Chad for the address!" uttered Emma.

Logan hurriedly searched Karpyn's phone contacts. He looked for 'Barrett'; and 'Andrew Barrett' and "AB"; and for 'President.' He found nothing. Karpyn had thousands of contacts and Logan didn't have time to go through them all. It had to be in there somewhere, maybe under a nickname... then it came to him, what about "POTUS," a common acronym standing for President of the United States.

He scanned for POTUS and found it!! Logan opened the contact card. It had no other identifying information except for the numbers 595-971-4368 in the Mobile Phone category; a D.C.-based telephone number 202-456-1111 in the Work Phone category; and the words 'Verf. 797843POTUS' written in the 'Notes' category. Logan took a screenshot.

At that same moment, Chad could stall no more. He read Karpyn the address from the yellow sticky note.

"Thank you," said Karpyn, hanging up the phone.

Logan disconnected the CyberSatanTLS app at the exact same time.

"Did you get it?" asked Emma.

"I got it!!" exclaimed Logan with a smile, earning a hug and kiss from Emma.

Emma sent a text to Chad telling him to text her when he was safe, but Chad was already long gone, having taken off as soon as he heard the sirens sounding in the background. He was nowhere to be found when the FBI arrived.

Now, it was time for Logan to do the same. After Emma took a photograph of Logan's screenshot of POTUS' contact info, Logan popped out his SIM card using a small paperclip that he brought with him to insert into his phone's pinhole-sized SIM tray. He put the miniature card in one pocket and his lifeless phone into the other. At least for the time being, no device that interacted with Karpyn's phone remained active for GPS tracking purposes.

Finally, there was only one thing left to do: head over to the White House to call the president. Emma and Logan left Lafayette Square and walked to Washington, D.C.'s most famous thoroughfare, Pennsylvania Avenue, a street that abutted the White House and connected the White House to the United States Capitol. When they reached the fence overlooking the White House's North Lawn, they sent a text message from Emma's cell phone to POTUS at 595-971-4368 that read:

> "Dear Mr. President – my name is Emma James and I am standing here with Logan West. We are high school students from New Jersey who have traveled a long way to speak with you ALONE about matters of national security and the future of humanity. We are standing outside the White House fence on Pennsylvania Ave. To prove that we are serious and have something of value to say, we know why time runs .0134 tp faster in the Copán Temple and why it is the same inside the secret hidden beneath the surface at Area 51. We know how they're connected and how to activate the mechanism inside the chamber. It is time for mankind to travel the stars."

Emma hit send. Immediately, a Verification notice popped up asking her to enter the 'Verf' number she wrote down a few minutes earlier, 797843POTUS. She did, and a message popped up saying, *"TEXT DELIVERED."*

"There, that should be enticing enough to get him to answer the phone," said an optimistic Emma.

They had done everything they could, laying their cards out on the table for President Barrett to see, including their real names… an irreversible display of trust, honesty, and hope. Their fate was in the hands of the president now.

President Barrett was in the Oval Office conducting a staff meeting when he received Emma's text message on his private cell phone. He read the message, instantly distracted by its contents. He sat there, trying to figure out how in the world two civilians had come to possess the most highly classified, top-secret piece of information in United States history, namely, what resided *beneath* Area 51. And as inconceivable as it was that *any* non-classified civilian would know what Emma's text claimed to know, he found it even *more* inconceivable that the authors of the text were just "high school students." He didn't believe that for a second.

Just as the president prepared to halt his staff meeting to call in the CIA to deal with the security breach and to figure out who he was dealing with, something else in Emma's text message caught the president's eye. There was an additional detail in there that he had not picked up on at first. When he put it together, he was even more stunned than before, if that was possible. He asked his staff to clear the room immediately.

After waiting for one minute, Emma dialed the president's telephone number... 595-971-4368. Again, she had to enter the Verification Code. She put it on speaker just loud enough for Logan to hear.

President Barrett answered, "This is the president."

"Mr. President, sir," said Emma, "may we come inside to speak with you?"

"I will give you two minutes. If you do not provide me with a satisfactory explanation for how you know what you do, I hope you understand you're both looking at prison time for illegally obtaining and possessing, possibly even stealing top secret classified information, is that clear?"

"Yes, sir," replied Emma.

"Good, stay where you are. The Secret Service will escort you in." He hung up the phone.

272

Emma asked Logan, "Are you ready for this?"

"Yeah, I'm ready."

Within seconds, four secret servicemen came up from behind them, appearing out of nowhere.

"Ms. James, Mr. West, please come with us," said one of the agents. Logan and Emma followed.

Meanwhile, President Barrett leaned back in his chair, deep in thought. He wondered if he was about to learn the answer to one of *the* most highly classified questions held close by American presidents since the government discovered the hidden cave in the Nevada desert more than sixty years ago. Many presidents had false alarms over the years but *somehow*, this time felt different. One way or another, he would soon find out, because he had just received word that the Secret Service had already scooped Logan and Emma up from Pennsylvania Avenue to bring them inside the White House.

Chapter 24 – Two Minutes

The Secret Service ushered Logan and Emma through the White House's N.W. Gate on Pennsylvania Avenue without waiting in the security line others were going through. They walked past the White House's superbly manicured North Lawn and veered right toward the West Wing which housed the presidential offices including, most importantly, their ultimate destination, the Oval Office. As they approached the double door entrance to the West Wing lobby, Emma started to get nervous. What if they couldn't convince the president that they were telling the truth?

"Logan," she said as the Secret Service escorted them up the West Wing steps, "whatever happens, I want you to know that—"

"I love you," interjected Logan before she could finish her sentence.

Emma smiled and with a twinkle in her eye, said, "I love you, too."

The Secret Service led them under the foyer through the doors into the lobby where they went through metal detectors, a security pat down, and an ID check. After they cleared security, the Secret Service guided them down a hallway past the Vice President's Offices, the Chief of Staff Suite, and the Roosevelt Room. Named after Presidents Theodore and Franklin D. Roosevelt, the ornate Roosevelt Room was the principal meeting room in the West Wing for all meetings that did not take place in the Oval Office, which was where Logan and Emma headed next.

As instructed, the Secret Service deposited them inside the Oval Office Sitting Area in front of the desk of the president's Executive Secretary, Regina Woulette. The renowned Rose Garden was visible through the windows behind her desk. After Logan and Emma settled into the comfortable waiting room chairs, the Secret Service stayed close by to monitor them. Ms. Woulette gave the overbearing security detail one of her famous looks of annoyance. She could tell from one glance at the petrified teenagers that they were no threat to anyone.

"First time at the White House?" she casually asked them, trying to ease their nerves. More than a little dazed and overwhelmed, they both nodded.

"You kids are going to do great, nothing to be nervous about. President Barrett is the nicest man in the whole world, I promise, or you let me know, I'll remind him to watch his manners."

Ms. Woulette had no idea why they were there or what they had done to warrant such a last-minute change to the president's afternoon schedule. She only knew it was important because any deviation to the president's schedule was rare.

They sat there for fifteen or twenty minutes before a device on Ms. Woulette's desk buzzed. The president was coming out. The door to the Oval Office opened and out walked the president, his Chief of Staff, Miles Garrison, and legendary five-star general, now Special Security Advisor to the president, General Warren Thomas Covington. The number of medals and distinguished honors on General Covington's dress uniform looked like they added ten pounds of weight to his uniform.

Emma and Logan took to their feet. General Covington, a serious-looking, older gentleman in his early sixties, approached them first. He was balding, with remnants of fraying dark gray hair circling his head.

"Mr. West, Ms. James, a pleasure to make your acquaintance," said General Covington.

"Likewise, sir, general, sir," responded Logan, anxiously shaking the general's hand.

"It's a pleasure," said Emma, holding it together more than Logan. She gracefully shook General Covington's hand.

On the way out, the general turned briefly back to the president and said, "Mr. President, I'll be in touch," referring to whatever business they were discussing back in the Oval Office.

When the general rounded the corner, President Barrett addressed his guests. "Ms. James, Mr. West, thank you for coming. I hope I didn't keep you waiting for too long. Please, come in."

The president gestured for them to follow him into the Oval Office. Inside, the president continued, "This is my Chief of Staff, Miles Garrison. I'm sure you've seen him on TV a few times - or maybe you kids don't watch TV anymore - or so my grandchildren have told me, not to mention a handful of frustrated network TV executives."

Chief of Staff Garrison interjected, "You'll have to ignore the president. He's the oldest 64-year-old you will ever meet. And he wonders why we failed to connect with the younger voters in the last election."

President Barrett chuckled. He and Mr. Garrison had been friends for nearly forty years and had a more-casual-than-expected relationship.

"Nice to meet you, Mr. Garrison," said Logan, shaking the Chief of Staff's hand. Emma did the same.

"Miles, we'll talk in a few minutes about the U.N. vote. Get the Senior Staff ready to roundtable the issue back here in a few minutes."

"Yes, Mr. President. Will there be anything else?"

"No, that will be all for now, thank you."

Mr. Garrison left the room, having completed the task the president had for him, putting one last set of eyes on the teenagers. Logan and Emma suddenly found themselves alone with the President of the United States. President Barrett was just under six feet tall, but standing alone with him in the Oval Office, he seemed much taller. He had wide, inquisitive blue eyes and light brown hair that was fighting a losing battle with time.

"Please, make yourselves comfortable," said President Barrett, directing them to take a seat on one of two comfortable couches in the middle of the Oval Office separated by an elongated glass coffee table. Beneath the coffee table woven into the carpet was the Seal of the President of the United States, which consisted of a shield with an American eagle holding an olive branch in one talon, a bundle of arrows in the other, and a white scroll inscribed "E PLURIBUS UNUM" in its beak. Encircling the entire Coat of Arms were the words "Seal of the President of the United States."

After the two of them sat down, the president wandered back toward his desk. "You know, in a situation like this, I usually like to know who I'm dealing with." He grabbed two thin files from his desk and walked back over to sit down on the couch across from Logan and Emma. He opened the first file and started reading.

"Immaculata James, born July 28, 1999, at Jersey City Shores Hospital to Robert James and Mary Rossi James. You wrote in your text message to me a few minutes ago that your name is Emma. Is that a nickname?"

"Yes, Mr. President. Immaculata is my legal name, but my parents have always called me Emma. Everybody calls me Emma or Em."

The president eyed her carefully for a moment, then, continued. "Your father's the managing partner at Britton & Barney in New York and your mother is a marketing manager at Dysons. You're in your senior year at Jersey North High School, top of your class, and you've already been accepted at Dartmouth, Columbia, Harvard, and Yale."

"Actually, I have only applied to those schools, I haven't been—"

"No, no, it says here that you've already been accepted. You just haven't received the acceptance letters yet."

"Oh," said Emma, somewhat embarrassed.

"An impressive list of Ivy League schools and I'm sure your Princeton and Carnegie Mellon applications will move through just as smoothly. Where is Carnegie Mellon, is that in Pennsylvania?"

"Yes, Mr. President," answered Emma. "Carnegie Mellon's in Pittsburgh."

"Why Carnegie Mellon?" wondered the president.

"Because it has one of the top-ranked cryptology programs in the country." Emma had applied to the Ivy League schools because of the pre-law and law programs at her dad's urging, but Carnegie Mellon was for her. Her parents didn't even know she had submitted the application.

"Interesting," replied President Barrett, intrigued.

"And you, son," said the president, transitioning to Logan's folder, "born May 3, 1999, in Queens, your mother Loretta Richards is the manager of one of my favorite restaurants in Manhattan, The Cityscape. And your father—"

"We can skip that, sir," interrupted Logan.

The president ignored him and kept going. "…Davis West, the founder of West Media Technologies, Inc. in Boston, now married to Hallie West, four children, living in the wealthy Boston suburb of Chestnut Hill."

The president's summary of the extent to which Logan's father had moved on from his life in every possible way clearly bothered Logan and Emma could tell. Logan never really spoke about his father and now, after listening to the president describe the situation, it was evident to her why. Emma put her hand on his shoulder.

"You haven't applied anywhere after high school, Mr. West. Why not?" asked the president.

"Can't afford it, sir. My mom doesn't make that much and my dad's a jerk. I'm going to start in community college and transfer if I can."

"You know, the Department of Education offers some pretty wonderful scholarship and loan programs you should look into," said the president, trying to sell his administration's commendable advances in education which he was very proud of.

"Thanks," Logan replied, sounding a bit dismissive.

"Seriously, you should look into it, I think you'd be surprised. Perhaps not as surprised as I was to get that text message earlier... and what I don't get is that until an hour ago, neither of you had so much as a blip on your criminal records or FBI tracking files. You," looking at Emma, "are probably going to be the valedictorian of your graduating class, and you, Mr. West, despite telling me you're not interested in going to a four-year college, still took the time to sit for the SAT and scored a near perfect score up in the upper 99th percentile."

Now it was Logan's turn to be embarrassed. Emma looked at him excitedly. "Logan, that's incredible."

"And yet, thirty or forty minutes ago, two outstanding students with bright futures conspired to hack into the cell phone of Russell Karpyn, the Director of the CIA in Europe, which explains how you got my telephone number... quite a gutsy and *illegal* thing to do to the CIA Director, although I must say, you outsmarted his agency with respect to who your third accomplice was."

Emma and Logan were both relieved to hear that Chad had gotten away without getting into trouble.

The president continued. "But what I'm trying to figure out is *why...* why would you both have jeopardized your futures like that? It seems obvious to me that you must have had a very good reason, because otherwise, why else would you have done it?"

"We do, Mr. President," assured Emma.

"Somehow, you've given us a lead that might help us capture one of the world's more notorious espionage thieves. I would've thrown you both in jail immediately if I wasn't so curious as to how you did it. And at the same time, that text message you sent earlier contained information known to only a handful of humans, most of whom probably have higher security clearance than me."

President Barrett dropped the file folders he had been holding onto the coffee table and leaned back in the couch, ready to get some answers. "I'm beyond baffled by all of this, and while I probably should just turn you over to the CIA, I'm going to give you the two minutes I promised you. Starting now."

Emma launched into it. "Mr. President, I know what I am about to say is going to be hard to believe, but I can only tell you that it is the truth and if necessary, we are prepared to prove it."

"You might just need to do that, Ms. James," replied the president.

"We know what's hidden inside Area 51 because we've seen it," said Emma.

The president doubted it. "That's not possible because that cavern's been completely sealed since the 1950's, long before either of you were born."

Emma was not done. "And we've spoken to the beings who left the cavern behind."

"The country's top scientists over the last half-century have estimated that cavern to be hundreds of years old, just a little bit older than you."

"It may be hundreds of years old from our perspective, but from the Vaniryans' perspective, time is malleable," she replied.

"Vaniryans? I'm not following," said the president.

Emma tried to explain. "They call themselves, Vaniryans. For tens of millions of years, they have traveled the galaxy on the waves of anti-mass subatomic particles called zeutyrons that blow past the speed of light, bending the space-time continuum."

"Okay, so you're talking about Einstein's theory of relativity or something like that," said the president, trying to understand.

"Yes, well, kind of, but it's more than that. When manipulated properly, the zeutyrons enable a person to not only travel faster than the speed of light but to move between space and time itself because the space-time continuum, which bends at light speed like Einstein theorized, can be bent to extremes at the speed zeutyrons move."

"What do you mean, extremes?'" asked the president.

"What I mean is, imagine if you have a long string and you bend it." Emma looked around and spotted a bottle of wine on the end table with a ribbon tied around its neck holding a card. She quickly stood up, walked over to the bottle and without asking, pulled the ribbon off of it.

"That bottle of wine was a birthday gift from the President of France, but sure, go ahead, I've already read the card…"

Emma looked at the bottle and realized that it was a 1799 vintage from Château d'Bordeaux in France. With November 9, 1799, marking the end of the French Revolution, Château d' Bordeaux's 1799 vintage was a world-renowned symbol of peace and a truly *valuable* gift of friendship between the two world leaders.

"Sorry," apologized Emma. "I'll put it back just as soon as I'm done." She returned, sat back down, and laid the ribbon out on the coffee table lengthwise, pulling it taut from end to end.

Using the ribbon as a demonstrative prop, she continued. "Now, you can pull the opposite ends of the ribbon together until they sit right next to each other." Using her index fingers to demonstrate, Emma dragged the ends of the ribbon downward and then pushed them toward each other until they were touching.

"Alright," said the president, following along.

"The space-time continuum is no different. It can be bent until two points along that continuum sit right next to each other. This allows a person to travel back and forth between the two points almost instantly. Inside the Copán Temple, the zeutyrons continuously move; they never stop moving. What your scientists have picked up in there is the bending of time by .0134 tp, caused by the zeutyrons, and that's just at the limited speed they move inside the temple. Imagine what they can do once they get out into space. It's the same inside the secret chamber below Area 51."

The phone on the president's desk buzzed. It was Ms. Woulette. "Mr. President, the Senior Staff is all here ready for you."

"Please tell them to hold for another minute."

"Yes, Mr. President," Ms. Woulette replied.

The president returned his attention to Logan and Emma. "None of this explains how you know any of this."

"We deciphered the map inside the Copán Temple…" said Logan. The look on the president's face said it all, but it was not nearly as priceless as when Logan followed that up by saying, "And we figured out what the Vaniryans left behind in Bologna for us to find."

Now *that* shocked the president. Bologna was as far as the U.S. intelligence community had gotten in their attempts to solve the Copán mystery. "And is Bologna where you encountered the Dealer?" asked President Barrett, piecing together how the teenagers had come across information about the Dealer's location.

"Yes," replied Logan.

The president looked like he was trying to think things through.

"Mr. President," said Emma, "we found the star in the heavens where the Vaniryans live, verifiable evidence of extra-terrestrial intelligence that you can pick up with your deep space telescopes."

"I know I'm not a scientist, but this star where you say these 'Vaniryans' supposedly live, obviously it would have to be many light years away, right? So, how is it then that you communicated with them?" President Barrett remained skeptical, but Emma offered up yet another unexpected answer...

"Through the zeutyron portals Logan and I went through. We visited their world," she stated. The president was speechless, so Emma kept going. "Mr. President, it is time for mankind to travel the stars, to prepare for the future. Like the dinosaurs, our time on this planet will not last forever. Maybe not tomorrow, but the future is inevitable for all of us, and the means to save humanity from what lies ahead starts with whatever's inside Area 51. We need to go to Area 51."

After listening intently, President Barrett stood up and paced. As ridiculous as *any* of it sounded, there were some things the teenagers had said that forced him to consider not only the ramifications of it all but also the potential. Deep down, he had always believed the universe was full of life and possibilities, which was one of the reasons why he always thought it was important for humanity to get its house in order. He walked over to his desk and buzzed Ms. Woulette.

"Yes, Mr. President," answered Ms. Woulette's voice on the other end of the intercom.

"Can you send Miles in?"

"Yes, sir."

The Oval Office door opened and in came the Chief of Staff.

"Yes, Mr. President."

"Miles, I know you're going to hate me," started President Barrett, causing Mr. Garrison to roll his eyes already dreading what the president was about to say, "but we need to clear my schedule for the rest of the day. I want to fly out to Los Angeles tonight. I would like wheels up on Air Force One ASAP."

284

"You're right, Mr. President, I do hate you," confirmed Mr. Garrison.

"I don't care what story you leak to the press. Just find a meeting for me to take in Los Angeles, maybe even schedule something with the mayor first thing tomorrow morning if you can."

"Actually, the mayor's been trying to schedule time with you to discuss federal water-shortage subsidies for Los Angeles anyway," said Mr. Garrison.

"Perfect. Let's also find an event for me to attend tonight, preferably a fundraiser. Clear it with the Secret Service, and once that's done, coordinate with General Covington for him, our guests here, and me to take a classified Priority–1 flight to Homey Airport after the fundraiser. I want no press tail for the Homey flight, so you'll have to work that out with the Secret Service so I can slip out of L.A. undetected for a few hours. I do *not* want the Homey flight leaked, not to anyone, not even Senior Staff."

"Understood," acknowledged Mr. Garrison.

"I want the staff working around the clock starting now on legitimate talking points for whatever fundraiser you squeeze me into tonight and for my meeting with the Mayor of Los Angeles tomorrow morning. I do not want any portion of this trip to look like a pretext, otherwise, the press will start asking questions, is that clear?"

"Yes, sir."

"And I want to be out of Los Angeles by early tomorrow morning so we can get back here and try to get back on schedule."

"Not sure we'll be able to put that Humpty-dumpty back together again, sir, but I'll try," said Mr. Garrison. "Also, you have that meeting with the Russian Foreign Affairs Minister tomorrow morning at 8 a.m. We've kicked it several times now. Minister Menputyn's not going to be happy."

"Over his *U.S. – Russia Science & Technology Sharing Agenda* proposal?" asked the president, somewhat confused. "I doubt Viktor's going to be upset over rescheduling *that*."

"I don't know why he would be put off either, sir. I just recall Viktor getting quite upset the last time we postponed the meeting. Practically caused an international incident."

"I had the flu for crying out loud," snapped the president.

Mr. Garrison did not disagree. "Either way, he was pretty insistent on getting the meeting back on calendar quickly."

"Well, just push him back to the late afternoon or later in the week. Tell him I apologize or whatever you think will get the job done. Tell him I have the flu again if you have to."

Mr. Garrison smiled. "I'll get right on it, sir. Will there be anything else?"

"No, that's all for now, Miles, thanks." Mr. Garrison turned and left the room.

After he exited, President Barrett turned back to Logan and Emma and said, "I know it's late notice, but how do you kids feel about taking a ride on Air Force One?"

They both nodded their heads.

"Good," said the president. "Then, I guess we have a few more phone calls to make." The president picked up the file folders he had been going through earlier and walked back to his desk. After thumbing through the first one, he dialed the phone. He waited patiently, and when a voice picked up on the other end of the line, he announced into the phone, "Mr. James, this is President Andrew Barrett…"

ΔΔΔΔΔΔΔΔΔΔ

For the next hour and a half, President Barrett's staff prepared for the unscheduled whirlwind trip to Los Angeles. Mr. Garrison busily worked on coordinating everything, and that included fielding irate phones call from senators whose meetings he had canceled. As for the Secret Service Director, whose team had no chance to vet the trip in advance, he just shook his head. It was just another day dealing with the head of the free world.

The president, meanwhile, after speaking with Logan's mom and Emma's dad, went off to speak with the First Lady while his aides went back to the presidential residence to gather some personal belongings for him. While President Barrett was gone, the Secret Service took Logan and Emma downstairs to run them through some extra security measures required for access to both Air Force One and Area 51. This included asking them more questions and verifying additional information, taking and running their fingerprints, providing them with detailed instructions, and educating them as to the possible criminal penalties, even for seventeen-year-olds, associated with breaching classified information protocols.

When the time came, Logan, Emma and the president boarded the president's helicopter, Marine-1, to head to Andrews Air Force Base where Air Force One awaited. Tonight, President Barrett planned to take the teenagers into the secret chamber below Area 51 to see if they could make sense of the mystery scientists had failed to solve over the last sixty plus years.

What was hidden beneath Area 51 was one of the most closely guarded secrets in United States history. In the 1950's, the United States government classified Homey Airport and the surrounding desert with the *highest possible security classification*; the government built a secure perimeter around the site, authorized the use of soldiers to guard the facility, and approved the construction of facilities above and below ground to conduct classified research. This allowed the government to legitimately conduct top-secret research at the site, feeding conspiracy theories as to what really happened there.

And *all of it* concealed the real secret of Area 51 buried deep beneath it all, the secret inner chamber. Over the last 60 years since its discovery, only a small handful of human beings had ever been inside of it. Of course, suspecting that Emma was one of them, President Barrett saw little harm in letting her see it again...

Chapter 25 – Time's Up

Bailey hung up the phone, annoyed by the angry protest she had to endure on the other end of the line. Still, she checked to make sure that her client wired the money anyway.

"What was that all about?" asked Uptin, who was playing cards with Bryant and O'Neal at the kitchen counter. All were very much alive since the shootouts in the Norwegian cave and at Stonehenge had not technically happened yet. Uptin got up and moved over to sit down next to Bailey, while Bryant and O'Neal retreated to the back bedroom to clean off their weapons.

"President Barrett blew Viktor off for some bogus meeting and Viktor's aggravated."

"So, what does he want us to do about it?" asked Uptin.

With a sly grin, she replied, "He said he'd pay us half a million to find out what the president's really up to."

"Damn, he's like the jealous ex that can't take a hint."

"For half a million, I don't care if he's crying over a breakup or planning World War III," said Bailey.

"Where are the professors?" wondered Uptin.

"They went back to their room an hour ago."

"We're getting nowhere with them, you know," said Uptin. "It's time to cut bait."

"I was planning to give them until the end of the month and get rid of them then if we're still staring at gravimeters or gravitometers or whatever the hell they're called."

"What's two more weeks going to solve? I'd rather just put them down now."

"Quimbey's on to something in the books," said Bailey, rolling her eyes. "Who the hell knows."

"Why's Viktor so worked up over Barrett canceling a meeting?"

"Last minute schedule change to fly to Los Angeles. Viktor's convinced the president doesn't do something like that on short notice unless it's important, and I agree." Bailey checked out the White House's most recent press bulletin. "According to the White House Communications Director, Barrett's landing in Los Angeles early evening, making an appearance at a fundraiser for the Helping the Homeless Campaign from 7:30 p.m. to 9:30 p.m. and taking an early morning meeting tomorrow with the mayor to discuss federal aid for the Angelino's water shortage crisis and other potential long-term solutions."

"The president's charitable, but he's not *that* charitable, and Los Angeles's been located in the middle of the desert since they named the city. None of that sounds 'urgent.'"

Bailey was way ahead of him, searching databases for evidence that the president might be doing something more interesting in Los Angeles than attending a fundraiser or meeting someone more interesting in L.A. than the Mayor. She looked for odd traffic advisories on the streets of L.A. and indications of possible incoming or outgoing classified flights at local airports. After a few minutes, she checked out the Airstrip Status Report for the Los Angeles International Airport (LAX). "*This* is interesting," she said.

"What is?" replied Uptin.

"Barrett's Helping the Homeless fundraiser is 25 minutes from the airport, and 25 minutes after it ends, LAX has already issued a flight delay notice on runways 6L and 6R." Pointing to her screen, she said, "Do you see it?"

LAX AIRSTRIP DELAY NOTIFICATIONS:

3:15 pm: 25L (7 min)

4:25 pm: 7R (35 min)

8:15 pm: 24L (5 min)

9:55 pm: 6L (10 min), 6R (10 min)

"Yeah, I see it," said Uptin.

"LAX's Delay Status Report clearly shows 6L and 6R shutting down for 10 minutes at 9:55 pm."

"Okay. So, what does that mean?" asked Uptin.

"Suspension of incoming or outbound air traffic on 6L and 6R is what LAX Air Traffic Control does when someone's using the Donovan Strip."

"What's the *Donovan Strip*?" asked Uptin. He had never heard of it before.

"William Donovan was the director of the predecessor intelligence agency to the CIA. Just north of runways 6L and 6R is a secluded runway strip named after him, reserved exclusively for discreet or classified flights."

"Okay, I agree, the timing's curious, but how do we know that delay is for the president?" asked Uptin.

Bailey poked around a little more. She knew Air Force One, a highly modified Boeing 747-200B, was too large for the *Donovan*, a short runway unable to accommodate the take-off or landing distance needed for a plane that size. If the president was heading over to the *Donovan* after leaving the fundraiser, she assumed he would have to be taking off in a plane *other than* Air Force One, likely a private or military jet or helicopter. If that were the case, there was no question in Bailey's mind that a military air-escort would have to accompany such a flight. Vandenberg AFB located just up the Southern California coastline near Santa Barbara was the closest air force base with the necessary complement of fighter jets to supply the air support a discreet presidential flight required.

"Let's check the FAA's flight notification database," said Bailey, referring to a Federal Aviation Administration ("FAA") database where all flight plans must be registered and where the FAA gives notices to all pilots to alert them of potentially conflicting air traffic or other advisories that might impact a flight route. While she did not expect Vandenberg or the pilots of a discreet presidential flight to lodge a public flight plan because that information would be classified, she *did* expect the FAA to issue advisories warning pilots to stay clear of certain airspace segments at select time intervals.

In this case, she was looking for airspace advisories along the route from Vandenberg AFB to LAX immediately prior to suspension of flight traffic on runways 6L and 6R, to see if a pattern emerged. Bailey entered the route, date, and time frame into the FAA database, and up came a list of domestic and military flight notifications. She started by checking out the notices issued for the first airspace segment along the route, and she saw exactly what she was looking for.

"There's a *military* no-fly-segment advisory from Vandenberg AFB to Lompoc for the fifteen minutes leading up to suspension of flight traffic on LAX's 6L and 6R," said Bailey. She checked for more flight advisory bans along the remaining route from Vandenberg to LAX, and sure enough, several additional advisories came up showing a tunnel of no-fly segments from Vandenberg to LAX along the flight path the fighter jets would presumably fly on their way to LAX.

"There's no doubt anymore," declared Bailey. "The president's flying out of the *Donovan* tonight. Now, the only question is, where's he going?"

"Can't you just check for more airspace advisories like you did from Vandenberg to LAX?"

Bailey shook her head and replied, "No. That route was easy because I knew the exact flight path to look for during a limited segment of time. But LAX could have hundreds of advisories going in a thousand different possible directions."

Uptin had an idea. "The FAA website classifies notices based on whether they are domestic or military in nature, right? Can't you just filter the search parameters to list *military* only?"

Bailey could do that, and that is exactly what she did next. When she did that, a short list of military no-fly-segments came up originating from LAX and overlapping with the same fifteen-minute period when LAX suspended air traffic on 6L and 6R. After plotting out the military no-fly-segment advisories, a noticeable flight path started to materialize.

"Here, let's get this up on the panel and map this out," said Bailey. Using a screen-mirroring feature, she projected her computer screen onto one of the computer-interfacing, oversized glass-panel maps standing upright in the living room. When her computer screen depicting the southwestern United States appeared on the oversized glass panel, visible from the front and the back, she told Uptin, "Grab something with a straight edge."

Uptin ripped off the folding lid from a cardboard box and handed it to Bailey. She held the lid's straight edge up against the glass panel map to extrapolate where the flight path was heading. With a red marker, Bailey drew a straight line along the cardboard lid's edge on the glass, tracking the path of the FAA's military-no-fly-segment advisories. To her surprise, the red line intersected with a target in Nevada she was readily familiar with...

"Huh... Homey Airport," uttered Bailey.

"What's that?" asked Uptin.

"Homey Airport is the U.S. Air Force base also known as *Area 51.*"

"*The* Area 51??"

"Yep."

"Interesting. That's got to be it. But why there?" wondered Uptin, familiar with Area 51's pop-culture reputation as a parking lot for UFOs. "Is he a UFO buff or something?"

"Log into the Russian Communications Sat-Intercept Platform," ordered Bailey. Victor had given them access to the secret Russian communications intercept platform that did things the United States Constitution prevented the U.S. from doing, things like reading and indexing private emails, texts, and social media posts from around the world. "Search the Sat-Intercept Platform for the terms Homey and Area 51, occurring over the last 24 hours."

He typed in the search parameters and within a minute, a long list of results came back identifying hundreds of hits from around the globe. While Uptin read through the results, Bailey moseyed over to the coffee maker to brew herself a cup of caffeine. She thought about the different ways she could dispose of the professors, whether killing or selling them. She doubted there was a market for their services anymore given that they had not proven themselves useful on the Copán project. One thing was for certain... returning them to Harvard wasn't an option.

Uptin, meanwhile, kept reading. Although he could not read Russian, he knew what to scan for, and one entry, in particular, caught his eye, a text message sent just a few hours ago in *Washington D.C.*, less than an hour before President Barrett canceled on Viktor. "Hey, look at this one about Area 51."

Результаты
Время:: 1830 угв 130
Источник:: мобильный, **551-555-0306**
Владелец мобильного устройства:: **Immaculata James**
Получатель #:: блокированный
Место, куда поступил звонок:: **Washington, D.C.**
Определены поисковые термины:: области 51
Сведения о полном текстовом сообщении:: Кликните
сюда

Bailey read Russian fluently, so she translated the Sat-Intercept Report for Uptin:

Results
Time:: 1830 UTC – 1:30 p.m. EST
Source:: Mobile Phone, 551-555-0306
Mobile Phone Owner:: Immaculata James
Recipient #:: Blocked
Location Call Placed:: Washington, D.C.
Search Terms Found:: Area 51
Full Text Message Details:: Click Here

They were on to something. She clicked on the link to read the whole text message sent by someone by the name of Immaculata James to a blocked number at 1:30 p.m. EST in Washington, DC, shortly before Barrett canceled on Viktor:

"Dear Mr. President – my name is Emma James and I am standing here with Logan West. We are high school students from New Jersey who have traveled a long way to speak with you ALONE about matters of national security and the future of humanity. We are standing outside the White House fence on Pennsylvania Ave. To prove that we are serious and have something of value to say, we know why time runs .0134 tp faster in the Copán Temple and why it is the same inside the secret hidden beneath the surface at Area 51. We know how they're connected and how to activate the mechanism inside the chamber. It is time for mankind to travel the stars."

Bailey laughed out loud when she read the text about the Copán Temple in Honduras. "You gotta be joking," she said. "High school kids outsmarted the Harvards. Alright, let's get all this intel over to Viktor right now… and when our wealthy minister calls back in a few minutes asking for more intel, I'm sure as hell going to charge him more than $500,000… seven or eight figures is more like it."

Uptin sent everything to Viktor.

"And one more thing, if you're done sending the intel, go bring the profs back in here. Let's feed them this information and see if it helps 'move' their research along. If it doesn't, get rid of them. They're no use to us anymore. Let's go get the kids."

Uptin smirked with approval. Just then, Bailey's phone rang. It was Russian Foreign Affairs Minister, Viktor Menputyn.

"That didn't take long," mocked Uptin.

Bailey answered the phone. "Viktor, this one's going to cost you $10 million—"

296

All of the sudden, the power in the building went out. Bailey heard the whizzing sound of a signal-blocking interference device approaching and striking the building to jam communications. She knew exactly what was happening and did not intend to go out quietly.

"Hurry, get the others. Let's arm up, hit the escape chute, and blow the floor. We're gonna have to fight our way out of this one."

"What about the professors?" asked Uptin.

"The CIA can clean them out of the rubble."

Chapter 26 – Full Triangle

The flight aboard Air Force One was every bit as unique as Logan and Emma thought it would be. The formality of it all, the gadgets, the sophistication, and the comforts completely lived up to the tax dollars the American people spent on the flying masterpiece. From the soundproofed passenger cabin that blocked out engine noise to the silver-plated wall décor and seat accents to the oversized reclining leather seats that swiveled, all the way down to the napkins embroidered with the presidential seal, flying aboard Air Force One was special.

Even though it was a last-minute trip, the flight was still full. Air Force One's normal crew complement, the Secret Service, General Covington, the president, his staff and, as usual, the press, were all on board. Treating it like any other West Coast trip helped to keep things looking "normal," although the Press Secretary still spent most of the flight answering questions about the president's sudden schedule change.

The Secret Service kept Logan and Emma isolated in a small sitting area, not guarding them *per se*, but rather preventing anyone else from talking to the teenagers. Everyone on the plane was curious as to who they were, what their connection was to the last-minute trip, and why they were on Air Force One, at all. Curiosity when met by silence and secrecy usually fueled rampant speculation among the staff, but in this rare case, Logan and Emma doubted the speculation surpassed the truth.

Logan and Emma reclined in comfortable chairs, holding hands. For the first time in a while, knowing that they were in good hands, they finally felt safe and relaxed.

"Can you believe we are actually sitting on Air Force One flying with the president to Area 51?" said Emma quietly, still trying to fathom how their simple class history project had led to this.

"You know, Emma, if we survive this, and don't get arrested… would you go to prom with me?"

Emma smiled and responded, "I mean, if you survive this and help me save the world, it'd be pretty hard to say no." She laughed, leaned over, and kissed him.

With a multi-hour flight and three-hour time difference, they touched down in Los Angeles at 6:30 p.m. local time. After the flight landed, a limousine picked up the president and some of his staff members to take them to a fundraising dinner for the homeless campaign, while Logan and Emma got into a black SUV with General Covington and four Secret Servicemen. They were being taken to a room at the Airport W Hotel where they would remain under guard until it was time for them to slip back out for the Homey flight.

Later in the evening, the Secret Service returned to take them back to the airport for their classified late-night flight. The black SUV drove them right up to a Gulfstream G500 private jet parked on LAX's secluded Donovan Strip.

They boarded the jet which had two pilots, one flight concierge crew member, four Secret Service Agents, the president, and General Covington already waiting on board. General Covington and President Barrett sat only a few feet away. After taking off, four F-16 fighter jets scrambled out of Vandenberg AFB flanked the Gulfstream on both sides, escorting it all the way to Homey.

With the president and general seated nearby, Logan and Emma could hear their names being mentioned occasionally. After a half hour, President Barrett brought them into the conversation.

The president swiveled his chair around and asked, "You kids, comfortable?"

"Very," said Emma. She stretched out her legs, enjoying a refreshing sip of sparkling water, her fear of flying seemingly cured by the events of the last few days.

"Good," replied the president. "Warren, why don't—"

Before he could say anything more, General Covington stopped him, leaning in to show the president something on his smartphone. In Italy, U.S. Special Operations forces working in concert with Italy's *Gruppo di Intervento Speciale* counter-terrorism unit had just completed a successful siege of the apartment building outside of Bologna where the Dealer and her team of mercenaries were hiding. The armed forces executed the operation with expert precision, surviving multiple explosive tricks up the Dealer's sleeve while rescuing Quimbey and Arenot in the process. While several US/Italian operatives suffered serious injuries, they sustained no casualties. After years of unsuccessful attempts to catch the Dealer, the U.S. finally 'had their man,' or in this case, woman, thanks to Logan and Emma.

Appreciative of their contribution to the Dealer's capture, the president shared the good news with them. "You'll be happy to know that U.S. forces, working with Italy's counter-terrorism operatives, apprehended the Dealer and two of her men tonight, rescued Dr. Jonas Arenot and Professor Jill Quimbey. There were a couple casualties on the Dealer's side, but no U.S. or Italian fatalities."

Emma and Logan were incredibly relieved to hear the news about the rescue of their friends, although technically, they had not met them yet.

"Congratulations, Mr. President," said Emma.

300

"We have you two to thank, young lady," replied President Barrett. Although the president did not say it, he was well aware that the successful outcome of the raid in Italy lent substantial credibility to Emma and Logan's incredible story about the Vaniryans and what they were flying to see beneath Area 51. The president looked at General Covington, ready to resume the conversation he started right before the general interrupted him. "Warren, why don't you show these two what you've got and let's see what they think."

The general got up out of his seat as did the president to relocate to the chairs next to Emma and Logan.

"You've both shown remarkable aptitude in discovering what you have, way beyond your years, and frankly beyond our country's brightest minds," said the president. "I thought we'd show you something else and see if you two can make some sense of it." Turning to General Covington, the president said, "Show them the Line."

General Covington pulled out a large tablet from his locked briefcase. He put his hand on the high-tech tablet screen which subsequently turned on. He pulled up several pictures of an island with enormous stone statues carved into human figures with oversized heads.

"Are you familiar with Rapa Nui?" asked the general. Both Logan and Emma shook their heads, so the general continued. "Rapa Nui is a remote volcanic island 2,300 miles west of the Chilean coastline, often referred to as Easter Island."

"What are those statues?" asked Emma.

"Those are Rapa Nui's prized possessions... nearly 900 statues called moai, created by the island's indigenous inhabitants during the 13th to 16th centuries, standing 13 to 30 feet tall and some weighing more than 80 tons," said the general.

"Fascinating," said Emma.

"There's no clear understanding as to how the inhabitants of the island moved these statues over the hill-laden terrain. Indigenous legends tell of the stones walking to their final destinations," General Covington added.

The general paused to allow Logan and Emma to ponder that while he pulled up the next image: a large red-rock face in Peru, with a doorway 25' high and wide carved into the solid rock, and a smaller door just under 6' in height, chiseled into the rock at the base of the larger doorway. "How about this site? Are either of you familiar with this one?" asked the general.

"No," they both said simultaneously.

"That is the Puerta de Hayu Marca in southern Peru discovered in 1996. The locals call it the Gate of the Gods. Ancient legends say the smaller 'door' is for mortals and the larger one is a 25' tall gateway for the gods."

"That's a gateway?" asked Logan.

"We were hoping you could tell us," said the general. "It's certainly tall enough for one of those moai statues to walk through."

Next, General Covington called up pictures of a moai statue laying on the ocean floor.

"What is that, another moai off the coast of Rapa Nui submerged in water?" asked Emma.

General Covington responded, "No. Actually, this statue was found in a twelve-thousand-year-old sunken city discovered in 1986 off the coast of Yonaguni Island, south of Japan. Some refer to the hidden city as the Japanese Atlantis." The general tapped over to a picture of Yonaguni. The Yonaguni Monument looked like an underwater city; it had staircase-like terraces with flat sides and sharp corners, structures, and other cityscapes.

"The submerged moai statue looks identical to the ones in Rapa Nui," said Emma.

"But for the fact that they were fashioned nearly 12,000 years apart, and thousands of miles from each other, they are," replied General Covington.

"But I don't get it," said Emma. "You're not anthropologists or archeologists. Don't you have people who study these kinds of things? Why the interest at this high level of government? Why *your* interest?"

"He's not done," said the president.

General Covington showed a map to Logan and Emma. "Rapa Nui is here west of Chile," said the general, pointing to the South Pacific Ocean.

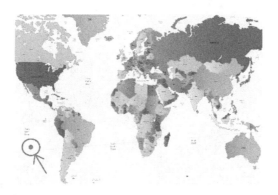

He continued. "And east of Rapa Nui, in the far south region of Peru, is Hayu Marca."

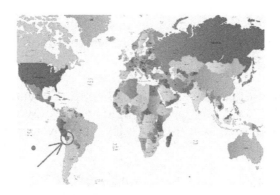

"And finally, south of Japan, northeast of Taiwan, is Yonaguni Island where divers found the submerged moai and ancient sunken city."

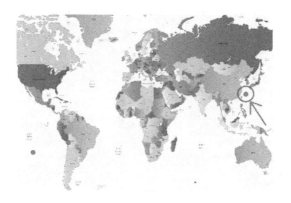

"Alright," said Emma.

General Covington continued. "If you look at a map plotting out all three of those locations, and draw a line from Rapa Nui to Yonaguni Island, you end up with a perfectly straight line starting at Rapa Nui, crossing right over the top of Hayu Marca and straight on to Yonaguni Island." General Covington conjured up a red line on the screen connecting all three points together so they could see it for themselves, a perfectly straight line from Rapa Nui to Yonaguni Island that crossed right over Hayu Marca, just like the general described:

304

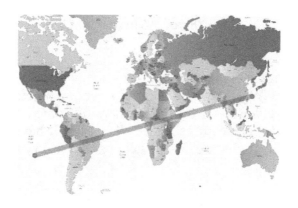

"That's interesting," said Logan.

General Covington kept going, "And there is a fourth archeological site right on top of the line over here—"

"That's enough for now," said President Barrett, stopping General Covington mid-sentence, much to Logan's and Emma's chagrin. "What do you think?" the president asked them.

"The straight line is interesting, but it's hard to know what to make of it. We would need to see more information," replied Emma.

"I couldn't agree more. If you two are interested, how about coming to Washington to help us out with these kinds of special projects, not the least of which is the one we are flying to see right now?" asked the president.

"Are you offering us a job?" asked Emma.

"I am. After high school graduation, I would like the two of you to consider relocating to D.C. for college and to continue working with us. Top Secret classified clearance."

"I'm sorry, sir, but are you serious?" Emma asked.

The president nodded his head and responded, "Quite serious. Brilliance is in high demand."

Logan appeared conflicted. "Move to D.C. for college? I'm not sure I can afford that, sir."

The president shared none of those concerns. "You don't have to worry, Mr. West. We're going to work something out with Georgetown for you to attend school there full-time on a scholarship while you work here with us. After all, I do still have some pull in D.C., or so Miles tells me. We'll take care of everything. What do you say?"

"Yes, Mr. President, yes and thank you!!" blurted Logan exuberantly. Emma excitedly hugged him. Logan could hardly believe what was happening. He never thought a college like Georgetown was possible. His path to a better life for himself and his mom had never been brighter.

"And you, Ms. James? We can work the same deal for you, too. After our little talk back in the Oval Office earlier today, I had my staff do some checking, and Georgetown's got one of the best cryptology programs in the country. With your eye for solving codes, puzzles, and mysteries, I can't imagine your government having nearly the same success studying special projects like the ones we've been discussing, without you. That is, if you're interested."

"Of course!" said an ecstatic Emma.

"Mr. President," said the captain over the loudspeaker, "We're coming up on Homey. Landing in about 10 minutes."

As soon as the Captain made the announcement, President Barrett's and General Covington's moods changed, perhaps because neither expected to return to Area 51 again during the president's administration.

Landing at Homey Airport was much like landing at Lakenheath AFB. Homey was a highly secure military facility with a multi-mile no-fly zone, secured perimeter, airmen stationed on the runway strip, and heavily guarded buildings on the premises. When they landed, airmen converged around the plane, after which the president, General Covington, Secret Service Agents, Logan, and Emma deplaned.

Airmen stood at attention and saluted their commanding officers while Air Force Lieutenant General Bernard Nemond came out to greet them. He was the highest-ranking officer at Area 51 and one of only three people on the base who knew the true purpose behind the president's visit.

"Welcome to Area 51," said Lt. General Nemond, saluting the president and General Covington. The president and the general returned the formalities. Lt. General Nemond acknowledged the teenagers but was otherwise ready to take the conversation indoors.

He guided them past the airmen and into Homey Research Building #2. Once inside, Logan and Emma found the building unexpectedly boring because none of the research offices had any windows to peek into. The lack of transparency was intentional, of course.

When they reached the elevators, Lt. General Nemond pressed the 'down' button. Now, Logan and Emma sensed they were going somewhere interesting, specifically, below ground. When the elevator opened, the Secret Service Agents did not enter with them. As the doors closed, Logan and Emma found themselves alone in an elevator with the military leaders of the free world: The Commander in Chief, Five-Star General Covington, and Lt. General Nemond.

"Well, this isn't intimidating at all," whispered Logan to Emma. He thought President Barrett chuckled, but he wasn't sure.

The elevator keypad displayed only four floors. Lt. General Nemond placed his thumb on a keypad scanner and pressed Basement Level 4. Logan and Emma felt based on the elevator's lengthy descent that they probably dropped the equivalent of ten stories before passing the 1st Level.

When they reached the 4th Level, the elevator doors opened, and they entered the floor nicknamed the "C.T." Floor, short for "Conspiracy Theory." They walked into a mission control-style command center with only two operators staffing the consoles at this late hour. Massive digital screens displaying global and orbital maps and data occupied the 25' tall wall at the front of the command room. Off to the right of the command center wall was an open hangar with large fragments inside of it.

"Are those from a UFO? The one they say crashed at Area 51?" asked Emma.

"No," the president replied with an amused laugh. "Those are actually interstellar fragments that crashed through our atmosphere in the Cloud Peak Wilderness area in north-central Wyoming in the 50's, in the Bighorn Mountains. We brought them over to this facility for research because of abnormalities in their shape and composition. Do you want to take a closer look?"

Knowing that of course, they did, President Barrett walked them towards the fragments with Lt. General Nemond and General Covington at his side. Some of the fragments looked like broken rocks from a meteor, while others had a smooth, metallic appearance and curvature that did not look natural. Logan crouched down to take a closer look, wondering if they were pieces of rock or fragments from a UFO.

The president answered Logan's question even before he could ask it. "We don't know whether they are alien technology or not."

"Our scientists have never definitively determined what some of these fragments are," said Lt. General Nemond.

"The shape... they're so smooth," said Logan.

"The elemental composition of this one here," said the president, pointing to a fragment beside Logan, "is unlike any on Earth. Its heat-tolerance characteristics actually led to some of the composite-technologies integrated into the exterior skin of the U.S.'s Stealth-2450B and some of our other high orbit assets."

"Incredible," said Emma.

"Kids," the president said, nodding to the generals, "it's time."

"Right this way, Mr. President," said Lt. General Nemond.

He guided them to the back of the command center and down a hallway where the offices for several other senior officers were located. Lt. General Nemond's office was the one at the very end of the hall. They walked up to it.

To enter his office, the security system required a handprint from Lt. General Nemond. After he provided it, the heavily sealed door opened. They entered, and the door closed behind them. There were no windows in Lt. General Nemond's office, only chairs, couches, an oversized desk with a computer, file cabinets, and two walls full of digital screens.

Lt. General Nemond opened his desk drawer and reached inside to press one more button. A trap door popped open at the back-left corner of the office exposing a staircase that went down. Lt. General Nemond led the way into the opening and the others followed. The staircase, which was dimly lit by overhead light bulbs every fifteen steps or so, wound down through ground-rock another fifty feet. It ended at a door.

"Here we are," said Lt. General Nemond. He flipped on a light switch and pushed the door open.

They found themselves inside a giant hollowed-out pyramid, several hundred feet wide and tall. The interior was massive, with the pyramid's four sides peaking at a point high above in the center. Its walls were smooth and white. They looked familiar, just like the walls Emma and Logan had seen in the Vaniryan pyramid when they went through the portal. Emma ran her hands over one of the walls. It was not made of stone. Rather, it felt *soft*.

Lt. General Nemond explained, "We don't know what the walls are made of or how long this pyramid has been here."

"There, in the middle," said Logan, pointing.

"*That* is the mechanism Ms. James referred to in her text message earlier today, and it's the reason we are all here," said the president.

In the middle of the floor sat a large, white metallic sphere.

"Have you been here before, Ms. James?" asked the president.

"No, sir," she replied. She had *seen* the sphere before, they both had, while in the cave in Norway. And when she visited TYC 129-75-1, the sphere was also one of the many images the Vaniryans had placed into her mind for her to see.

"Are you sure about that?" responded the president, leading the group closer to the five-foot-tall sphere.

"Yes," Emma replied. "I am sure..." She paused. Up close to the sphere, she suddenly realized what the president's questions were all about. Inscribed near the top of the sphere were words that read: "*It is time for mankind to travel the stars – Emma J.*" Those were the same words Emma had written to the president in her text message earlier in the day.

Emma's eyes enlarged. So did Logan's.

"Is that you?" asked the president, asking the one question every president had wondered for the last sixty years.

310

"But how is that possible?" whispered a confused Emma.

"Do you know how it works?" said the president, patting her shoulder with his hand.

Emma replied, "I think so."

"Generals, what happens here today does not leave this pyramid," instructed the president. "That is an order."

"Yes, sir," said the generals.

"Ms. James," the president said, gesturing toward the sphere, "the floor is yours."

Emma approached the sphere. As soon as she touched its surface, it lit up, revealing an image of the Earth's geography outlined by radiating blue lines on the sphere's surface. This was as far as the United States' best scientists had been able to get with the Vaniryan sphere over the last sixty years.

Like Emma did in the cave back at the *Hvit Fuge Stranda*, using the tip of her left index finger, Emma touched the globe in order: first, she touched the location of Falaise, then Storfjorden, Stonehenge, Giza, Tiwanaku, Copán, Area 51, and lastly, Falaise, again. She did not remove her index finger from the sphere after touching Falaise last. Instead, she left it in place and watched as the mechanism activated.

The walls and floor of the secret pyramid disappeared and the galaxy and its billions of stars holographically appeared. Billions of stars hovered around them like fireflies. Looking down, up, and around, it appeared as if they were floating in outer space. Whatever they were standing on was completely invisible. The sphere remained fixed beside them with Emma's left index finger remaining in contact with it. If she let go, the stars would disappear, and the pyramid's walls and floor would re-appear.

"Sir, it has never done this before," said Lt. General Nemond to the president.

"Indeed," replied President Barrett, equally taken aback by the developments. "Please, Ms. James, continue."

With her free right hand, Emma pointed toward a star off in the holographic distance and a blue line extended from her right index finger all the way to the star until making contact with it. Instantaneously, they surged forward in the holographic galaxy, warping through the stars in the blink of an eye. They found themselves orbiting the star she selected amidst a solar system of six circling planets. It was as if they were there.

Orbiting closest to the star was a small red planet. Second out from the alien sun was a slightly larger gray world. The third planet out was a small blue sphere, followed in orbit by a large blue-green planet. The solar system's fifth planet was a massive, stark white globe, probably frozen to the core. And finally, far off in the distance orbited an icy gray-blue planetoid.

Emma pointed her free index finger toward the tiny red planet orbiting closest to the blazing star. A blue line again extended from her fingertip until reaching the red planet. A ten-foot-tall and twenty-foot-wide rectangular portal materialized in front of them. It revealed in crystal-clear detail what waited for them on the planet's fiery surface, a hostile, burning landscape completely inhospitable to human life. With the planet's tortured surface appearing close enough to touch, they could almost feel the scorching heat from the blistering temperatures on the other side of the portal burning the skin on their faces. Emma tapped the sphere with her right index finger, and the portal disappeared.

Next, while keeping her left index finger on the center sphere, Emma pointed toward the fourth planet in orbit, an inviting cerulean blue-green sphere with swirling white clouds. As before, a large rectangular portal appeared before them. This time, through it, they could see the lush multi-colored plant life of another world and hear strange squawking and chirping, the sweet sound of indigenous life on another planet.

Emma let go of the sphere, which would not deactivate as long as the portal was open. If she tapped the sphere again, the portal and everything around them would disappear.

"Astonishing," said the president. "And you understand the technology behind all of this?" he asked her.

"I can see it," she replied. "I don't have words for all of it yet, even some of the concepts, but I know the knowledge is there."

"So, what do we do now?" the president asked, looking to the 17-year-old for guidance.

"We explore, Mr. President. We explore."

Chapter 27 – Black Monday

"Thank you, Ms. Lynnette, Ms. Vázquez, and Mr. Goldberg," said Mr. Jackson as the three students returned to their seats. Their oral report on the mythology and history behind Stonehenge on the first day back from Thanksgiving break (otherwise referred to by students as "Black Monday") left out many details Emma and Logan now knew to be true about Stonehenge. Nevertheless, Mr. Jackson seemed to enjoy their report.

"I liked the research your group did to compare the astronomical and agricultural properties of Stonehenge to the 1,000-year old megalithic stone circle found near Calçoene, Brazil," commented Mr. Jackson. "The analogy to crop cycles works for both sites and your report made a solid argument that the indigenous people arranged the stones the way they did not only for worship but to track astronomical observations for agricultural purposes. Well done. Now, it's time for the next report. Logan, Emma, you're up."

All eyes turned to them. Logan and Emma stood up and walked to the front of the classroom. Logan connected his laptop to the overhead projector and Emma prepared to speak. Before she could begin, Mr. Jackson chimed back in.

"Class, this next project is a reminder of... how shall I say it... the flexibility of history. Never forget that history is always told from the eye of the beholder, from the perspective of those who wish to retell the story, or in this case, to profit from it. Okay, Logan, Emma, *now* you may begin."

Logan punched up a picture of the Copán Ruin's broken stone palace, and Emma started talking. "So, we did our report on something called the Chamber of the White-Eyed Star God, discovered by a Harvard professor named Dr. Jonas Arenot around six years ago. He found it hidden inside a Mayan temple in the Copán Ruins in western Honduras." Emma stopped to allow Logan to take over as part of their alternating presentation.

Logan went next. "The Mayan city of Copán was *the* capital of the Mayan kingdom for approximately 500 years from the 5th to the 9th centuries. The city actually lasted for hundreds of years beyond that and was discovered by the Spanish explorers. The Mayans organized the city to allow great processions to honor their rulers, building a large procession-way in between the dozens of structures that made up Copán. There was a central plaza, an adjoining acropolis, a series of surrounding step pyramids, temples, palaces, and houses."

Logan stopped talking and called up a picture of the Copán Temple on the screen. It was Emma's turn again.

She pointed to the picture and said, "Our project took us inside the Copán Temple. There are thousands of hieroglyphics carved into the sixty-two steps leading up to the step-pyramid's flat top, earning the steps the nickname, the Hieroglyphic Stairway of Copán. Dr. Arenot, after supposedly deciphering a cryptic hieroglyphic message carved into Step #34 West, discovered a secret chamber inside of the Copán Temple called the 'Chamber of the White-Eyed Star God,' with thousands of mysterious hieroglyphic numbers carved into the walls. For years, experts speculated as to what the numbers meant. Were they a map leading to treasure or a tomb? Did they count the number of days until the end of the world? Turns out it was none of those things. Unfortunately, there was no mystery here, at all. The whole thing turned out to be a hoax."

The class jeered, cheered, and laughed. Mr. Jackson settled everyone down and said, "While Ms. James and Mr. West's project may not have gone as planned, everyone should remember that learning is achieved by going through the steps that lead to discovery, no matter the end result. Learning is about the process, not the outcome."

"Well, *our* outcome," said Logan, "after weeks of researching the Copán Temple, was the coincidental timing of a press release by the FBI and the FCC's Internet Fraud Division a few weeks ago, declaring the Copán Ruins mystery to be a hoax."

"How did they figure it out?" asked Beck Raymer.

Emma explained, "The press release didn't say because the investigation remains ongoing, but the Honduran Silvicultura Departamento upset by the perverse exploitation of its national monument has closed access to the Copán Ruins to all outsiders for the time being, except for those pre-approved by the Honduran government."

"Any other questions?" Mr. Jackson asked the class. He looked around for hands. Seeing none, he said, "Thank you, Mr. West and Ms. James." Logan and Emma returned to their seats to the sound of several more laughs. Once they sat down, Mr. Jackson said, "Okay then, next presentation."

Chapter 28 – *Who Are You?*

President Barrett walked out of the doors leading to the presidential residence's second floor Truman Balcony, named after President Harry S. Truman. It was constructed during Truman's presidency in 1948 and overlooked the White House's South Lawn with a clear view of the 554-foot-tall obelisk-shaped Washington Monument in the distance. President Barrett inhaled the brisk air of a November morning in Washington. He took a sip of his morning coffee, waiting patiently for General Covington to arrive.

When General Covington emerged from the residence a few minutes later, President Barrett spun around to greet him. He reached out to take hold of a manila folder the general was carrying.

"Did Karpyn's men do it?" asked the president.

"Yes, they altered the shield in the Archiginnasio and removed the microfilm from the municipal library's archives."

"Good," said President Barrett. "Did anyone see them?"

"No, sir."

President Barrett turned around and started reviewing the folder.

"What are you looking for?" asked General Covington.

"Not sure yet," replied the president.

"My people did a full genealogical work up like you requested."

The president glanced at a few more pages and said, "Thank you."

President Barrett walked up to the balcony railing and leaned on it. He looked up at the moon which was still hovering low in the morning horizon. With his back to the general, he said, "You know, ancient civilizations used to believe that the cosmos depicted their history and destiny. They didn't see the stars as scattered matter careening through the galaxy, originating from the Big Bang like scientists do today. They believed the gods arranged the constellations the way they did to tell the story of their people, their past, their present, and even to tell their future."

General Covington stepped up to the balcony railing to join the president. "And what do you believe, Mr. President?" he asked.

"I don't know. After what we've seen, I'm just not sure of anything anymore."

"Have either of them put it together?"

"I don't think so," replied President Barrett. Looking over at the general, he added, "Have we?"

"Do you think she's human?"

"Of course," replied the president.

"Should we at least restrict her Pentagon access?"

"No. That won't be necessary, at least not yet," said the president.

"Are you sure?"

"Yes. We'll talk to Dr. Arenot and Professor Quimbey after they arrive about keeping an eye on her. And we're also going to have surveillance set up on them both. That should be good enough for now. Let's discuss this later following our afternoon briefing, once I've had a chance to review the file some more."

"Thank you, Mr. President." General Covington saluted as he exited.

The president sat down in a chair and placed his coffee cup on an outdoor coffee table. He opened the folder General Covington had given him earlier to a page containing a map of the seven global coordinates associated with the Norwegian Albo. He stared at the map.

Taking his right index finger, he drew an imaginary line from the Area 51 plot point in southern Nevada, down through the Copán region of Honduras until he reached the coordinates for the Gate of the Sun in Bolivia. It formed a straight line:

"Immaculata," he said, referring to the letter "I" that he had just drawn from Area 51 down to Tiwanaku.

Next, he placed his finger on the Storfjorden cave in Norway, drawing a line down to the Great Pyramid of Giza in Egypt, then looping to the left and back up through the Château de Falaise and ending at Stonehenge. It formed a not-quite-so-perfect letter J:

"Immaculata James," the president muttered to himself, studying her initials "I J" embedded into the coordinates map. "Who are you...?"

The End of the beginning...

To receive updates on the upcoming <u>sequel</u> to, *The Coordinate*, please go to http://marcjacobsauthor.com/sequel/

Leave A Review

Thank you for buying THE COORDINΔTE, and I truly hope that you enjoyed it! If you enjoyed THE COORDINΔTE, please consider leaving a review and/or rating it, so that others can discover THE COORDINΔTE and join in on the adventures of Emma James and Logan West. I would love to hear your feedback. Leaving a review anywhere would be great, but also, please considering leaving a review at the following sites:

https://www.amazon.com/

https://www.goodreads.com/

About Marc Jacobs

I have always looked to the stars as a reminder of humanity's minuscule place in the universe. I find inspiration in the science fiction genre because it feeds the imagination and keeps people believing in a greater world of possibilities. In my debut science fiction novel, THE COORDINATE, I explore a question that I have wondered about my entire life, one that has remained unanswered throughout the history of mankind, "Are we alone in the universe?" I live with my family and work in Los Angeles. Proving that no moment in life is to be wasted, I wrote THE COORDINATE while driving to and from work every day, dictating the story into my iPhone Notes App. Now, that's making good use of time!! Thank goodness for the heavy traffic on the streets of Los Angeles. And the bad-good news is, my commute has not gotten any shorter, meaning, look out for the upcoming sequel! Lots more to come!!

Contact Marc and Receive Updates

If you would like to contact me – *readers, fans, agents and publishers all welcome!!!* - I would love to hear from you. Please visit my website at www.marcjacobsauthor.com or shoot me an email at marc@marcjacobsauthor.com. Also, if you would like to receive updates on the upcoming sequel to *The Coordinate*, please visit www.marcjacobsauthor.com to join the mailing list and to look out for updates.

Thank you!!!

Marc

There's More!!!

If you've read this far, why not keep going? There is a lot more to see and enjoy at my website, www.marcjacobsauthor.com!! In addition to learning more about me, there are ancient mysteries for you to solve, pulled together from a collection of age-old discoveries that, to this day, scientists, archeologists, and historians can't quite explain. Can you? There's also a quiz on the website to see if you have alien DNA. I mean, let's face it, don't you sometimes find yourself thinking people just don't get you and wondering if some part of your DNA might come from another world? I thought so. I look forward to seeing you at www.marcjacobsauthor.com.

Praise for The Coordinate

Kirkus Reviews – "Two teenagers embark on a school project that turns into an exciting, dangerous, and globe-trotting adventure in this YA sci-fi novel. ¶ In his debut novel, Jacobs tells a Dan Brown–style adventure story for a high school audience—one that's full of puzzles to decode and bold, perilous actions... Jacobs keeps the plot moving throughout by introducing unexpected twists. ¶ Entertaining on several levels, and sure to win fans for a planned series."

San Francisco Book Review – "Marc Jacobs' novel, The Coordinate, will not disappoint your high expectations. With action and unsuspecting twists throughout the story, you'll be viewing the wonders of the world in a completely different way than before and will be reevaluating your thoughts about the state of our current world."

Self-Publishing Review – "The idea that there are hidden secrets about humanity's past will continually fascinate readers, and it is done to great effect in The Coordinate. ... The novel is a great work of adventure, as if we're following a team of Lara Croft and Indiana Jones as teenagers. ... Jacobs does a wonderful job towing the line between a whimsical adventure that is far from reality and an engaging plot that feels relatable to a younger audience. From abducted Harvard professors and cryptic puzzles to FBI raids and secrets hidden in the stars, this relatively fast read will keep you turning pages until the last one. ... The Coordinate is a thrilling adventure from an ambitious and creative author."

IndieReader – "IR Verdict: A thrilling cross-continental Dan Brown-style action adventure that blends sci-fi and ancient conspiracies seamlessly into an intriguing plot..."

Your Review – Your turn. If you enjoyed THE COORDINATE, please consider leaving a review and/or rating it. I'd love to hear from you."

Credits

Cover Image Photo Credit: korney-violin-54739-unsplash

Cover Design Credit: Alfredo Sarraga, Jr. and Marc Jacobs

World Map Image: shutterstock1249221784 by Andrei Minsk

Cover and Interior Images of the Stars: shutterstock 1202146780 by Matsumoto

Cover Image of the Pyramids: David McEachan

CPSIA information can be obtained
at www.ICGtesting.com
Printed in the USA
BVHW041301230719
554165BV00007B/33/P